SERIAL
MONOGAMY

KATE TAYLOR

DOUBLEDAY
CANADA

Doubleday Canada and colophon are registered trademarks of
Penguin Random House Canada Limited

LIBRARY AND ARCHIVES CANADA CATALOGUING IN PUBLICATION

Taylor, Kate, 1962-, author
Serial monogamy / Kate Taylor.

Issued in print and electronic formats.

ISBN 978-0-385-68562-7 (bound).--ISBN 978-0-385-68563-4 (epub)

I. Title.

PS8589.A896S47 2016   C813'.6   C2015-906516-X
                                              C2015-906517-8

This book is a work of fiction. Names, characters, places and
incidents are products of the author's imagination or are used
fictitiously. Any resemblance to actual events or locales or persons,
living or dead, is entirely coincidental.

Book design: Jennifer Lum
Cover images: (Marbles) © Dvmsimages | Dreamstime.com,
(background) © Tolga Tezcan | Dreamstime.com
Printed and bound in the USA

Published in Canada by Doubleday Canada,
a division of Penguin Random House Canada Limited

www.penguinrandomhouse.ca

10 9 8 7 6 5 4 3 2 1

Penguin
Random House
DOUBLEDAY CANADA

For Joel

These pages are for you. I want you to read them. And after that it's up to you, the two of you, to decide. File them away and forget about them. Burn them if you want. Publish them if you think that's useful. I had no specific plans for them; I suppose I just wrote them for myself, these various bits and pieces. But I have brought them together here for you.

My darling daughters. It breaks my heart that I cannot know who you are as you read this. My bright-eyed Goli. My wavy-haired Anahita. What did you study? Did you stay in Toronto? Have you chosen professions? Is Goli still my gentle girl? Anahita, the stubborn one? Have you found love? Perhaps not yet. You are still young. There's lots of time and when it arrives it's always complicated. You'll see.

Please don't think I wrote this to take revenge on your father. If he betrayed me once, he has also stuck by me again and again. And don't let these pages poison your relationship with the woman who I imagine is now your stepmother. I bear her no ill will for events that already seem long in the past. Whatever I may have written here, the truth is that I have too little time now to indulge in extraneous emotions. But I want you to know me and I can think of no other way.

Has your father kept these pages safe for you? Are they still as crisp and white as they were when the printer churned them out yesterday and I squared them into a tidy pile? Or are they now yellowed and dog-eared, time-worn for all their waiting? I suppose you still have paper, do you? Perhaps printers have been replaced by some lovely new technology. Just six or seven, you girls would laugh at me. Egged on by your father, you would joke that I barely had a phone and then would forget to take the pathetic thing I did have when I went out for a walk and nobody could reach me. You couldn't believe that when I was a girl phones were anchored to houses and we would venture outside the range of communications for hours every day. I suppose by the time you read this all those devices will be implanted directly in the brain. There are some things I really don't mind missing.

I am a writer. Of course, I am a mother, your mother. And a wife, your father's wife. A lover before that, I suppose. But before it all, underneath it all, I am a writer. I don't know if you will have read any of my books. There's a whole shelf of them in the living room. All the different editions. It wasn't my idea—I would have happily kept them in my office—but your father liked to see them on display. He was always amused by the notion I had been translated into Swedish.

But perhaps the shelf is not there any more and you all moved to another house. Did the books make the move? Did he take these pages with him?

I wonder if you will remember that I was writing that story for *The Telegram*, during those good months we had before I got sick again, a serial for a newspaper, a historical piece. It was a bit of a crazy idea. It won't be sitting on any shelf, but I have included it here. And then I've added some other chapters along the way, things I've been working on that were never intended for print.

I hope you'll understand as you read it. Sometimes I misjudge my audience, tell them stories they are unready or unwilling to hear. Do you remember how I tried to tell you tales from *The Thousand and One Nights*? It's an impossible project, you'll understand now; the Nights are filled with sex and violence, sadism and sodomy. They are wholly inappropriate for little girls, but I so wanted you to know about Scheherazade, the woman who could save her own life and those who might have followed her simply because she could seduce a man with a story. I wanted you to have that piece of your father's culture; he said it could wait until you were teenagers at least, but I wanted so much for you to hear those tales. Maybe I somehow knew that I would not be there to tell them to you when you grew older.

It's been a while since we've had a session. I am too tired these days, but remember how we would squeeze together into the bottom bunk of your pink bedroom: Goli squished against the wall—how you would squeal, Goli: "You're squeezing me!"—and Anahita giggling as she all but fell off the edge of the bed. And I would lie in between you, repeating the tales from memory and bowdlerizing like mad, turning vengeful tyrants into loving husbands and giving the magic genie a merciful disposition, until I would see your eyelids growing heavy and I would stop wherever I was.

You always loved the ending, always the same ending, ". . . and so, Scheherazade stopped her story there. The King begged to hear more. 'What happens next?' he demanded. But Scheherazade would not be swayed. 'It is almost dawn, you must sleep,' she said. 'I will tell you the rest tomorrow night.'"

t was a warm night in late spring. 2010. The end of May, I think, or maybe it was early June. It was already hot; we'd turned on the air conditioning and it blew gently into the room, a motor sounding a deep note somewhere in the background, far away. I was wearing some skimpy little nightgown or T-shirt and had pushed the sheet down to my midriff. With one hand I was lazily caressing my chest, my fingers sliding underneath the thin cotton. Perhaps I was wiping the day's sweat away from between my breasts; perhaps I was vaguely thinking I might like to have sex with my husband. Maybe it was both, that sense of end-of-day achievement giving way to nighttime pleasure. I can't remember exactly why I was feeling my breast but afterwards, after it was known, after it became a thing that was out there between us, my recollection of that disastrous first moment, that horrible, sickening sense that something was wrong, was always associated in my mind with the not unpleasant feeling of the slightly damp skin beneath my caressing fingertips.

"I have something to tell you." My husband sounded unrushed, unalarmed. I remember those first words but not how he phrased what came next. The student, the one who was doing the research. They had become close. He had crossed a line. I do remember those words. He had crossed a line. It sounded so benign, so insignificant. So I had to ask, "What does that mean?"

"You know," he said. "Gone, well, further than . . ."

He was having an affair with one of his students. I lay there numb, shocked, unable to believe the gap that had opened in my life, the gap between five minutes ago, the pleasantly minor drama of an early heat wave, the barely registered sound of the air conditioning, the drops of perspiration on my fingertips and the lazy thoughts in my mind, and now, him, our girls asleep across the hall, and me. Who was I? Well, clearly not someone he was about to have sex with. I gathered up my pillow and stumbled out of the room.

"Oh don't . . . Don't go. Surely we can talk this through," he said. I had no idea what words he thought we might have used. I lay on the living room couch, covered by a shawl I found in the hall closet, until finally at dawn my tears began. I cried for weeks.

I spent the next day wandering the house in a daze, throwing myself on the bed, weeping until the sobs shook my body, eventually snuffling them back and getting up, making tea or a sandwich, running a bath or trying to read the paper, until the sight of Al's shoes in the front hall or the thought of picking up the girls from daycare would set me off again. Al had said nothing more that morning and had left with the girls, walking them to school before heading to the office, so we had not exchanged another word except for "Have you seen Anahita's backpack?" and "You can leave the milk out. I want some in my coffee." I thought the twins, who were in their final weeks of kindergarten, would surely notice their mother looked anxious and their father vacant; I choked back tears, bit my lip and answered their prattling with monosyllables. I could not imagine any adult walking into that house and not seeing that things were terribly wrong. In one night our seemingly happy, well-regulated home had some-how metamorphosed into something melodramatic and tawdry. In the weeks to come, I would often wonder if Goli was crying because she sensed something was amiss or Anahita was in a temper because she knew her father did not love her mother and then be brought up short when Goli tearfully confessed that Emma was no longer her best friend or Anahita revealed she did not think she would ever learn to read. Their lives, their joys and their fears occupied them utterly; mercifully, they could barely glimpse the pains and pleasures of the adults around them. Meanwhile, I felt oddly distant from the events of my life, no matter how much pain they were causing me.

I was in a fog of disbelief and at certain moments I would split in two, my one half leaning back and observing as my other half gave in to tears. It was only on the second day I realized that, if this was actually happening, I could at least call Becky.

"He's what?"

"Having an affair."

"With who?"

"Well, you may know her. One of his grad students."

"Oh, not his research student! Jeesus, Sharon. Not our Al. I thought we could trust him."

"Apparently not."

On the other end of the phone, Becky sighed deeply and made the little clicking sound she does when the world has disappointed her. She has a sunny, optimistic view of things, so the world, a place of darkness and pessimism, often disappoints her. She never says so, never likes to utter a judgment of anything or anybody, so she just clicks her tongue. She must be the most patient and forgiving person I know, always giving everybody the benefit of the doubt. So very different from me.

Becky has been my closest friend throughout my marriage. I met her in grad school when she was the newest hire in Al's department, imported from the States to improve the gender balance and teach American lit. She is small, red-headed and soft-spoken; a peaceable character who others rely on and often underestimate. She is the kind of person who is always getting praised for bringing cookies to meetings instead of her breakthrough work on Nathaniel Hawthorne's guilt complex. As the department grew fonder and fonder of her committee work, the chair seemed to forget very quickly they had hired her because she was the most promising English Ph.D. in her year at Berkeley. I had lectured her on her professional strategies often, but she just shrugged and said, "I like making cookies." It was hypocritical of me anyway, since I relied on her too, if not for her baking then for talking me down and balancing me out. This phone call was just the first of many filled with my lamentations and her words of comfort.

"How old is Al now? Forty-five?"

"Yeah. Forty-five."

"And she must be twenty-six or twenty-seven. Men are such clichés." She paused, then added, "It'll blow over."

"Do you think so?"

"It's not going to last. She'll make him miserable."

"Right now he's making me miserable."

"She'll start to push; he'll get panicky and cut and run."

"Maybe she is already pushing. He chose to tell me about it . . . He's not trying to hide it. I think he's going to leave."

"What about the girls? He's not going to leave the girls."

"I don't know. I don't think he has even thought about the girls."

"Well, he will. He'll think about leaving, moving in with a twenty-five-year-old and then he'll realize what it might mean to the girls and he'll go buy a sports car instead."

He didn't buy a sports car and he did leave home, despite his daughters' tears. But then he came back. What choice did he have under the circumstances?

The Dickens Bicentenary Serial: Chapter 1
Staplehurst, Kent. June 9, 1865

Nelly was looking down at her skirt when the accident
happened.

She had been gazing out the window, the way one does
on trains, watching the gentle Kentish countryside unfold.

And then she had looked back at Charles with a quick,
small glance of intimacy that expressed both an enduring
bond—for good or for ill, she would not have been there
without him—and a fleeting anxiety over their impending
separation. Another hour or so and they would reach
Charing Cross and they would be off in their own directions. She would never have dared tell him that, in their
early days together, if their bags were light, her mother
would sometimes simply pocket the fare for the hackney
that he gave them and add it to the housekeeping while
they squeezed onto an omnibus. But now they travelled like
grand ladies, with hat boxes and trunks, and would require
one of the four-wheeled coaches that would be waiting

outside the station to transport them in style. Charles would tell an attendant on the platform that he believed the ladies in carriage five required the services of a porter before he slipped into the crowd, leaving them to find their own way to their lodgings. Once there, they would make do with an egg for supper and take to their beds early. They led a different life when they were not with him.

But for the moment they were with him. Nelly was wearing a day dress that had been bought on the Rue de la Paix and could not stop admiring the sheen of the fabric, a pale blue silk. It was an utterly inappropriate thing to be wearing on a railway journey, with all the soot and the grime in the carriages. Her mother had said as much when she appeared at breakfast that morning before they left for the station. But the dress was new and Worth was the latest thing, and Charles had said, "A beautiful dress for a beautiful girl" as he bought it. Nelly had felt thankful to still be a girl, and she wanted Charles, when he said goodbye that day, to remember her that way.

There had been a time when she would never have imagined owning a dress from Paris. Her sisters, perhaps. More talented than she; more forceful, certain to be leading ladies on the West End someday, with fame, fortune and Paris gowns to follow. She had dreamed of it for them, even if it had not come to pass, but she never imagined it for herself. In truth, after the events of the past year, she did not know what to imagine for herself and preferred on the whole not to think of it. This day she simply concentrated on the joy of wearing a beautiful dress; it must mean a fresh start, and at that moment she was looking down at it with some kind of thankfulness. And so the crash, the horrible lurching, the ghastly backward tugging and all the hard metallic sounds around them and the cries of horror and despair became forever associated in Nelly's mind with the ripple of the folds in a piece of powder blue silk.

It began with a noise, a persistent whistle, raising the alarm. There was something panicky about the way it was repeated on a higher and higher note, but it was only in retrospect that they read it as a warning of what lay ahead. At the time it just sounded like the engineer's whistle calling to the brakeman and indeed the train began to brake, strongly at first and then violently, with the screeching of metal on metal and, as they looked up at one another in surprise, the train began to lurch from side to side.

Nelly screamed, and clung to Charles, sitting on the seat beside her. They had the carriage, all six seats, to themselves—Charles always arranged this privacy for them—and her mother, discreet as ever, had been sitting across from them and in the far corner, facing the engine. As the train started shifting, her expression of concern changed to horror and she now flung herself across the narrow space between the two rows of seats and into

Charles's arms. So, there the trio clustered, with the gentle-man sandwiched between two hoop skirts, his linen suit pressing against blue silk on one side and a sensible purple muslin on the other, all three of them clinging to one another as the train seemed to settle briefly back into a regular forward motion before suddenly there was the most horrible grinding and screeching, like the braking but worse. They could hear cries from other passengers in the compartments on either side of them, but these were soon drowned out by a ferocious series of crashing sounds, one after another, as though some giant were striding through a warehouse full of wooden crates, knocking down towers of them as he went. But this awful noise was not the worst of it. It was the sensation that accompanied it, that the passengers were being pulled backwards, jerked back down the track. Later they would say to one another, when trying to remember the exact order of things, "It all happened so fast," and yet that moment also unfolded appallingly slowly, the three passengers sitting there in horror, wonder-ing how far the carriage would slip before it stopped.

Suddenly, they were falling, all three flung from their seats to the floor as the other side of the compartment collapsed down in front them. Nelly tried to stop her fall with her hand but could feel something sharp cutting into it while Charles's larger body fell heavily against hers. And then, with one final crash, it all stopped.

They sat up and found themselves clutching one another on the floor of the carriage, tumbled together in one corner like gumdrops at the bottom of a paper bag. The seats they had occupied were now several feet higher than the ones across from them: the crash had left the compartment at a forty-five-degree angle, and as the immediate shock passed, Nelly became aware not only that her hand was bleeding profusely but also that their carriage kept shifting slightly, as though trying to settle into its improbable new position.

Outside, there were voices, some yelling instructions and demands, others simply calling for help, but in the compartment it was oddly silent as the three passengers waited for the movement to stop. Charles seemed to realize their predicament first. He turned to his older companion. "Are you hurt, Mrs. Ternan?"

"No," she replied. "I think I am fine. I'll just see if I can stand . . ."

"I wouldn't do that. Stay down and try to move as little as possible. We don't want the carriage to fall any farther."

"Nelly's bleeding," she said, noticing her daughter's hand for the first time.

"It's all right. I've just cut myself. There's broken glass."

Charles pulled his handkerchief out of his breast pocket and wrapped it around her hand and then, very gingerly, sat up high enough to raise his head above the window. He looked about in both directions.

"I think I can climb down here," he said. "The embankment looks to be within reach. I'll see if I can jump down and get help."

He turned the handle of the compartment door, pushing it outwards and up into the air, and then carefully crawled into the opening and peered down.

"Should be able to manage it," he said as he began to swing his legs into position and attempt to shimmy himself up and out the opening without making any sudden movements. He was in his fifties now—only a few years ago Nelly could not have imagined such an age as anything but decrepitude, but today she recognized it as the prime of mature life—and he was still athletic, sprightly when he needed to be. He seemed to have found firm footing beneath him for he slipped himself down from his perch and, as his head disappeared from view, they could hear the thud of his feet landing on the ground.

"Are you all right, sir?" Amid all the other noise, the voice that greeted him sounded close at hand. "Why, I know you . . ."

"Do you now?" Charles's response was almost jaunty.

Inside the carriage, Nelly froze.

"Sure I do. It's Mr. Dickens."

And it was then that Nelly knew they were sunk.

Dickens wasn't really my thing. That was Al's subject area. He was the big man in comp lit, the expert on Dickens' reading of *The Thousand and One Nights*, the prof whose devastating combination of an olive complexion, a Persian surname and a slight English accent—picked up when he changed planes at Heathrow en route from Tehran to Montreal aged thirteen, I guess—attracted a bevy of admiring under-graduates, girls with long tresses who had thought they might like to do a master's thesis on Jane Austen until they met him. But people often assume you share your spouse's interests.

The Dickens serial was first proposed to me at a Christmas party. In retrospect, I wondered if the whole thing had been a set-up, the party organized so the pub-lisher could suggest his project in circumstances where it would be difficult for me to refuse. At the time, how-ever, I just thought Frank Randle was trying to be kind.

He is the book editor at *The Telegram*, and I write reviews for him from time to time.

I gave up academia and all pretense of a serious interest in Dickens a decade ago; I wrote my first novel, a silly little thing about a girl obsessed with Jane Austen, and when a publisher took it on, I quickly abandoned scholarship. Without anything else to do and a promising advance, I managed to produce a second one in two years. It was published straight to the international best-seller lists a few months before the twins were born. Public taste is always something of a mystery to me—perhaps readers liked the happy ending and the fact I kept it short—but the sight of me on the daytime talk shows, eight months pregnant and promoting yet another hit, certainly contributed to the notion women can have it all. I was able to hire a nanny and returned to writing before the girls were three months old. I was soon making more money than a comp lit prof, much to Al's annoyance, I suspect, although he always said he was proud of me. His colleagues at the university, on the other hand, found it difficult to hide their contempt. My books aren't romances per se; they don't even necessarily feature happy endings any more, they just conclude with hopeful moments that allow the reader to decide whether widows have the strength to go on or divorced dads find love for a second time.

Frank, meanwhile, assigns me impenetrable literary experiments about which I dutifully rave or sexually explicit novels penned by writers covered in tattoos that I defend against anticipated slights. I get to prove my intellectual credentials and he gets to parade my name through his pages. It's a mutually beneficial arrangement.

That was not, however, why he had invited me to a drinks party in the cramped Victorian he shares with two cats and thousands of books. It was a rare bit of entertaining on his part and I assumed I was there because he felt sorry for me. That had made me all the more determined to go, determined that I was going to feel well enough on the night, that I could do something perfectly normal, maybe even enjoy myself. Al was convinced that it would only be unnecessarily exhausting, but when he failed to dissuade me, he decided he had better come along too, chauffeur me there and lend support. That was fine; I'd put a brave face on the whole situation, show everybody I didn't need their pity on any score. My hair was just growing back; I had a little buzz cut that Al said looked sexy, which was just him trying to be nice. Every woman in the room knew I was too old for anything so radical and guessed the reason behind it if she did not already know the gossip. I was the woman whose husband came home only because she had breast cancer.

So there I was, parked in the living room with some other authors whom I didn't recognize, trying to remember to nurse the soda water I had been reduced to, only so that

I didn't need to run off to the bathroom, and pretending I had read some article in *The New Yorker* although Al had let our subscription lapse after he moved out and we had never got around to renewing it. We were debating whether Alice Munro might be overrated. It was the literary crowd behaving as though it was still the 1990s, as though nobody had invented the Kindle, as though nobody need remember the name of that woman who self-published a book about vampires and got it on *The New York Times* best-seller list, as though every citizen in the land still had half a pound of newsprint landing on the doorstep with a satisfying thud every morning. I was trying to think of something knowing to say when a big, square man with a flattened face that made him look a bit like a bull terrier approached the group.

"Sharon . . . Great to see you."

I hadn't a clue who he was, but Frank now appeared helpfully at my elbow.

"Sharon, you remember Bob Stanek, our publisher."

"And a huge admirer of your work . . ."

I couldn't imagine *The Telegram*'s publisher ever reading my work; usually men like him are more honest and tell me their wives are fans.

But he persisted and was surprisingly convincing. We had a discussion of the plot of my last book—he seemed to remember it a lot more clearly than I did—before he eventually came around to the subject of Dickens. Turned out he was an aficionado. He had read every one of the novels. Even the ones nobody reads, like *Barnaby Rudge* and *Our Mutual Friend*. He was one of those hard-nosed businessmen intent on proving to you they have a literary side or artistic sensibilities. The type who are Sunday painters and wish to discuss Tolstoy. I kept trying to shake him off, saying, "You must talk to my husband; I think he's in the kitchen," and looking about for Al, who had not reappeared since he'd gone off to refill his wineglass. Frankly, I hear quite enough about Dickens at home, but Stanek wasn't taking the hint and burbled away until he came up with a brain wave—or made his pitch, depending on how suspicious I want to be. The next year would be 2012. The bicentenary of the novelist's birth. Dickens wrote serials. All of the novels originally appeared as serials. His genius was in somehow maintaining narrative integrity in something written in instalments. Newspapers need new ideas. So, a popular novelist, the Dickens of her day— I tried hard to compose my face into the correct expression of outraged modesty at this bit of sycophancy— writes a serial for the newspaper. A few thousand words a week, say twenty or thirty weeks' worth of instalments. Am I up to the challenge?

"Um, I'll think about it," I mumbled, intrigued but not sure what to make of the proposal. And just then Al came into sight, raising a "Do you want to go home now?" eyebrow at me from across the room, and we left soon after.

We didn't talk much in the car. I told Al I had met *The Telegram*'s publisher, and he repeated the kitchen's assessment of the newspaper's chances of surviving beyond 2020. He was right: standing was tiring; talking was tiring. We hadn't stayed much more than an hour and I was exhausted. But it was a good tired; I was pleased with myself and just a little bit excited. I had gone to a party, and someone wanted me to write something.

When we got home, the girls were still up, an hour past their bedtime, but I sympathized with the babysitter, a teenager from across the street. Their young memories of our six-month separation might be fading, but their father had been back in the house less than a year and I had been sick through most of that. We tried hard, shelving our differences to get our fragile family through the days, but there must have been an undercurrent of instability all the time; they weren't going to nod off to sleep unless both parents were safely accounted for.

I kissed them and Al sat with them while I got ready for bed but I found I was now too stimulated to sleep. It was work I knew I could do. Immediate. Contained. When Al came to bed, I told him about Stanek's suggestion.

"You aren't thinking of accepting? It's way too soon."

"Lots of people go back to work as soon as they're clear of chemo."

"You have to be careful. You don't want to wear yourself out."

"I'm tired of being sick. I want to do something."

The serial sounded a whole lot better than vomiting up breakfast two days out of seven, so I agreed.

The Dickens Bicentenary Serial: Chapter 2
Staplehurst, Kent. June 9, 1865

"I'm sure he will be back soon, dear. He's probably help-ing other passengers." Mrs. Ternan tried to sound com-forting but stating their predicament only made Nelly feel worse. Her hand, which she had barely noticed in the first moments after the crash, was throbbing badly and an alarming amount of blood was still seeping through Charles's now sodden handkerchief. It had been a quarter-hour since he had left to get help; soon after he had disap-peared from view, she had checked the little pocket watch he had given her the Christmas before last, and then checked it again, and again. They could hear all kinds of noise outside, shouts and moans, the sound of which convinced them they were much better off than some. They debated whether perhaps they should clamber up to the door in their turn; Mrs. Ternan pointed out that even if they could not climb down from the carriage in their skirts, at least they could call and get someone's attention.

But Nelly forestalled her; Charles would want us to wait, she said. Neither said out loud what they were both thinking: the novelist would mainly want them not to draw attention to themselves as his travelling companions.

Nelly shifted her weight a bit to lift her hand, causing the carriage to move slightly as she did so. She winced, and her mother now noticed how stained the handkerchief had become.

"Let me look at it, dear."

"It's fine."

"It's not fine. It's still bleeding." Mrs. Ternan leant over to grasp her daughter's hand. Nelly tried to draw it away and this time, with her sudden movement, the carriage swayed perceptibly. They both gasped but Mrs. Ternan did not let go.

"Nelly. You need a better bandage. Maybe I could use my petticoat."

"No, Mother. Don't. You'll spoil it."

"It's a petticoat, dear. We can always get another. I don't suppose I am going to be able to reach my sewing scissors. Where's my dressing case?"

Mrs. Ternan looked about the jumble of bags in the carriage and spied her dressing case up on the luggage rack, wedged in between two other cases in one corner. Thankfully most of their belongings had been on the rack above her head in what was now the lower side of the compartment so the bags had been forced back on themselves rather than tumbling on top of them as they landed on the floor. It was mainly their hat boxes that lay about them; Nelly would not trust her new bonnets to the luggage van where their trunks were stored, so the hat boxes had travelled with them.

"I'm just going to have to rip it. Let's see if there isn't a seam loose," said Mrs. Ternan as she lifted her skirts and began to examine her petticoat. And it was at this awkward moment that they heard various sounds outside the window and saw a hand reaching up to rap on the glass.

"Ladies? Are you all right?" a male voice called through the door.

"Yes," Mrs. Ternan called back, hurriedly rearranging her skirts, "but my daughter's hand is cut."

"Right. We'll get you out of there. Are there two of you?"

"Yes."

"I found 'em, Dan," the voice now called back to someone else. "Ladies, if I may, I will need you to try to open the door for me. I can't quite reach the handle. Can you do that?"

"Yes. We'll try to open it."

"I'll just stand back then."

Mrs. Ternan now inched her way over to the door, reached up to the handle positioned well above her head and opened it up into the void as Charles had done before. There was a bit of puffing and panting and finally the man's head and torso appeared at the floor of the doorway. "Ladies," he said, "we heard you might be needing a hand down."

He helped Mrs. Ternan down first but their progress was slow. Clambering up to the ledge in her crinoline and getting her legs over without exposing her underthings was a tricky business and made the carriage shift alarmingly "Gently does it, gently . . ." their rescuer kept saying. He was evidently a rail engineer or perhaps a platelayer, since his blue overalls were tolerably clean. Mrs. Ternan finally succeeded in getting herself modestly seated on what was the bottom of the doorway into their compartment. Steeply angled upwards by the position in which the carriage had settled and without a station platform beneath it, it was elevated well above the ground and the man could hardly be expected to lift her by her waist like a girl. As Mrs. Ternan sat there, waiting to negotiate her descent—Nelly could not see how far a jump she had to take and it was only when her turn came that she realized the engineer had reached them by standing on several wooden crates that had been dragged into place—she looked back over her shoulder and called out to her daughter.

"Nelly, my dressing case!"

Nelly looked at the precious dressing case, still sandwiched up on the luggage rack.

"I can't safely reach it, Mother. You'll have to wait."

"Don't worry, miss. We will come back for all the baggage," the engineer reassured her, but later, when she saw what awaited them outside, she came to doubt anyone would care much about the fate of a dressing case or hat box. Still, her mother's concern brought her back to the practicalities of the moment, awakening her to something other than her throbbing hand and soaked bandage. She looked at her hat boxes lying on the floor and she looked up again at the rack where the dressing case was stuck. The bag on the outside of it was her own dressing case, smaller than her mother's, a dainty ostrich-skin cube that Charles had given her for her birthday the winter before last, at a moment in their relationship when, if she were honest with herself, he had bestowed on her so many gold trinkets that the idea of yet another held little appeal. But it was the bag on the other side that was important: the largest of the three, it was wedged in against the far wall of the compartment. It was Charles's battered old grip, a large rectangle of solid brown leather sitting upright on the luggage rack. And inside it, there was the manuscript, a good five dozen pages written in his flowing Italic hand that comprised the next two months' instalments of the latest serial, the first due at the printer's the following week. As her mother and the engineer began to discuss how it was the older woman would make her descent down to the ground, Nelly, carefully, gingerly, trying ever so hard not to move the carriage any farther, stood up and began to climb onto the seat that she and Charles had been sharing on the train.

She got onto it and managed to stand, but as she began to reach toward the luggage rack she realized she only had one hand at her disposal to pull down the heavy bag. She looked back; her mother was still in sight but absorbed by the task of descending into the arms of her rescuer, offering loud encouragement from below. Looking above her head, Nelly stretched up and grasped the handles, which were almost out of reach. She managed to grip them firmly enough to tip the bag onto its side, pushing the two dressing cases out of its way, but she certainly did not have the power in one hand to bear its weight as she swung it down off the rack. Standing back, she took a breath, tensed the muscles beneath her corset and tugged. The bag budged a little. She tugged again and again, and finally edged it to the lip of the rack. She tugged one last time, it teetered and, as she stepped aside, it fell with a thud that coincided with Mrs. Ternan's leap toward the embankment. Nelly clambered down and, with one hand, hauled the bag toward the door.

Soon enough a friendly face reappeared there.

"I can just lift you down, miss, if you'll permit the familiarity," the engineer volunteered. "I warn you, the ground's soft underfoot. You'll get your shoes muddy, I'm afraid, but there's not much for it."

"I don't care about the shoes, but I have a bag with me," Nelly replied. "Can I perhaps just throw it down ahead of me?"

"Just pass it to me, miss, I'll take it," he replied.

"Thank you. My mother and I are much obliged to you."

"Not at all, miss. Least anyone can do for you after what has happened. I hope your mother is not too alarmed."

"No. She is quite calm, thank you."

It was after she had passed over the bag and began to settle herself on the ledge provided by the bottom of the compartment door that the engineer noticed her bloody bandage.

"Why, you are hurt, miss. I had not realized."

"It's all right. I just cut myself on some glass. I only need a fresh bandage."

"We will get you a doctor soon as we can, miss. There are poor souls who are in worse need, I'll tell you true enough, but we can't leave you to bleed."

Nelly and her rescuer both braced themselves and he simply lifted her down to the crate he was standing on and from there to the ground. It was soft and muddy, as the engineer had warned; Nelly found herself standing in what seemed like a marsh area, a good ten feet below the track.

As soon as she was clear of the carriage she began to recognize just how lucky they had been. The front of the train stood on the rail ahead as though nothing had happened but the back carriages had failed to cross a low viaduct that covered the width of the wetland and lay in a shambles in the low ground in which Nelly now found herself standing. The carriage she had just climbed from was the last to have remained on the bridge but dangled at a precipitous angle, which explained the discomfiting swaying they had felt.

"If you just move this way, miss. We are trying to lay some boards." The engineer indicated a few planks that had been laid so they could reach the far side of low land, where the last cars of the train still stood on the rail.

"What happened?" Nelly asked, pausing to puzzle out the derailment as she stepped onto the planks ahead of him.

"We were working on the track, miss. Had a section right out midway through the viaduct there."

"So the train didn't clear it? Why didn't someone warn the engineer?"

"Oh, we would have, miss, in the usual manner of things, we would have had the missing section all back in place and shipshape. But we didn't expect the Channel train until four o'clock."

"But I don't think our train was early. We left Folkestone about five minutes late . . ."

"I don't rightly know, miss." His voice became strained now as he tried to justify the unthinkable. "We weren't expecting the train, that's all." He stopped there and then said more firmly, "I'll carry this across for you, if you go ahead. Your mother is just on the other side." He shepherded her over to a drier area that Mrs. Ternan had already reached on the far side of the viaduct. Nelly thanked him, and taking the precious leather bag, she stumbled up the embankment.

When I first started chemo, Al or Becky came with me and sat and waited while the nurses dripped the magic poison into my veins. But with the girls to be picked up from school and housework and cooking to be done, it soon seemed stupid to have another adult taking several hours off work to be there. It was more useful to have Becky do our groceries than come to my medical appointments. By my third cycle, Al was dropping me off at the hospital's front door and I was taking a cab home. For my three-month checkup, I took the subway for the first time in almost a year. I was rather proud of that, another milestone, like Frank's party. There was a huge Christmas tree in the hospital's atrium, sparkling with oversized silver balls; the doctor said, "That all looks fine," and I stopped on the way home to pick up a gift I wanted for the girls. It was a good day.

Al hurried into the front hall as soon as I came through the door.

"Where were you? I thought you'd be home by now."

"I stopped to do some shopping."

"So?"

"So far, so good."

"All good?"

"Yup, all good. That's what she said."

He folded me into his arms, hugging me tight, but after a moment I pulled back to look at his face. He was smiling. He looked relieved and happy. What else did I expect? It's not that I thought he wanted me dead or anything; on the contrary, he may have wanted me to get better really fast. Once or twice in the first months after he came home, the phone rang and someone hung up when I answered. Maybe it was just a wrong number. I mean, if she was calling, surely she'd just call his cell. But I got a horrible little reminder of what it felt like when he first told me of her existence, the twisting doubt at every turn, the gut-wrenching assumption about every unexplained gap in his schedule; the ugly temptation to pick his phone up off the kitchen counter and read an incoming text. We had agreed to set this stuff aside, concentrate on my getting better. Of course, I asked him about her. Once, he said, "She understands," which wasn't very encouraging, and another time he said, "It doesn't matter. You don't need to worry about it," which sounded better, but mainly I had been too sick and tired to pursue it any further. It's been a year since he came home, but I can't help wondering if she's still waiting for him. If I get better, will he leave?

"We should go out to celebrate tomorrow night, get a babysitter," he said.

"We'll never get one at this time of year. And I'm busy tomorrow; remember, I asked Frank for a drink. I want to strategize about the serial."

At that Al just raised an eyebrow.

"A good Christmas. That will be our celebration," I promised.

Despite the approaching holidays, there was a whiff of fear in the newsroom when I dropped by to meet Frank the following day: it took me a second to recognize it, but it was a familiar odour. The chemo clinic smelled of it too. There, everybody was slow and shuffling, almost languid in their pace but terrified nonetheless. *The Telegram*, on the other hand, seemed to survive in an atmosphere of barely controlled panic; the place was full of scurrying bodies and bent heads, all the editors and reporters engaged in a desperate busyness that suggested they were bailing the *Titanic* rather than simply putting out tomorrow's paper. In the brew pub across the street, where Frank and some of his cohort often go for a beer, the gossips reported that subscriptions were in free fall; advertising was down and traffic to the website where readers scarf up the content for free was not beginning to make up the difference. Stanek, like some tyrant who can't believe that nature won't bend to his will and so blames his underlings for famine and floods, had just fired a perfectly respectable editor and replaced him with some roving social media executive who promised to turn everything around. One of Frank's witty buddies said the guy was just working in newspapers the way hipsters affect porkpie hats. It's retro and fun and hey, the next big thing should be on its way soon.

They continued in this bitter vein for some time and it took me a while to get Frank on his own.

"You know about this Dickens serial idea?"

"Emm."

"If the publisher is so keen on new media, why am I being commissioned to revive a nineteenth-century form? Nobody publishes fiction in newspapers any more. Do you think people will read it?"

"I'm not sure people read newspapers period, so why not give it a try?" he asked. "Stanek is an eccentric; marking the Dickens bicentenary is a pet project of his. And the serial is counter-intuitive; he likes that aspect. On the one hand, you've got one-hundred-and-forty-character blasts appearing on your phone every second; on the other, wait a week to run out to the good old newsstand and buy the next gripping two-thousand-word instalment."

"I'm not sure it'll work," I said.

"Then why did you agree?"

"I don't have anything else on the go, and I like the idea of something so contained and written to such a tight deadline. I can be pretty sure I'll live to see it through."

Frank swallowed and said nothing. People don't want to hear that you might not get better; they tell you there are all sorts of fabulous treatments these days, as though maybe you didn't know that already. I have an aggressive triple-negative breast cancer, triple-negative because it lacks all three of the common receptors they target with those nifty new drug treatments. The doctors never say much about the prognosis and on that night I was just trying to hold on to the previous day's optimism. I quickly filled the awkward pause.

"You guys are offering me pretty good money. And it's a flat fee. You pay me whether the readers buy it or not."

"Yes. But you'll care how it does . . ."

"That's true. I was really hoping you would edit it, but some assistant called me and set up a meeting with the weekend editor. We are supposed to have lunch after the holidays. What's he like?"

"Jonathan Torres? Decent-enough guy once you get to know him. You'll figure him out. You're going to love the challenge. Publishing fiction weekly, just like Dickens used to. I bet you've already got something mapped out."

I just smiled; it had been only two weeks since Frank's party but by this point I was already deep into research on the Staplehurst railway crash. "I should get home to the girls. Guess you'll see me in print."

———

In my book, "decent-enough guy once you get to know him" is code for unprepossessing and not too bright but harmless. On meeting Jonathan Torres two days into the new year, I was not at all sure, however, that the man was harmless. He is tall and fit looking with curly black hair and would be good looking were it not for rather thick glasses that seem to displace his gaze by a few inches so that it is almost impossible to make natural eye contact with him. From the start he took a hearty tone with me that was audibly false. He came across as simultaneously awkward and smarmy. How appropriate, I thought, he's a Uriah Heep. You could almost imagine him rubbing his hands together.

Once we had shrugged off our heavy winter coats and settled ourselves in the cheerful French restaurant that offers about the best food you can get within walking distance of *The Telegram*, he read the menu quickly, picked out a steak, let me order a salad, and made a sound in his throat to indicate business will now begin.

"Fabulous project the publisher's got you working on," he said. "Great idea. Love it. Do you know what you are going to write? I mean, I know you know what you are going to write. You're a novelist, an awesome writer. Love your stuff. I haven't read that much but what I have . . . I mean, the publisher loves your stuff and you've done this before obviously. Not quite in this form but I am sure you have ideas; I just mean . . . Well, do you have the plot worked out? We don't want you to get going and then not know . . . Well, I guess novelists always know what their ending is . . ."

I listened as he tied himself in knots. He seemed to feel I was important enough that I had to be flattered but probably not good enough to actually do the job. I wondered if his world was full of people who were more powerful than talented. Or perhaps power was the only coin he recognized.

"Yes. I have an idea, and a plot."

"Great." He sounded very relieved. "Can I ask what it is?"

"I thought since we are reviving a nineteenth-century form that I would set the story in the nineteenth century."

"Love it. A Victorian story. Sounds good."

The food arrived and we ate for a bit before he seemed to realize he had not got what he wanted.

"So, you say a Victorian story."

"No, you said that actually."

"But you did say that it would be set in the nine-teenth century? You just said that."

"Yes. Nineteenth-century England, so that's Victorian. And France too. There will be a few scenes in France."

"Great. So, France and England in the nineteenth century. So, um, what's going to happen?"

I took pity on him finally.

"Well, it's the Dickens bicentenary; the story will be one from Dickens' own life."

"From his life?"

"Yes."

"You mean the story of his life, an autobiography."

"No, not really a biography," I said, trying to hide any note of condescension as I corrected him. "Just an episode from his life. An episode in which he played a role, but he's not the protagonist."

"So Dickens appears as a character, but he is not the main character?"

"That's right. It will be about people around him."

"Good. Sounds great. Love it. Can you tell me a bit more?"

"Why don't you wait until you read it."

"Emmm . . . Okay. I know Bob settled the fee with your agent. He told me you'd agreed to a minimum of fifteen instalments."

"Yes, at least. I think it may take me more like twenty. I tend to underestimate how long anything is going to be, but once we get started, I can give you a final count."

"You'll need to start soon, won't you?" He sounded alarmed. "We were hoping to begin publishing before the end of the month. I mean, it's 2012 now."

"Don't worry. We'll be fine. I've already written two instalments. I am just beginning a third."

The Dickens Bicentenary Serial: Chapter 3
Staplehurst, Kent. June 9, 1865

They sat on a grassy bank for several hours before another train was finally commandeered to take them in to London. In other circumstances it might have seemed a pleasant-enough spot to wait, a sunny bank overlooking a marsh-like riverbed alive with bird calls and butterflies on a June day, but their vigil felt only like a second nightmare after the horror of the accident itself. Half the train had fallen from the track into the low-lying land; behind their carriage, a jumble of others lay in a broken heap that looked as though some petulant child had smashed its train set. Various men, some railway employees, some passengers apparently, were busy extracting people, and the results had made a battlefield of the low land. Bodies, it was not clear whether dead or alive, lay on wooden planks that had been turned into makeshift stretchers. Cries of help could be heard from the tangle of metal and moans of pain from those who had been brought outside. Nelly noticed one man lying on the ground bleeding from a gash that ran the entire length of an exposed calf and another figure, its clothes so ripped and its face and head so covered in blood she was not sure whether it was a man or a woman. "Don't look, Nelly; please, don't look," her mother whispered urgently, tugging at her arm—but try as she might to look away at the sky or the ground, she found she could not stop her eyes from returning to the scene.

So, she watched the men, at a distance of perhaps one hundred yards, as they busied themselves about the wreck like ants on an anthill, bringing up planks, lifting out bodies, in some instances even prying bits of twisted metal out of the way of their efforts. After perhaps half an hour of this, she noticed a woman lying on the ground with a man on his knees beside her—Nelly was not sure how long this couple had been there; perhaps the woman had been freshly removed from the wreck during one of the moments when Nelly had succeeded in following her mother's example and had averted her eyes. The man seemed to be talking to her, comforting her, and as he looked up for a moment from this task, she recognized Charles. He stayed with the woman for several moments but then dropped her hand, got up slowly and moved on, walking amid the other passengers and stopping again to offer help. She was puzzled by him leaving the stricken woman, even if there were many others in need. And then as the motionless body continued to lie there, it occurred to Nelly that perhaps the woman had just died in Charles's arms.

Now that Nelly had noticed him, she could spot him easily, his trim figure moving about in the wreckage helping where he could.

Her mother, noticing her silent concentration, looked up from her skirt and followed her daughter's eyes.

"There's Charles," she said quietly.

"Yes."

"Helping . . ."

"Yes."

They were one of many little clusters of survivors too stunned or too injured to help, merely watching as more and more hands gathered around the train. Locals from the village and surrounding farms began to arrive, the men carrying boards, shovels and crowbars with which they clawed at the wreckage, the women offering bandages and food. One harried doctor, identifiable by his bag, moved among those lying around the wreck while an efficient sort, perhaps a clergyman's wife or a teacher, tended to those on the bank. She removed the blood-soaked handkerchief from Nelly's hand and wrapped it very firmly. The bleeding had slowed so that the wound was now visible and Nelly could see a deep, ugly gash.

"You'll want to get that looked at when you get to London, my dear," the woman suggested.

"But when will we get to London?" Nelly protested.

"They are bringing up another train, I think. Shouldn't be too long."

But it was long. Later, a young woman approached them shyly, a farm girl in a stained skirt with a basket over her arm.

"Would you like some milk, miss, and some bread? And the old lady too?" Nelly and her mother gratefully accepted the simple food, both drinking straight out of the earthenware jug before handing it back to the girl.

Finally, the new train did arrive, shunting itself very slowly up to the front of the wreck. Men began unloading bags from the cars that still stood on the track to transfer them to the new train, and a conductor approached the bank where they sat and directed them back across the makeshift boardwalk. Nelly had long since lost sight of Charles, but as they made their way to the train, she saw him again, hurrying toward the dangling carriage that had been theirs. He clambered up onto the crates that still stood there from their own rescue before an official reached him and stopped him. She could not hear what was said but he was arguing with the man, gesturing toward the carriage. She supposed the sight of baggage being removed from other cars had awakened him to the fate of his own. She stopped herself from crying out to him but instead hurried in his direction, carrying his bag in her good hand, willing him to look up. She was about fifty feet away from him when he did see her, stopping in mid argument as he stared across the space between them.

He looked at her with anguish in his face but made no move toward her. She looked down at the bag she was carrying to draw his eyes to it. He gave her but the slightest nod of recognition. It was such a small look that passed between them, neither the railway official, relieved to see he no longer had to argue with the gentleman who had been insisting on climbing back into a dangerously positioned carriage, nor the other passengers now all moving back toward the track would have realized that the gentleman and the young lady even knew each other. Charles turned without a word. She bit her lip and looked down at her dress. The skirt was badly stained with blood and soot and torn in several places while the hem, which she had caught on the ledge climbing out of the compartment, dangled beneath it. Her fresh start hung in tattered silk around her. She looked up in time to see Charles's back as he moved slowly toward the head of the train and she wondered now at the price she had paid for Paris gowns.

f each of us is the protagonist of his or her own story, then surely we must all graciously acknowledge that the hero dies in the end. But not at thirty-seven. With two school-aged daughters.

I'd like to say that the possibility of premature death has taught me to appreciate life more, filled it with days of smelling roses and sipping tea. The truth is the treatments make you so sick and exhausted, you don't have the energy to savour anything.

And then afterwards . . . afterwards . . . Well, I do try to value what I have. Sometimes I do this mental exercise, this little game to remind myself how lucky I am. I pick the happiest day of my life. I guess a lot of women might still say that their wedding day was the happiest. Ours was a small affair at Toronto's city hall followed by dinner with our two families who did their best to conceal their mutual distrust. I remember it mainly as anxious.

The night the twins were born stands out, but more

for drama than joy: the rush to the hospital; the hours of pain; the excitement of their arrival—and then the aching pleasure of seeing those little scrunched-up faces and tiny hands and knowing they were mine. But it was a feeling so rapidly displaced by the logistics of sleeping, nursing and diapering, a highly practical project made to feel oddly abstract by the time that fog enveloped it, that neither the word *day* nor the word *happy* really seem to apply.

I think of ordinary days instead. I see images of my family in my mind's eye, and I remember an afternoon—the girls must have been about four—when we walked the Scarborough Bluffs.

Al and I were never outdoorsy. We had begun our courtship as earnest academics debating Dickens' use of narrative voice into the small hours. As I recall our first years together, any time not spent working was spent at the kitchen counter with a glass of wine or, better yet, in bed. I think that in the first place we shared—before the twins were born and we moved to our current house—there were a few pots of flowers on the porch. I suppose I must have bought them and put them there, but gardens, let alone parks, were something beyond our horizon.

The arrival of children forced us outside, walking the streets to soothe them to sleep or visiting the local playground with plastic spades and pails jammed into the bottom of the big double stroller. As their toddling legs grew longer and stronger, we explored farther afield.

On the weekends, the four of us began to walk down into the ravines near our house, dark, magical places where Al would marvel with the girls at every twig and every pebble. Perhaps it was because Al had not grown up in Canada that he became so intrigued by what seemed to me the most pedestrian of local species. Soon, he had taught the girls to name all the trees they saw: "That's a red maple" or "That's a spruce," a four-year-old would announce, to the surprise of any passersby in the vicinity. And I learned to welcome the treasures they busily collected from the ground and handed to me for safekeeping. I did put my foot down and ban sticks and stones from the house, so we kept what was soon an overflowing basket on the front porch, occasionally topping it off with a prized bird feather. I think it was my idea to explore geology. Al had often explained to the girls that the hill that we drove down any time we went to Daddy's office at the university or paid a visit to our friends Becky and David was the shoreline of a lake that had been there back in the days of the dinosaurs. I'm not sure the chronology of that is quite right, but they were excited by the idea that all of downtown Toronto used to be under water and that dinosaurs used to roam a shoreline located at the bottom of their backyard. Al began explaining glaciers and, wanting to be a sport and contribute to the project, I said, "If you want to see rocks, let's go to the Bluffs."

And so one day—I think it was spring; it was windy

and cold; I remember us all complaining about it—we bundled into the car and drove across town, out Kingston Road, and stopped at Bluffer's Park. I'd been there once before, dragged out there on a moonlit night by an enthusiastic boyfriend who wanted to show me the eroding cliffs that stretch eastwards along the Lake Ontario shore.

We played on the beach at the bottom of the cliffs, throwing pebbles into the lake and running along the sand, and then drove back up to the top to get the view. You cross a bit of parkland to reach the edge and Anahita set off at a run with Al right behind her, Goli struggling to keep up and me bringing up the rear. I remember seeing the three of them, strung out in front of me like three frames of a moving image: Anahita's small figure racing ahead, her long hair flying all over the place, and Al's slender back leaning forward, one arm outstretched as though to catch her, and Goli's compact little body chugging along in pursuit, legs churning like an old-fashioned egg beater. There were the three things dearest in the world to me, fanned out before my eyes like a gift, and I slowed my pace and fell back to admire them. Al, as though sensing the moment too, turned back to look and caught my eye over Goli's head. He did not call out or urge me to catch up, he just smiled at me. Al's smile is usually a small, conspiratorial thing that draws you seductively into his ambit, but this was the biggest, silliest grin I'd ever seen on his face, as though he too could not believe his good fortune.

I reached them as they stopped at a barrier with signs warning that the cliff edge was dangerous. Before I could protest, Al, who often scoffed at Canadians' obsession with public safety, was lifting the girls over the wire cable and clambering after them. Each of us grabbing a child's hand, we approached the edge and peered down the cliff face, the girls oohing and aahing at the sheer drop. It did feel unsafe, and the second they had glimpsed it, Al and I quickly backed up, pulling the children away, lest our most precious achievement fall into the void below.

I don't remember what happened on the drive home. Perhaps Al recalled springtime in his grandparents' garden in Tehran, as he did for us sometimes, or Anahita and Goli sang a song taught them by Ms. Batra, the kindergarten teacher they both adored. Or maybe there were tears because I vetoed ice cream on the grounds it would spoil supper.

Perhaps when we arrived home, Al and I prepared a nice meal and everyone remembered how to use their forks and knives. And after dinner, Al did bathtime and I did storytime and once the children were asleep, we found ourselves together in our adult bed with a few moments to spare.

Or maybe we were late and tired, and I was increasingly short-tempered and we ate takeout pizza straight from the box. And after dinner, Al mumbled something about end-of-term marking and spent the rest of the evening in his tiny office in the attic, ignoring a temper tantrum or two on the floor below.

Perhaps it was one of those family occasions when at least the adults managed to be their better selves, embracing life's simple pleasures with serenity and facing its many frustrations with patience, remembering that they loved and were loved in return.

Or maybe we were selfish, competitive and angry.

I don't recall the rest of the day. I just hold on to that image of the three of them running ahead of me through the grass, knowing that there I had achieved a peace that the happiest of my characters might have envied.

The Dickens Bicentenary Serial: Chapter 4
Doncaster, Yorkshire. September 20, 1857

Nelly could not think where Fanny and Maria had got to and here was Mr. Dickens, come all the way from London, and needing conversation.

"Shall I ring for some tea, Mr. Dickens? It's almost eleven. I'm sure my sisters will be here any moment," she said, trying gamely to play the role of the gracious hostess in the unprepossessing surroundings of the boarding house's front parlour. They had only arrived the day before yesterday and she was not at all sure that either the landlady or her maid of all work would respond to a bell, although there was a small brass one sitting on the mantel.

"There is no hurry, child. No great hurry. I suggested to your mother we might all drive into the country for a picnic lunch."

"That would be lovely. Such a beautiful day," she said, not indicating that her mother had already told her of this plan before she had hurried back to the theatre to see if the manager and, more importantly, his helpful wife might not join them and so provide a second chaperone for the girls. The previous evening, the manager had been effusively grateful when he had been introduced to the writer after the curtain, so the couple seemed likely to agree. Nelly already had her bonnet and gloves at the ready on the hall table.

"Oh, quite beautiful. Indeed." Mr. Dickens leaned back in his chair and smiled at her. She smiled back and pondered what to say next; this was just the sort of situation in which she relied on her older sisters to take the lead; Fanny was always so clever and Maria had got on famously with Mr. Dickens when they were performing his new play together in Manchester, and had clearly impressed him. Indeed, Nelly secretly suspected it was largely thanks to Maria's captivating talents that the great man had bothered to stop in Doncaster to watch them all perform at the Theatre Royal on his way south from a walking holiday in Cumbria.

For her own part, she had thoroughly enjoyed the performances in Manchester the previous month and found Mr. Dickens easy enough to talk to when there was theatre business to be done, the discussions of blocking and voice and lighting and costumes that she had known all of her life. Indeed, the whole experience had been joyful and friendly; she had only a minor role in the main event but did appear in the little farce that closed the evening in which Mr. Dickens himself played an old man ridiculously in love with his young ward. Nelly played the ward and found her co-star not the least bit grand, despite his fame; there was much chatting and easy laughter during rehearsals and after the performance. Now, however, that he appeared not as a colleague with work at hand but as a gentleman paying a courtesy call, she felt much less sure of herself.

"I hope you enjoyed last night's performance," she tried again.

He laughed.

"I enjoyed your performance."

"Oh, but Maria is really far more gifted than I. Her singing was so lovely; I do envy her her voice," Nelly said, trying to stick with the topic that she supposed interested him the most.

"Your sister is a remarkable performer, but I don't think you need envy her in any regard," he replied.

He sat there, saying nothing, smiling benignly at her. The silence lengthened, but it did not seem to bother him for he just kept smiling. Nelly was thinking hard about what to say next when her mother came into the room. "Oh, there you are," Mrs. Ternan said to Nelly with some annoyance. "I thought you had gone with your sisters." She then remembered herself. "Mr. Dickens. How do you do. So kind of you . . . "

"I didn't know where they were, Mother," Nelly replied over top of Mrs. Ternan's belated niceties.

"It's my fault, Mrs. Ternan," Mr. Dickens said, advancing to take her hand. "I sent her sisters off to the High Street to fetch us a picnic before Miss Ellen had appeared. You must forgive me; in my eagerness to depart on our excursion, I decided we should not waste any time."

Nelly felt caught out and wondered why he hadn't told her Fanny and Maria were off shopping but supposed she hadn't actually asked him.

"Well, no harm done," said Mrs. Ternan, reclaiming her composure. "Mr. and Mrs. Eliot have agreed to accompany us."

"Have they? How kind of them," Mr. Dickens replied.

"Very kind. Mr. Eliot knows the environs well and has suggested the best route to be taken to reach Conisbrough Castle."

"He will prove invaluable then. What a good thing that I have rented two carriages."

After some discussion, it was agreed that Mrs. Eliot would join Mr. Dickens, Nelly and Maria in one barouche while Mrs. Ternan and Fanny would sit with Mr. Eliot in the other. Nelly felt badly for Fanny that she was not to share the honour of the famous writer's company at such close quarters as her younger sisters, but she supposed her mother, who had been sent into a flurry of calculations and preparations by the suggestion of a drive into the country, was right and that it would not have been proper for the three girls to ride unaccompanied with Mr. Dickens. It was an impression confirmed when Mr. Eliot winked broadly at Mr. Dickens as he helped his wife up, saying, "You're a lucky devil, Dickens." At first, she thought he was jokingly boasting about the company of his own wife whose arm he was holding as he said these words, but then, to her shame, Nelly saw him nod knowingly in her own direction.

It was not that such a disagreeable remark shocked her; the theatres were filled with gentlemen who presumed and her mother was filled with useful advice about how best to deflect their little remarks or their unwelcome glances, but it did surprise her in Mr. Eliot, who had seemed so deferential to Mr. Dickens the previous evening. Now he all but elbowed him in the ribs as though the two men were old friends out on the town. Mrs. Eliot laughed raucously. Nelly blushed for them both, but as their carriage moved forward, Mr. Dickens talked so amiably about the Yorkshire countryside and so knowledgeably about the history of the ruined castle they were about to visit that the awkward moment quickly passed.

Two hours later, she found herself edging her way up the narrow spiral staircase of the castle's keep, glad she had worn stout shoes for the outing. Sir Walter Scott had set some of the action of *Ivanhoe* at Conisbrough and

Mr. Dickens was delighted by the literary connection. After they had picnicked on the grounds beneath the castle with its huge cylindrical keep looming over them, Mr. Dickens had led the party up the earthworks that would have once formed the castle's moat and into the ruins proper, recreating for them as they walked the miraculous appearance of Aethelstane of "Coningsburgh" at his own funeral. Mr. Dickens fairly pranced about from crumbling wall to ruined tower, calling on them to imagine what the place must have looked like in the twelfth century, its mighty portcullis opening to receive the funeral procession of solemn knights and weeping ladies who believed the heir to the Saxon throne had died in battle.

However, once they arrived at the entrance to the keep and looked inside, their eyes adjusting to an interior lit only by the occasional shaft of sunlight coming through narrow slits in its walls, the party was divided.

"I am not going up that," Mrs. Eliot declared frankly as she peered disapprovingly at the steep staircase of worn steps and missing stones.

"Looks unsafe," agreed her husband.

"But just imagine the view if you did manage it," Mr. Dickens encouraged.

In the end, Mrs. Ternan reluctantly agreed that she and the Eliots would stay below while Mr. Dickens accompanied Nelly and her sisters, who were all eager to try the stairs. So, they departed with a reassuring promise they would turn back if it became dangerous.

They climbed a piece, what felt like a storey if not two, but it was hard to tell on the narrow spiral and the going was slow. They picked their way gingerly up each step with Mr. Dickens taking the lead, urging them on and warning the sisters of any rough footing ahead. Eventually, they emerged in a large chamber with the remains of a huge stone hearth, which he knowingly declared to have been the great hall. Peering out its few narrow windows, they could catch tantalizing glimpses of the surrounding countryside, but when they approached the next flight of stairs hoping to go higher for yet better views, they found the first steps had entirely crumbled away. Mr. Dickens nimbly scrambled up the remains, all but hoisting himself up the tight walls of the staircase to reach a step that was intact. From there he peered up and around, promising, "It gets better from here. I can give you each a hand up."

Maria demurred and hung back while Nelly stepped forward. In the middle of the three, Fanny put out a hand to restrain her younger sister but by the time she did so, Nelly had caught Mr. Dickens' hand and, despite her long skirt, vaulted herself up to where he stood.

"Nelly . . ." Fanny protested, but Mr. Dickens overrode her, saying, "Nothing to fear; we will just see how far we can climb. We'll stop if there are any more gaps." And with that Nelly and Mr. Dickens disappeared from sight.

They could not, it turned out, go far; within another turn of the staircase, they found its roof had fallen in and they were facing an insurmountable wall of rubble. They turned and picked their way back into the room where Maria and Fanny were waiting, eager to get out of the cold castle and back downstairs into the September sunshine.

As her sisters pushed on, Mr. Dickens, so bold in climbing up the stairs, now hung back, taking the steps very slowly and continually turning back to Nelly, who was following him, to offer his hand.

"Careful," he said. "Down is always more tricky than up."

Soon, Fanny and Maria were out of sight around the next turn and Mr. Dickens stopped altogether. He just stood there for a moment, then he took a big breath and turned back to her.

"Nelly," he said emphatically, as though reassuring himself he had got the name right. ". . . I hope I may call you Nelly."

"Of course, Mr. Dickens."

"And you must call me Charles."

"I couldn't possibly, Mr. Dickens."

"Why not?"

"It would not be right."

"Pray, what could possibly be wrong if I have invited you to call me thus?" He sounded a trifle put out and Nelly hurried to explain her thoughts, although she found it odd to be having such a conversation in the confines of the castle's crumbling staircase. "You are too great a man for me to take such a liberty, Mr. Dickens. It would be too familiar of me."

"Nonsense. I want you to think of me as a friend, some intimate with whom you may dispense with unnecessary formalities."

Nelly found her heart beating a little faster at the notion that such a man as this should take such a friendly tone with her and thought hard how to respond correctly: "I would be honoured to consider you thus," she said. "My sisters and mother and I are a small family—I think you know my father died when I was just a girl—and your friendship would be a most welcome addition to our little circle."

Mr. Dickens, for that is how she would continue to think of him for some time, looked slightly discomfited by that.

"I am so glad . . ." he said.

"I am sorry, I have been hasty in my enthusiasms. I did not wish to burden your friendship with my family with undue expectations."

"No, no. Not at all, Nelly. It's just I had hoped . . . well, I am still a young man. This may sound odd to you, but inside I feel I am but a boy."

In the gloom of the staircase, she looked at him in puzzlement: it was hard for her to see any boy in a man of his achievement and wealth, a writer known throughout the Empire, a father and husband who lived in some palace in London that could house his wife, his sister-in-law, his many children and all the servants it must take to care for such a ménage. Such a personage seemed very far removed from both her meagre theatrical engagements and her youth. "A boy?" she repeated.

"A boy." He looked at her fondly, and reaching up to her on the step behind him, he took her hand in his. "Your boy," he said and leant toward her, craning his neck upwards to get his mouth level with hers.

Her dawning horror must have shown plainly in her face for, before his lips reached any closer to hers, he stopped and recoiled with an expression of pain as shocked and pure as if she had just bit his hand.

To make matters worse, someone was coming. They could hear heavy breathing and the rustle of skirts from below, and Mrs. Ternan's head now appeared in view as she struggled her way up the stairs. Evidentially she was not best pleased with how far behind her sisters Nelly had fallen. As she saw the pair above her, she stopped only long enough to catch her breath before saying point- edly, "I hope there is no misunderstanding, Mr. Dickens."

"None at all. None at all," he said as he turned from Nelly to resume his descent, but his face remained dark.

On the way home, Fanny took her turn sitting with Mrs. Eliot and Mr. Dickens while Nelly and Maria rode back to town with her mother and Mr. Eliot in silence. By the time they reached their lodgings, it was the hour to change and get ready for their evening's performances, for they still had several nights to run in their Doncaster engagement. At their door, Mrs. Ternan, as if to compensate for any lack of civility shown by their earlier encounter, thanked Mr. Dickens most warmly for his generosity in planning their outing and, not wishing to presume he would be attending the theatre again that night, asked whether he would be staying in Doncaster much longer before he returned to London.

"Not long," he replied. "I'm for the overnight train."

"Where's my blue shirt?"

"Which blue shirt?"

"The striped one, the one I always wear when I present a paper."

"I have no idea."

That was how one of our worst arguments began, inconsequentially, over an unlaundered shirt, although I suppose it was about bigger things. The girls were small, three or so, and we still had a nanny in those days; we kept her until the girls started kindergarten. As I recall she usually took the bag of Al's shirts to the cleaner's after he or I asked her to, but that was not how Al understood the matter.

"Sharon. I have to leave early tomorrow. Where the fuck's the shirt?"

I stared at him, uncomprehendingly. Did he really think this was my problem?

"Maybe it's in the laundry bag still," I said, taking

the bag off the closet door. It was large and stuffed. Apparently, the shirts had not walked themselves to the cleaner's. I opened it up, rummaged around and found the one in question. "I guess . . ."

"Can't you keep things organized around here? I mean, you have help . . ."

"I don't quite understand why this is my fault."

"Well, whose fault is it?"

"It's your shirt."

"I don't believe you. You know how hard I have to work; you're at home all day."

"I work at home."

"Okay, sure. But the book's finished. I mean, if you don't have time to run the shirts to the laundry, the least you could do is warn me . . ."

"Why are you obsessed with this one shirt? Wear a different one already."

And so it went on like this, this ridiculous argument over who should take responsibility for his laundry; he was at his worst, haughty and dismissive, and I wouldn't back down because I thought he was in the wrong and I'm stubborn. He eventually accused me of failing to support him in his career, which I pointed out was completely untrue, and we wound up lying in bed in the dark in a sulky silence unable to apologize until exhaustion finally overtook us and we fell into an uneasy sleep. And the next day, in the manner of many married couples, we just moved on and forgot about our fight, without ever clarifying whose job it was to take the shirts to the cleaner's, let alone figuring out what that was really about.

You always think, when you hear about some woman running off with another man or somebody's heart-breaking separation, that the marriage must have been a disaster, the couple must have known they were headed for the rocks; they were battling ferociously or barely on speaking terms or something. You think you'd get some warning, if such a thing were ever going to happen to you. I swear I had no warning, no warning at all. I thought the bond between us was steely strong, forged with passion and burnished by children. I thought if we occasionally disagreed about trivial things, it was merely trivial. A fight about a shirt was just an irritation, a diversion. Everybody has bad days; those times when you snap at your spouse only because she's the nearest person at hand. Al did not really expect me to wash his clothes. But I guess if I look back, if I have to pick a time where I had some inkling that we might be in trouble, or saw for an instant, quickly to be discarded, that there was a real problem here, it was the night before the fight over the shirt.

It was at a party, a party to launch my third book; we had taken over a restaurant not far from the house. Waiters passed around glasses of wine and trays full of cute little appetizers; I had bought a sleek new dress for the occasion; my publisher made a pretty and flatter-ing speech. I stood up to thank her and everybody else. I pulled out a bit of paper because I can't be trusted not to ramble at these things and needed to stick to a script. As I was straightening out my sheet of paper, I looked out at my audience, readying myself to speak, and I saw a man who wasn't looking at me; instead, he was staring off to one side. In a fraction of a second, there were three things I noticed about him. The first was that he was so handsome, heart-stoppingly good looking; the second was that he looked annoyed, put out somehow by the proceedings, as though he wanted to be somewhere else. And the third thing I noticed was that this man was Al.

Perhaps to put it in that order is overstating what happened; perhaps I should just say that Al looked unhappy, like an awkward outsider at this party, and that there was this millisecond before I recognized him, probably because he was standing in the shadows. At any rate, I had this tiny moment where he felt like a total stranger to me, a man I had never seen before in my life. Occasionally I have had hazy flashbacks to that night, fleeting moments when I look at Al and see someone else and then have a feeling of déjà vu, that I have known him as a stranger before. I think back to the first time I saw him at the front of a classroom, lecturing on Dickens, the sense of excitement that swirled around this unknown man, but then I realize that's not it. And I think of the shock when he told me he was leaving, my image of him standing at the front door, ready to go, and I know that's not it either, that was a time too full of my anger and sorrow over his behaviour for him to feel unfamiliar. And then I remember the night of the party.

Perhaps I'm exaggerating here. Everybody experiences those occasions when you look at the man who you have slept beside for a decade and wonder what the hell he's thinking.

This Saturday, he's looking puzzled, or maybe it's disgruntled. He's sitting at the breakfast table with the weekend paper spread out before him. With much fanfare *The Telegram* has announced a literary event and begun publishing a serial novel by the distinguished (their word, not mine) novelist Sharon Soleymani to mark the bicentenary of the birth of Charles Dickens. The first four weekly instalments have been received with a deafening silence, except for a few emails from Dickens enthusiasts and cranks, making suggestions about future instalments, soliciting advice on their own projects or sharing stories about the first time they chortled their way through *The Pickwick Papers* or wept at *Bleak House*. God bless them for their interest because Jonathan Torres has had nothing to say about the publication of this fabulous project that he so loved until I run out of patience and send him an email asking how he feels it has been received. He takes three days to answer with two words, "Good response," the terseness of which makes me suspect the opposite is true. There is no word from Stanek either. Typically, dear Frank fires me off a congratulatory missive the first Saturday morning, but I am feeling decidedly unloved at *The Telegram*.

But that's not what hurts. We still have the paper delivered but Al shuns it and always reads the news on his tablet. *The Telegram*, however, has decided to run the serial only in print—this may be an exceedingly clever bit of marketing, or not, we will find out soon enough. I showed Al the first instalment—"Oh, Staplehurst. Very smart," he said—and I assume he has read the next two. I pick the paper up off the porch every day, weekdays and weekends, and leave it on the kitchen table when I'm finished reading. But so far he has said nothing more. It's mid-February, and I'm growing increasingly nervous. I want him to like it; I know he thinks I should be husbanding my strength, babying myself, but I need to work and want him to see that, to see the old me, the clever one who could match him at his own game.

And now finally, as the fourth instalment appears, he is visibly reading. Ostentatiously reading, sitting in the middle of the kitchen with a cold cup of coffee, frowning at the paper and rustling it occasionally as he does so.

"I always thought that story was greatly overplayed."

"Overplayed? There was practically a conspiracy to keep the affair secret until the 1930s. Don't sully the name . . . "

"Yes, but recently it's been so overdone. So he had a mistress. Lots of men did."

"And still do," I say, before remembering I'm not supposed to do that.

"Hey, we agreed . . ."

The phone rings, interrupting our conversation. Marriage, in my experience, is full of conversations you never manage to finish. It is the lovely Jonathan on the line. He sounds panicked.

"Is this just going to be about this Nelly person?"

"Is that a problem?"

"Did you get my email?"

"I haven't got to my desk yet."

"Don't you have a BlackBerry?" He sounds as contemptuous as my daughters, continually petitioning for a smartphone.

"I'm thinking about going Samsung," I lie.

"Anyway, I sent you an email. I thought the serial was supposed to be about Dickens. Is this Nelly person his mistress or something?"

"Yes, his mistress. I did tell you Dickens was not the chief protagonist."

"Yes, but I told the publisher it was going to be about Dickens and he isn't sure about this direction. We hoped after all that stuff about the train crash you would move on to another topic. Follow the people he rescued or something. He thinks what you are doing is unfair . . ."

"Unfair to Dickens?"

"Yeah. Like you're slandering the man when he can't fight back."

"I think the legacy of anybody who wrote *A Christmas Carol* can look after itself."

"But you're making out like he's some pedophile or something."

"He was forty-five. She was eighteen. That's a fact."

"Yeah, but you don't have to emphasize it."

"You read it and edited it. Why didn't you raise these concerns earlier this week?"

"Well . . ." He clears his throat and attempts a decisive note. "You are going to need to tone it down for next week. We'll have to talk about a new direction. You'll need to come into the office."

"The direction will be what I decide it to be. Flip me Stanek's email address and I'll deal with him."

"I don't know. I'm the editor on the project . . ." He is getting whiny now.

"But he's the one with the problem. Send me his email and I'll respond to his complaints. Politely."

"Okay." He sounds relieved.

I am just composing my polite email to Stanek, saying I heard he had some concerns about the fourth instalment and would be happy to talk to him that afternoon after my daughters' ballet class was over, when the phone rang again.

"Sharon. Bob Stanek. Is this just going to be about Ellen Ternan?"

"No. Not exactly . . ."

The Dickens Bicentenary Serial: Chapter 5
London. February 16, 1858

There was consternation at Park Cottage. Mrs. Dickens had left her card.

Or, rather, her coachman had left her card, stopping the brougham in the middle of the street—to the annoyance of the coalman waiting in his cart to get by. The coachman had lifted the knocker and, when Mrs. Ternan had opened her narrow front door herself, handed her the small, engraved rectangle of Bristol paper. If he had expected a servant to answer or was surprised at finding himself in the further reaches of Islington, he gave not the slightest sign of it and, despite the gesticulations and shouts of the coalman, took time to give her the lowest bow before returning to his vehicle.

"What are we to do now?" Mrs. Ternan asked her daughters that evening.

"Does she want to visit?" Maria asked.

"No," said Fanny, "but her husband wants her to visit." Maria giggled.

Nelly caught the censorious look that her mother shot her sisters.

"Why would he want her to visit?" she asked.

"To show the world that we are ladies!" Fanny replied.

"We are ladies," Mrs. Ternan said firmly.

"Yes, but there are gossips who say Mr. Dickens' interest in Nelly is not altogether gentlemanly," said Fanny.

"Fanny!" her mother cried out in reproach at her boldness.

Nelly, recalling a recent walk on Hampstead Heath, a gold bracelet and a welcome audition with the previously unmoved manager in Drury Lane, blushed fiercely and burst into tears.

"It's not my fault!" she protested.

"Of course not, dear. You are blameless," Mrs. Ternan said.

"You were always the beauty," Fanny said. It was not an envious or malicious remark; it was accepted family wisdom that if Fanny and Maria were the clever ones, Nelly had inherited her mother's looks.

"So what are we to do now?" Maria asked. "Invite her to tea?"

"I suppose I must," Mrs. Ternan said. "Leave a card with her indicating an hour I will be at home."

"Do I have to be at home?" Nelly asked.

"I think we all have to be at home. That is rather the

point, isn't it?" Fanny said. "Maria and I can drop the card in. Or do you think we can trust Colleen?" Colleen was the char lady who came in daily to shovel coal and clean floors.

"That is sweet of you, dear, but I suppose Colleen can go if we give her good instructions on how to find the place. And I will just pour the tea myself."

"They live in Tavistock Square. It must be a palace," Maria said. "What will Mrs. Dickens think of us, without even a girl to open the door!"

"She doesn't have a footman to accompany her coachman," Fanny pointed out.

"Girls." Mrs. Ternan drew herself up and spoke in a voice trained to carry to the back row: "Mr. Dickens is an artist. He has bought his fine house with his fine talents. But we are artists too, and have also worked with our talents for everything we own. That is not something that may be said of Mrs. Dickens. We have no reason to feel her inferior."

And so Mrs. Ternan waited precisely two days and then hunted out one of her seldom-used visiting cards and wrote on it in her finest hand "*Mrs. Ternan finds herself at home with her daughters on Tuesday afternoons.*" Fanny and Maria walked Colleen to Tavistock Square to hand it in, and the family prepared itself to receive a visitor.

To that point Nelly had not given much thought to Mrs. Dickens. She had met her briefly, nothing more than touching her glove and bobbing a little curtsey, after the opening in Manchester. Mrs. Dickens had registered only as a vague maternal figure in the midst of the large retinue of servants and children that accompanied Mr. Dickens. It was her sister Miss Hogarth who seemed to take charge of all practical arrangements while Mrs. Dickens presided benignly if a bit blankly over the proceedings. Used to her mother's organizational skills and lifelong work, Nelly was unaccustomed to anyone permitted the luxury of inactivity and paid Mrs. Dickens little heed.

When she showed up on their very small doorstep the following Tuesday, however, Nelly mainly felt sorry for her. It was a wet and windy day and she was a large woman clothed in a voluminous rain cape, struggling to manage an umbrella and her wraps as she alighted from the brougham. She looked flustered and uncomfortable, and if she had wished to appear as their social superior condescending in paying this call, she rather ruined the effect by knocking over the umbrella stand with her cape on her way into the cottage's tight little vestibule. This seemed to upset her equilibrium yet further, and as Mrs. Ternan righted the stand with a few sorrowful comments about the size of the premises, Mrs. Dickens kept saying, "Yes, how awkward. How very awkward it all is." It was an annoying reaction that made the situation worse rather than better and yet Nelly could not think ill of her. It was clear she dearly wished herself anywhere else and yet it was also clear, during the social call that followed, that she was a kind-enough soul that she did not want to give offence.

"I don't believe you have met my eldest," Mrs. Ternan began when they were finally standing in the cramped parlour. "Mrs. Dickens, may I present my daughter Fanny."

Fanny bopped nicely; Maria brought tea and they all sat down, with Nelly positioning herself as far into a dark corner as the small space would permit.

"Two sugars, thank you."

"It was such a pleasure to meet you in Manchester last summer," Mrs. Ternan said. "I hope your return journey went smoothly."

"It was uneventful as I recall," Mrs. Dickens replied.

"So often the trains are late."

"Our train arrived right on time, and the journey was without incident, I am glad to say."

"I am relieved to hear that. Did you spend Christmas in the city?"

"No. We have recently bought a house in Kent."

"How pleasant. It is always so invigorating to breathe country air."

"Our house is cold and I find that country air exacerbates my catarrh."

"I am most sorry to hear that. The cold can be very trying. May I offer you a biscuit?"

"Oh no, thank you. I make a rule of never eating between meals. I am afraid it does not agree with me. I am a martyr to my digestion."

And so the delicate biscuits Mrs. Ternan had purchased specially from Fortnum and Mason sat uneaten while the conversation continued.

"What a cozy parlour this is and how prettily you have decorated it."

"Thank you. It is small but it suits our needs. I am afraid, however, I cannot take much credit for the decorations. They mainly belong to the landlady."

"Oh. I find it so comforting to be surrounded by one's own things."

"Of course, but in the theatre we travel so much. One gets used to keeping a few mementoes in a suitcase."

"How brave of you. I can't imagine living without my own furnishings, and the piano, of course."

"Yes. A piano is such a joy. Do you like music?"

And so they continued in this vein for ten minutes, at which point Mrs. Dickens declined a second cup of tea and indicated she had several more calls to pay that afternoon.

"Tuesdays are such a popular day, don't you find?"

"Very much so," Mrs. Ternan lied, eager to let Mrs. Dickens extract herself as soon as possible without further incident. "My compliments to your husband," she added as she opened the front door and saw her guest out.

For three miserable months during the summer that culminated in our separation, Al lived in the house and slept on an inflatable mattress in the basement, his own solution to the impossibility of my getting any sleep if we remained in the same bed. I suppose he had been managing to fall asleep beside the woman he was betraying for some months—he was evasive when I asked when his affair had begun—but in the first few nights after his announcement my anger kept me tossing about, seething in silence or starting up bitter denunciations until he quickly removed himself to the living room couch. The basement, a dank, unrenovated space filled with stray pieces of hardware and boxes of musty books, was not a comfortable alternative, but the girls seldom ventured down there so Al could go to bed after they were asleep without alerting them to the situation.

In the morning he would rush off to the campus, although he wasn't teaching any summer courses, while

I took the girls to the various day camps for which I had signed them up back in the winter, a lifetime ago. I would make their sandwiches and smear on their sunscreen and drop them off with cheerful hugs—and the minute I pulled the car back into the driveway, I would burst into tears. I couldn't work; my own emotions trumped those of my latest characters; so I would fill the days with long, sad walks or shopping trips for things I didn't need. I had decided these were much safer occupations than staying in the house after I had spent one morning hunting through Al's desk drawers and unsuccessfully guessing possible passwords for his university account because I had discovered you couldn't instantly call up his office email on his home computer. The thought of what I might have found in his email had I read it frightened me, leaving me with a nasty churning in my stomach, and I was mainly relieved I hadn't managed to get into it.

Whenever I found myself alone with Al, I alternated between ostentatious silence marked by heavy footfalls or the loud manhandling of objects and noisy attempts to draw him into a discussion of our relationship, which he avoided as best he could and which usually ended with me in frustrated tears. I would demand to know if the affair was still continuing, if he did not love me, if we should not try marriage counselling, questions he mainly answered with sorrowful silence since he knew I wasn't going to like the answers he might give. Marching down to the basement to confront him at night, I would denounce his betrayal, or begging him to stay behind on his way out the door in the morning, I would demand we discuss our marriage. I would quote to him statistics about the failure rate of relationships between older men and younger women, I would tell him his faults and admit to mine, I would insist we work things out. I could not possibly, for my own sake as much as the girls', just show him the door.

I would persist with talk in the face of his silence, clawing away at the subject, growing more and more desperate as I sensed I was losing the argument, that neither my angry passion nor my reasoned pleading was carrying the day. He would give me a hearing, as though that were his duty, but his answers were brief and unrevealing, little more than "I don't know" or a shrug of the shoulders. I had this panicky feeling of being outflanked or arriving too late, like one of those dreams when you run into a station with a half-packed suitcase only to see the train pulling away from the platform. I would try to draw him back into old arguments because at least if we were arguing, he was still here. But he would close down my approaches by saying, "It's too late" or "I think you just have to accept we aren't compatible."

"Compatible. What does that even mean? Nobody is compatible. Every person is different from everybody else."

"Well, some people seem to get on better than we do. We're too much alike to be together."

"I thought you said we weren't compatible."

"Yes, because we are too much alike. We both have these egos that need . . . I don't know . . . Air? Space?"

"Fuel. Your ego just needs fuel . . ." My voice was rising. He never yelled; he could be hurtfully dismissive in an argument but he never lost his temper. These days, he would go very quiet and look sad, which made me feel all the more desperately certain I was losing.

When I was furious, he always seemed a bit surprised, taken aback that things might possibly get ugly. It was as though he had not anticipated my anger, or at least did not have any particular plan, any idea about what happened after you tell your wife you're sleeping with one of your students. I wondered if she was pressing him hard for a resolution, just as I was, and if his preference might not have been to never tell me at all, and to keep going in the old-fashioned way, with a wife at home and a mistress in an apartment, for as long as he possibly could. A strong, decisive figure who had always exuded self-confidence—we'll be going here; we'll be doing this—he now seemed at a loss, unable to take control of a situation he had created.

It was an impossible, miserable time and we got a brief respite when I took the girls out to Nova Scotia to visit my mother for a week, but since I did not confide in her what was going on at home, the holiday had a surreal quality for me as I played at being the happy mother and dutiful daughter.

Still, the break from immediate, daily anguish calmed

me and I returned determined to have it out with Al, to fight to give our marriage a second chance and our girls the home they deserved. Of course, in retrospect, I can guess he probably spent the time in the arms of his grad student, strengthening his resolve to leave, but after weeks of obsessing about her obvious lack of character and manipulative wiles, I happened at that moment to have achieved a bit of distance on the subject of Al's lover. She was just a symptom of some middle-aged malaise that Al and I could fix together. I went home almost hopeful.

And at first things seemed better. Al greeted us cheerfully off a midday flight and I unpacked while he mucked about with the girls. Did the bedroom closet seem a little less stuffed than usual? I suppressed my rising panic and kept going with my chores. Dinner seemed normal, filled with the girls' accounts of the seaside, but as soon as they were asleep, Al was waiting for me downstairs.

"We need to talk," he said. "This isn't working."

"Of course, it isn't working. How did you possibly expect it to work?"

"I think I should leave."

"I think you should break off this nonsense so we can try to fix things."

"It's too late. You know that; there's nothing here."

"How can you say there is nothing here?" I ask, gesturing around the living room where the girls had scattered the new toys their grandmother had given them. "Our life is here, the girls' life, my life."

"Okay, but life has got to be about more than houses and junk, and ours has become about nothing else. Whose turn it is to pick up the girls, whose turn it is to empty the dishwasher. We wind up arguing about trivia. Do you remember that day last winter when we had that fight in the appliance store about whether we needed a front-loading machine? I mean, I really don't care what kind of washing machine we buy and there I was arguing about it. I don't even remember why."

"We can work on these things," I plead.

"What, you want to work on how to have more constructive discussions about washing machines?"

"We can work on making more room for things that aren't trivial. I can put the new book on ice," I offered. It wasn't getting written anyway. "If you feel I'm not paying enough attention to you, let's take a break, get away somewhere."

"That's not going to solve anything. I just don't think this was meant to be."

"You used to say I was the other half of your soul."

"Okay. Maybe we've changed or something. I don't know, people say things like that when they are falling in love. Or they think they are falling in love."

"Are you saying we were never in love?"

"I think we were both trying to escape things."

"And now somebody else is your escape. How do you know it's love this time?"

He had no answer to that, or perhaps he had an answer he couldn't give me.

Finally he said, "I just want to leave. I've found an apartment. I can move in Wednesday, the first of the month."

I tried to dissuade him, tried to get him to promise to wait a bit. The girls were entering grade one in a week's time; it's a big transition, I argued, they'll need stability at home. Better to get all the changes over at once, Al replied.

"I survived changing schools and changing countries. They'll manage," he said with uncharacteristic toughness.

He went down to the basement and I went upstairs, feeling numb. I opened the closet again; yes, there were fewer clothes. He left for campus early the next morning and didn't come home that night, phoning to say we should eat without him and not to wait up. I told the girls he was busy preparing for the start of term and when he finally showed up the following afternoon, we quietly agreed that we needed to tell them Daddy was going to live in his own apartment for a bit. I wanted to yell and scream and beg, but I didn't want to frighten the children. I was trapped into good behaviour, forced to remain calm to protect them. Everybody says you have to maintain a united front, never battle it out in front of the kids, that's what will really damage the children of divorce, although I was damned if I was going to tell the girls this was my idea. When we sat them down the following evening, I let

Al do the talking. He seemed surprised when the girls began to cry, and he tried rather lamely to reassure them.

"It will be fine, girls. I still love you—as much as ever. We'll see each other all the time."

The girls were barely six. Al adored them and had treated them as mini adults almost as soon as they could speak. Now, the more they cried, feeding off each other's alarm, the more he tried to reason with them, until their tears overwhelmed his attempts. Anahita flung herself at him while Goli clung to me, and as we sat there, each with one child in our arms, petting and kissing and comforting, he gave me this helpless expression as though somehow this was a situation from which I could rescue him.

To stop the flood, Al quickly agreed he wasn't going anywhere that night. He slept in the basement again and ate breakfast with us the following morning, disappeared for a few hours during the day and then returned in plenty of time for dinner. But then, after the girls were asleep, he got up to leave.

"I have to unpack some stuff at the apartment. Maybe I can come and get them for a bit tomorrow and take them over there. Get them pizza. They'll think it's fun." He paused a moment and we just stared at each other. "They'll get used to it. Kids are resilient." His confident self seemed to be returning now that he had made a decision.

"What about me? How am I supposed to get used to it?"

"You'll be fine, Sharon," he said. "You always are."

The Dickens Bicentenary Serial: Chapter 6
London. February 21, 1858

"Oh, look, Mr. Dickens, there they are." Nelly touched his sleeve and gestured toward a patch of daffodils fifty yards away from them across Hampstead Heath. It was February and they were out looking for signs of spring.

"Yes, right you are," he agreed and began striding toward the flowers, set in a little dell that must have been providing shelter from the winter cold because elsewhere on their walk they had encountered only snowdrops. "I do wish," he said as they continued, "that you would call me by my Christian name." It had become his familiar request now, a not-altogether-happy joke between them.

"Oh, perhaps someday," Nelly said, shaking her head with a little laugh.

"Someday soon?"

"Well, I am not sure what you mean by soon," she answered. "And really there is no point to my agreeing to a future time when I might call you by your Christian name. At that rate I might just as well do it right away."

"So why not do it right away then?"

"Perhaps I feel that you need something to look forward to," she said.

"You lead me a merry chase."

"Oh, no. I think you are the one leading."

"Right then, a chase for daffodils," he said, grabbing her hand and running with her the last few yards toward the dell.

"There you go, milady, I present you with spring."

"Lovely. So thoughtful of you to have arranged it. It always is my favourite season."

It was not the first time they had walked out together; the first time had been a few weeks previously when he had suggested to her that she might like to join him on his family's regular Sunday walk on the heath. When she had alighted from the carriage he had sent for her, she was not altogether surprised to discover that he was the only member of his family present. They had walked all afternoon, two hours or more, and he had talked to her of the novel he was planning.

"How fares the French novel?" she asked now as they continued their way uphill beyond the daffodil dell.

"It fares very well," he said. "Thank you so much for asking."

"And did you decide why the doctor was imprisoned in the first place?"

"Well, it's something to do with the aristocratic family, some secret of theirs he might expose, but I was thinking it need never be spelled out."

"Won't the reader want to know?" she asked.

"Yes, I suppose so, but I think some readers will realize that it's a thing of his past and that his past is gone; he isn't really that person any more."

"You mean people change?"

"Yes, and also that we can't fully know other people. We only know ourselves. He is a man who has been imprisoned. That is all we can see of him."

"How very wise that sounds. Each of us a book closed to others."

"Perhaps not entirely closed but hard to read. I certainly find your thoughts mysterious," he said.

And yet he was often all too transparent to her, Nelly thought. But she replied nothing and was glad he did not pursue the topic as they were forced off the path to negotiate their way around a muddy patch.

"Let me give you my arm here," he said. "The frost has made the ground slippery."

"Did you hear from our friend in Drury Lane?" he asked as they started up again.

"Not yet."

"Perhaps I might write him another little note."

"Please don't. I wouldn't want him to give me a part because he felt obliged to you."

"Of course not, my dear. I would never wish to interfere. But you will excuse me if I am convinced you will shine in a Shakespearean role if only given the opportunity your talents deserve."

"Yes, well, let's wait a bit to see if the manager agrees with you. And in the meantime"—at this she struck a melodramatic pose—"No, Mr. Waterspout, it was the parrot."

He laughed. "Yes, you have a great feel for that material too. No doubt about it. I am sure you have numerous admirers at the stage door every night."

"Oh, dozens. A queue of them all the way down Haymarket."

"And a special one in a little red waistcoat?" Suddenly his tone was sharper, almost nasty.

"I'm not sure what you mean."

"Clean-shaven young man. Red waistcoat. He was there the other night." Mr. Dickens had collected Nelly at the Theatre Royal the week previously and taken her and Mrs. Ternan to supper.

"Oh." She almost guffawed in recognition. "That's only Robby Strachan."

"And who is Robby Strachan?"

"Mary, who plays the maid, her brother."

"Oh, yes, the little Scot. But I don't suppose the fellow has only come to the theatre to see his sister."

"I have no reason to believe otherwise."

"No? Really?" He turned and studied her face for a minute and seemed to find the answer he wanted there. "Well then, that's a relief."

"Why so?" She taunted him now.

But he wasn't to be teased out of his jealousy and replied sadly, "Because it allows me to hope."

She pouted a moment at that, and then said lightly, as though there were no connection, "My mother was honoured to receive a visit from Mrs. Dickens on Tuesday." She paused before adding, "Perhaps it is me who has to wonder if I can hope."

"Oh my dear child. Yes. Let us both hope."

He suggested they might keep walking as far as The Spaniards Inn and take some refreshment there before finding her a cab. She knew it would be unwise to enter a public house alone with him, but only said that she was already a little footsore and thought they should turn back. In truth, she was tired, but it was the conversation as much as the walking that she found taxing. She was previously unacquainted with the game she now found herself playing and unsure of what outcome might be expected or desired. She knew, as she laughed at a good joke, basked in a compliment or admired a new trinket, that she did not want this excitement to end, but she also found it difficult to achieve the right balance of encouragement and discretion. She had only the barest advice from her mother, who had said on the occasion of this second walk, "He can do much for you, Nelly, but make no promises as to what you might do for him."

They were walking back downhill toward the entrance to the heath, admiring the view of the city laid out before them, when Nelly felt her companion stiffen and heard him suck in a short, tight little breath of unpleasant surprise. He said nothing and kept walking the same path without pausing; she looked ahead wondering what might have alarmed him and saw only a young man, his head bent, his gaze concentrated on the ground at his feet, walking straight toward them. As he came closer, Nelly recognized him although his head was still down; she had, after all, rehearsed with him in London and appeared on stage with him in Manchester; it was Charley Dickens, his father's eldest son. Neither father nor son deviated from the path and now Nelly wondered, as he still did not look up, if Charley had not actually seen them but was choosing to avoid eye contact until the last possible moment. That area of the heath was open; neither party could change route without making it apparent that was what he was about and so, with an agonizing inevitability, they came up to each other. As he approached, Charley stepped off the path they were walking, a tract worn into the sandy soil of the heath, and paused to let them pass. He raised his hat as they did so, saying, "Miss Ellen. Father," without any intonation whatsoever. His father, meanwhile, grunted slightly but said nothing, neither then nor afterwards as he and Nelly continued downhill. He chatted amiably enough as he found a cab for her, and exchanged some final pleasantries in a friendly tone as he handed her in. He gave the driver precise instructions as to the route he was to follow to Islington and paid him handsomely before stepping back and raising his hat to Nelly, waving discreetly from the cab window. The moment he was out of sight, she leant back thankfully on the hansom's stiff, narrow seat. In a way, she thought with some bitterness, it had been a family walk after all.

n all my life, I had never known anger like this. A passerby drops a cigarette butt into your front garden. Your spouse forgets the teacher's name again. Your sister-in-law makes one of her little remarks. Brief annoyances; simmering resentments, they blend together and leave you self-pitying and sharp-tongued at day's end, ready to throw an uncooperative corkscrew across the kitchen counter or snap unfairly at a recalcitrant child. But what I experienced in those weeks after Al first left was something not merely of a different magnitude but also of a different quality. This was murderous rage.

I saw her pretty face, that face I had glimpsed once at some university Christmas party where I was the glamorous wife, the established author, the exotic adornment who confirmed for them all that the professor lived a charmed life in some rambling old house where his spouse presided graciously over the comings and goings of friends, children and contractors. And the pretty face was just another grad student suffering through a Ph.D. in a studio apartment she shared with a cat. Did I detect then an unearned note of self-consciousness? Did she seem a trifle too aware of herself, as though she thought she had some larger role to play or knew something I didn't? If there was a ghost of some complication there, I put it down to snobbery, hers, not mine: I assumed she had realized, like Al's university colleagues before her, that the novels I write are of the type that feature a gauzy picture of a woman's face on the cover. Still, she must have impressed me in some way because, from that one encounter, I could remember her face and see it as I imagined the laundry bleach pouring down her throat or the garden spade crushing her skull.

In the first weeks after Al had left, when my confused and tearful little girls had finally gone to bed, I would go down to the basement to empty their cotton panties and pink T-shirts from the dryer and, out of earshot of children and neighbours, I would find that I was raging to myself out loud. Yelling and cursing her name, spitting it across the cracked linoleum floor, turning it into some horrendous expletive again and again, until I would break down, choking on my tears.

I would wonder at myself sometimes. I had become a cliché, the scorned woman so furious that Hell itself has no place for her. In rational moments, in daylight hours, I would think surely we can all come to an understanding; we must do what is best for the children; they are what matters, after all. Or I would resign myself and say, What is all the fuss about? He no longer loves me; I am not sure I love him. It happens all the time. Families reconfigure themselves. We just need to be civilized.

But at night, I was a different beast. I would lose touch with the sensible woman who walked her daughters to school and promised them they would see Daddy tomorrow. I understood now all those stories, the murders, the suicides, the babes slaughtered by their own warring parents, the gawking neighbours insisting they always seemed like such a nice family. I could kill.

I wouldn't, of course. My daylight self held me back; I had not yet relinquished all sanity and all control. But I knew the feeling well enough to think it through. So I murder her. I probably won't get away with it. I would think of various methods—mainly I would imagine that I might travel to an insalubrious neighbourhood where I suppose one might be able to buy a gun, go to her apartment and fire off several bullets—but I couldn't think of any way to hide the crime. Say I just leave her body there, or manage somehow to drag it to a nearby dumpster, the most cursory police investigation will surely find her professor, some emails, and start to take a look at both the professor and the professor's wife. I'll be arrested. My brother will get me a good lawyer, but I'll probably have to plead guilty and wind up spending at least ten years in a women's prison. The girls will grow up knowing me only from conversations through a glass screen. Or perhaps they let children visit in the same room with the prisoner. I think I saw that in a movie once. At any rate, I will have separated myself from my children, traumatized their young selves, done the very opposite of what I want and left them entirely to their father and her, their new stepmother, their young, pretty . . . Oh, except she would be dead because I murdered her. Well, he would probably find another one, and I would be the crazy woman, the jealous wife locked up in a jail cell.

And with that thought, the unfairness of it all would descend on me with a weight that threatened to crush my spirit and my rage would begin again.

Some nights, I did my best to contain it. I tried to read a book or concentrate on chores. I talked myself down; warned myself not to make myself sick, not to wake the children, not to lose control. I searched the Internet for helpful articles that would explain my emotions to me. And other nights, I simply felt them raging through me like a disease I could not fight.

The days were better. At least I could call Becky and recount the latest outrage or speculate how long Al could possibly remain enamoured of a glib graduate student while ignoring his young daughters' evident distress.

"Oh the babies," Becky would say and make her clicking sound. "I just don't know what I would do if David . . . "

Soon after she arrived in Toronto, the gentle Becky had married the equally amiable David, a med student she had met in the athletic centre who was now our pediatrician and Al's regular squash partner. They have three little boys who, as if to compensate for their soft-spoken and kindly parents, are utter hellions. My girls, a year older than their eldest, adore them, pet them and encourage them in much mischief. Our family parties are uproarious. The last one I remember we had to stop the older kids from putting the baby—Becky's youngest—in a bucket they were dangling down the third-floor stairwell with a rope. Or at least our family parties *were* uproarious. We had not had one since Al had dropped his bitter bombshell.

"I'd probably just kill David," Becky joked, not knowing how close she came to my own thoughts—although it was not Al who was the target of my murderous rage.

Of course, I felt angry at him too, cursed his pride and his stupidity, but it was a different kind of anger. I knew him; I had loved him; he wasn't just some voodoo doll I could poke with pins. Part of me longed for his return, for normal life to resume, for forgiveness or at least forgetfulness to work its soothing charms, and somehow I must have known that if I gave full voice to my anger against him there would be no going back. I had ranted, I had raged, both at him before he left and to myself now that he was gone, but I had never said anything irreparable, those burning phrases that might end a marriage on the spot. I had held back from even thinking the things that would take me to the point of no return, the final, bitter judgments of his character that would close the door on our relationship for good. This, however, made discussing his departure with my outraged supporters rather difficult.

After he had actually left the house, I had to tell people other than Becky what was going on. People like my mother, who had lived, since the death of my father a few years before, in a small condo in Halifax with a nice view of the Atlantic, and my brother, whose Vancouver condo gave him a nice view of the Pacific. A cool and sometimes prickly lot, we weren't close and it seemed typical that the three of us had wound up about as far apart as Canadian geography would permit without one of us moving to the Arctic. My father was an insurance adjustor who had died from an aneurism the year of his retirement, as though he was just another statistic from the actuarial tables on which he had built his career. He had been the family peacemaker, the gregarious one who compensated for my mother's reserve, the one who called on birthdays and hauled my mother across the country to share turkey in Toronto or Vancouver in alternate years. Since he was gone I made a dutiful call to my mother once a week and took the girls down East every summer; her reaction to Al's departure was sorrowful but distant.

"I'm so sorry, dear. That must be very hard for you. But maybe it was to be expected."

"Why expected?"

"Well, he isn't like us, is he? I'm sure they do things differently where he comes from . . ."

I didn't bother contradicting her or pointing out she had always appeared flattered by the charm offensive Al had launched at every meeting with his mother-in-law. She was seventy now; I was not going to change her casual but ingrained xenophobia.

I didn't do much better with my brother. We have not seen each other in several years and communicate mainly by email. A lawyer recently elevated to the bench, he has a busy career and a demanding young wife whom he married in his forties. He's preoccupied. He knew something was wrong when I actually called.

"What's up?"

"Al's left. He's been having an affair with one of his students."

"The bastard. When did that happen?"

"He's been gone a week. He told me about the affair about three months ago."

"What a jerk. I never did like him," my brother said.

I am the aggrieved one, the one who has been hurt, but this isn't exactly what I want to hear. My brother the judge, always as comfortable with moral certainties as he is with legal niceties, happily rushed to judgment in the language he uses at home because, I have always supposed, he can't use it in a courtroom. "A real asshole."

"Why didn't you like him?"

"Too charming, especially with women. That Middle Eastern thing. The ladies love it but it's so phony."

Apparently Al was perfectly right to complain my WASPY family did not welcome him. I had always told him he was imagining it; we were just not effusive where we came from.

My brother asked after his nieces, offered words of sympathy and cursed Al several more times before I eventually hung up annoyed and dissatisfied. I was the one to judge Al, not others. If they had always distrusted him, which I suspected was merely hindsight, why had they not said something to me before our marriage? If they truly disliked him, which I doubted since most people found his urbane manner and ready smiles easy enough to like, what did it say about my judgment? If they were so quick to write him off, did that mean I must abandon all hope of his return? They could be outraged on my behalf, but not more outraged than I was. I wanted their sympathy but not their pity. It was a delicate dance; most people got it wrong and I resented them for it. In the first weeks after Al had left, I had unsatisfactory calls with a high school friend and my motherly agent; a troubling email exchange with another mother from the girls' school, a disgruntled drink with Frank at *The Telegram* and a bitter lunch with my editor. And I almost walked out on my hairdresser of fifteen years after he had the gall to say, "I always thought that one was a bit off."

My audience was always frustrating me, denying me the particular vindication I sought, yet I felt compelled to rehearse my story for any intimate who would listen, telling once again my version of events.

The Dickens Bicentenary Serial: Chapter 7
London. June 7, 1858

As the red velvet curtains dropped, Nelly sat forward in her seat, raised her gloved hands and applauded with all her might. She felt Maria and her colleagues had acquitted themselves admirably and needed the encouragement; the audience had proved boisterous and inattentive that afternoon. She clapped as the secondary players took their bows and, as the leads came forward, reserved a little brava for Maria. Maria was followed by Mr. Rawlings, who bowed low before the spectators as though they had just received his Lear in reverence rather then prattling their way through a farce. Nelly eased up as Mr. Rawlings brought out his leading lady; she had nothing against Miss Banks but felt no actress, except perhaps her sister, could really prove herself worthy of the magnificent Mr. Rawlings. Nelly had been sweet on him ever since she had seen him play James Wilder in *The Red Rover* at the Lyceum the winter before and had decided he was the very personification of the heroic officer of the Royal Navy. Gracious, noble, high-minded, he appeared to her as a man whose physical beauty surely reflected his intellectual and moral superiority. When the audience began to shuffle out of the theatre, she made her way to the front with anticipation: she was to meet Maria backstage and her sister had promised she would do her best to arrange an introduction to Mr. Rawlings himself.

Backstage, she greeted the stage manager and explained she was there to see her sister; he gave her an appraising look but said nothing, simply nodding in the direction of the ladies' dressing room and watching her as she quietly knocked at the door. Maria's voice rang out, inviting her inside, where she squeezed into a corner, making herself as small as possible while her sister and two colleagues removed their wigs and makeup. Miss Banks, she knew, had her own dressing room next door but the rest of the female cast members had to make do with a tiny room with only one table. Nelly would have waited out in the hall had the stage manager seemed a friendlier sort, but she did not like his fishy eye. Maria introduced her to the other two actresses as she hurriedly sponged off the makeup and brushed out her hair. If they were to bump into Mr. Rawlings before he left the theatre they couldn't dawdle; the men in the company always took less time than the ladies to get back into street clothes and out the stage door. The others were still working away with sponges, cloths and brushes as Maria picked up her bonnet and shawl and ushered Nelly back into the hall.

Sure enough, Mr. Rawlings was there, chatting to the stage manager and the watchman as he prepared to leave. Nelly only recognized him because Maria gave her a nudge; apparently, his curly blond locks were entirely the inspiration of the wig mistress for his real hair was a rather dull brown and receded at his temples; without benefit of his costume, meanwhile, his shoulders appeared slightly stooped. He looked older and more tired than he did on stage. Nelly scolded herself for her stupidity; it was not as though she was unacquainted with the purpose of wigs, makeup and costumes. The trio of men barely glanced at Maria and Nelly as they approached and did not stop their conversation; the watchman had a rolled-up newspaper clasped in one hand and was gesturing with it to make a point.

"The old devil," he said, chuckling.

"I haven't read the thing myself," Mr. Rawlings replied. The hallway was narrow and the ladies could hardly pretend not to hear but Maria said, in a friendly manner, "Don't mind us," as they prepared to squeeze past.

"Miss Ternan," said the stage manager, belatedly standing aside. "We were just discussing Mr. Dickens' letter in *The Times*."

"Letter?" asked Maria blankly.

"Explaining to the world why he has abandoned his wife," the stage manager said.

"Awful thing," added the watchman with relish.

"Indeed," Maria agreed, although Nelly expected that, like her, her sister had no idea what letter they referred to.

"It's well known that he prefers his wife's sister," Mr. Rawlings offered.

"Well known! That's a vicious accusation," Maria said, rounding on him.

The three men looked momentarily taken aback by her vehemence, but Mr. Rawlings recovered himself quickly and said, "Well, Miss Ternan, I have heard you are good friends with Mr. Dickens yourself." A smile spread across his face while the other two men laughed. Maria, now flustered and red-faced, grasped blindly for Nelly's hand and the two women hurried out the stage door and onto the street, walking home in silence.

Installed in Islington for the foreseeable future, Mrs. Ternan had done something Nelly had never known her to do before: she had taken out a subscription to a newspaper. It was enough to have your mail chasing you from one end of the country to the other, without adding your newspapers to the packet, so, on the road or in London, the family always relied on the newsstand. But Mrs. Ternan planned to stay at Park Cottage, know-ing her own career would require her to turn her hand to elocution lessons soon enough while still hoping for the imminent triumph of the girls on the West End. London would be their base and to make the cramped quarters of Park Cottage feel more homey she had planted marigolds in a box that could just perch on the windowsill outside the parlour. And she had begun taking the paper. The result was a stack of old copies of *The Times* tucked away in a corner of the kitchen where they came in handy for washing windows, clearing coal out of the grate or packing up vegetable peelings to carry out to the bin. It was there, the following morning, sneaking down before her sisters were up, that Nelly found the previous day's paper. She slipped into the parlour and was about to start reading it when she heard her mother on the stairs. She dropped *The Times* underneath her chair and went back into the kitchen to start the fire and boil the kettle.

Settled at the breakfast table with her mother an hour later while Maria and Fanny, who had both had engagements the night before, slept in, she finally dared to pick it up again.

Her mother looked up vaguely from the morning mail.

"Isn't that yesterday's paper? Today's is here," she said, indicating the chair beside her. Apparently she had not read whatever letter it was that had Maria's company talking.

"That's all right. There was something I missed yesterday," Nelly answered as she scanned the pages of *The Times*. She found the letter soon enough, under the headline "Personal. A message from Mr. Dickens."

The first sentences did nothing to calm her. The writer stated that, some domestic trouble of his having become a source of public discussion, he was compelled to explain that his separation from his wife was amicable and mutually agreed upon, and to denounce false rumours about innocent people dear to his heart. Nelly's nervousness, which had made even dry toast an impossibility that morning, now gave way to a lurching queasiness. She had experienced enough of Mr. Dickens' affection for her to suspect there might be rumours about her.

The next bit reassured her somewhat. Perhaps wishing to forestall any criticism of her role in his household, Mr. Dickens praised his sister-in-law to the skies, saying she had done everything in her power to prevent his separation from his wife and cared ceaselessly for his children. Maybe this was the source of Mr. Rawlings' crude remark; no matter how vile, the gossip was only about Georgina Hogarth, Nelly thought with relief.

As for his wife, he said their marriage had been unhappy for many years and that she herself had often suggested they separate. Nelly puzzled over this for a moment. Mrs. Dickens had seemed an agreeable-enough character if hardly very interesting when she had come to call the previous winter, but surely a man of Mr. Dickens' talents and stature deserved better than a woman who paid little heed to her appearance and seemed much inclined to complain of her health. Besides, no outsider could know what transpired in a marriage; if only nineteen, Nelly was not so naive she did not realize that, and she supposed that Mrs. Dickens, a rather soft-spoken person as far she could judge, might be a veritable shrew in private.

Nelly knew Mr. Dickens to be a kind and charitable man and no doubt he had been a model of forbearance in his marriage. And yet she was made uneasy by what came next. He added that he had been very generous in his settlement with his wife, but also stated that she did not love her children and suffered from a mental disorder that he did not specify. Nelly recalled Mrs. Dickens had seemed perfectly sane when she had visited Park Cottage, but perhaps her mental health wavered according to her tribulations. How difficult it might be to live with a woman who was often in a low or worse yet violent mood. Still, Nelly did sense something untoward about such statements perhaps because she realized that whatever burden Mrs. Dickens might place on her family members, it was not exactly gentlemanly to complain about it to one's correspondents.

But what followed was worse. Again, Mr. Dickens denounced malicious gossip, and this time defended a pure and innocent soul as blameless as his own daughters. Apparently, an innocent who might be compared with his own daughters was being attached to his name. Nelly's queasiness was suddenly replaced by a surge of heat as an uncomfortable flush rose up her cheeks to the roots of her hair, leaving her breathless and perspiring.

She did believe she was innocent. She was certainly pure. She had not looked for scandal; she had not flirted. At least, she did not think she had flirted. Meeting Mr. Dickens as a fellow actor and manager of a production in which she was appearing, she had perhaps been less overwhelmed than other girls might have been, and thus more easily established a rapport with him. Her mother had permitted their occasional walks on the heath, and surely there was no shame there; they were always in full sight of dozens of people and she had never taken so much as a cup of tea alone with him. She had accepted gifts; it would have seemed rude to refuse them, but nothing more than a few tokens a manager might give an actress at the end of a successful engagement. He had put in a word for her in Drury Lane, but she had certainly never asked for such a favour and he had done the same for Maria too.

If she knew full well the implication of his attentions, Nelly was certain her own response was proper; she had never made him any promises nor told him what he must do. She could reassure herself that she was not the cause of the Dickenses' separation with a certitude she found deep in her soul, but she also thought it hard to believe that Mrs. Dickens was an unloving mother with a mental disorder. The letter seemed improbable and unwise: if his domestic affairs had been the subject of rumour and innuendo, such a statement would surely only inflame the gossips rather than tame them, while also bringing news of his separation to all sorts of people previously ignorant of it. The genial and big-hearted man she knew was full of captivating tales that would hold any audience spellbound, yet this writer seemed a cramped and unconvincing character more likely to delude himself than his reader, whoever he intended that to be. How could he have ever written such a thing, let alone allow it to fall into the hands of a newspaper? For the first time in her acquaintance with Mr. Dickens, Nelly began to question if their friendship was really wise.

As she stared unhappily at the newspaper in front of her until she could no longer read the words, Mrs. Ternan now looked up from her correspondence with a smile.

"There's a very kind letter from Mr. Dickens, Nelly."

"Oh?"

"He thinks Fanny should go to Italy. He truly believes in her talent and it is really the only place for voice training. I wonder . . ." Her mother hesitated. "I would need to go with her. I wonder if you and Maria would be all right here on your own for a few months? I don't like to leave you alone in town, but it's such an opportunity for Fanny. He's offering to pay for the lessons and all our expenses."

During the autumn that Al was absent from the house, I had to acclimatize myself to the horror that is alternating weekends. Every other Friday, I would pick up the girls from school, remove the half-eaten sandwiches and crumpled art projects from their backpacks to be replaced with nighties, toothbrushes and clean underwear, and remind them that Daddy would collect them before dinner. This is what we had agreed, with frigid civility. We tried to avoid making practical arrangements in front of the children, reminding each other when voices grew nasty or my tears began that we could not risk them seeing this kind of thing. Al took the girls one weeknight and every other weekend, but perhaps this was just temporary. He had said he wanted joint custody: I had pointed out he didn't have enough room in the apartment to keep the girls all week and was desperate at the idea they might one day encounter his girlfriend. My brother had told me I needed a lawyer and provided several names. I hadn't called them yet and Al hadn't raised the possibility of divorce. Now that he had got out, he mainly tried to avoid more arguments. Occasionally, one of the girls would say she didn't want to go for the weekend. When pressed the children would always agree they wanted to see Daddy; they just did not want to sleep over at his apartment.

"Why?" I asked, uncertain that I wanted to hear the answer.

"It smells funny," Anahita said. I instantly imagined the worst and felt my anger rising. What kind of smell? The smell of a new perfume? At my pleading, Al had promised that, for the time being at least, he would hide all signs of his student from the girls and I, thankfully, had never seen her. She was this invisible, unknown malignancy.

"What kind of smell?"

"Soapy. Like medicine."

"Like medicine? It's probably just he cleans with a different kind of cleaner than Mummy is using. That's all, sweetie. Just a different cleaner." I didn't know if I really believed that, but whatever it was, the place doesn't smell like her home.

"Yes, it smells," agreed Goli, backing up her sister. "And Daddy buys the wrong kind of milk."

"What kind does he buy?"

"He buys the blue one, the one that you always drink, and we drink the red one."

Al was feeding six-year-olds skim milk. He never uses milk himself, takes his coffee black and doesn't eat cereal. Maybe the student was buying skim.

"Did you tell him it was the wrong kind?"

"Anny told him and he said to stop fussing." Goli stared up at me. Her lower lip trembled.

"He said milk is milk," Anahita added. "But you always say it's different and that kids should drink the one in the red box."

"I'll tell him you need the right kind of milk. Tonight, I'll tell him when he comes, I promise."

"Why can't he just stay here tonight?" Anahita wheedled.

"No, Ana, you know. We've talked about this. You need to see Daddy at his place."

After they left, the house would be overcome by an unwelcome hush. In the quiet, I could hear an odd mechanical hum that I had never noticed before. It sounded ominous, as though some system were malfunctioning. I would hunt about for a bit and then realize it was only the fridge. The phone would ring and I would start up with fright. It was only a telemarketer. I swore at him and banged down the phone. I had never noticed the quietness of an empty house before; I mean, before Al, before the girls, I lived alone in a variety of houses and apartments and they never seemed empty. I was sometimes lonely, I wanted some larger life outside the confines of the small spaces I inhabited but I never felt uncomfortable in them.

Now, I would roam about, picking up a magazine and casting it aside, retrieving a stray pink sock from under the couch and finding myself in tears.

The days of those empty weekends were tolerable; they were just like my regular work days and I would keep working to fill them even if I was struggling with the novel I was supposed to complete that spring, uncertain how the characters might ever extract themselves from a disintegrating marriage. The nights were worse, much worse. I could barely tolerate myself or the house after dark. I tried to make sure I had something planned; sent out emails to every other single woman I knew seeing if she wanted to go to a movie Saturday night. Friday, I would usually just go to a mall, buy the girls too many Christmas presents or spend a long time in the bookstore browsing the self-help section, skimming through titles about infidelity and mid-life crisis. Sometimes, Becky would manage to book off from family responsibilities and we would have the luxury of an evening out together in a restaurant. It felt odd to be alone on a Saturday night without our children, strange like the empty house, but—as long as I didn't drink too much wine—less tear-jerkingly sad.

We tended to have long conversations in which Becky patiently allowed me to revisit old haunts again and again. "Al said we were never suited to each other. That we're too different."

"I thought he said you were too alike."

"He's said that too. He's not entirely consistent."

Becky pondered the question and then offered, "I don't think you're all that alike. Al is very likeable and—"

"And I'm not?"

She laughed.

"Of course you're likeable, sweetie. I was just going to say that Al wants to make a good impression; I think he wants people to like him."

"And I don't care whether people like me?"

"Well, you don't, Sharon. You are so wise and gentle with your characters but you can be really tough with real people. You're rude sometimes."

Becky wasn't being cruel, just repeating our accepted wisdom; she was good cop, I was bad. Al charmed people; I got my hands dirty. I was rather proud of my status as the tough one in the crowd, the person who could be counted on to complain if service was slow or fire the neighbour-hood teenager who was supposed to shovel the snow but missed the big storm.

"Al got himself in a bind this time. Any way he moved he was going to piss somebody off."

"Yeah. Backed into a corner. He couldn't please both you and . . . what's her name again?"

"I don't believe I remember her name."

Becky laughed again.

"Underneath his charm, there's a certain superior-ity . . ." she said, pensively.

"Oh yes."

"So, underneath that there must be need. People who bother to be charming do it for a reason."

Was it need? He certainly made himself interesting. He first seduced me with stories of the Iranian revolution, romantic and frightening tales that made him seem so heroic. Even though he was only a boy at the time, even though he isn't Muslim and his family eventually fled Iran, he described Tehran in those years as a tantalizing place, full of both promise and danger. By day, the city throbbed with heat, anger and displays of the Shah's military might, but by night the cool air was alive with forbidden cries of "Allahu Akbar." In his push to create a modern society, the Shah had outlawed Islam, even forbidden the veil. His secret police were everywhere, but nobody could find let alone stop the people who cried their protests from the rooftops. I guess that story didn't turn out so well in the end, but Al just seemed to regret that pulsating moment of hope and fear, and it all sounded fabulously exotic compared to sneaking cigarettes in the girls' washroom at Halifax West High School. Al wanted my attention and he got it.

At some point in these conversations, I would usually remember my manners and ask after Becky. On one occasion she said she'd had a bad week; she had a paper to prepare for a conference and two of her boys got head lice, first one, then the other, so she had kids sent home from school two days running. She had spent two nights in a row washing and combing so she could send them back the next morning.

"They are so bloody hard to see. You'd think a doctor would be good at it, but David was no help at all, and he says the treatments often don't work. If we haven't got rid of them by the weekend, we'll just have to give the two of them buzz cuts."

"At least with boys you can do that. When the girls got them, we had such a battle over it. Goli agreed to have her hair cut a bit shorter but Anahita refused. And she can be so stubborn and her hair is so thick for a little kid's. Al had a huge argument with her over it." The girls are fraternal twins; Goli has my hair, fine and straw-coloured the way mine was when I was a child. She will probably go dirty blond when she's older too. Anahita's is blond too but already a bit darker, and wavy and thick. Picking lice out of it took forever.

"Yeah. Al told David that he must have spent hours brushing her hair when you guys had lice."

Becky paused, realizing she had spoken out of turn. I suppose I had just assumed they weren't in touch; assumed if Al had fallen out of my life, he had also disappeared from the lives of my friends, that he was the guilty party and would be ostracized accordingly.

"When did he tell him that?" I asked.

"I guess they were talking about it this week."

"Oh." Really, what had I expected? That David would drop his squash partner on moral grounds?

"It's not true. I combed her hair. Al wouldn't go near either of them; he was disgusted by it." He associated the lice with filth and poverty and was appalled by the episode, despite my attempts to reassure him that all Canadian school kids get head lice at some point. I read somewhere it's something about the cold weather, they come back again every spring even stronger, although I have no idea if that's true.

"I guess maybe David misunderstood him or something," Becky said, trying to brush the topic away.

"Maybe. More revisionist history. Playing the sensitive guy, the perfect dad, for the new girlfriend."

"Let's talk about something else."

"What else is there to talk about? I don't know how that bitch can live with herself, two small kids, like encouraging someone to abandon—"

"Sharon." Becky's voice had a small warning note, pulling me back from the precipice. "You don't know she's encouraging him; it may be all his idea."

"Then why is she going along with it?"

"She wants to be you, sweetheart. She wants to be the wife in the nice house with the kids. She's lonely and she's hoping and waiting . . ."

"I just think she's a bitch . . ."

"Sharon, use your imagination. Think what it must be like to be her."

hay sat on the edge of the unmade bed idly flipping through the pages of a cookbook. Chocolate crème. Cabinet pudding. Charlotte russe. In the pictures, the desserts looked simultaneously airy and luscious but the recipes sounded rather complicated, and Shay had never been much of a cook. She sighed and put the book aside, thinking she really should be getting dressed.

It was ten o'clock and usually by this hour she was sitting at a reader's desk at the British Library. She would have managed to eat two slices of toast and pull on a pair of jeans and a sweater, even if she had left the bed unmade and her plate sitting in the sink with the dinner dishes from the night before. It was a mighty effort just to get out of the house, but her work was a tonic that provided her with direction and purpose. Except that, if she were honest with herself, she had to admit her research was boring her silly, and for the past few weeks she had often spent mornings in bed, crying intermittently. Sometimes in the afternoons she had dragged herself into the library but sometimes she had stayed home and read crime novels. It wasn't so much that the pain of separation was any greater than it had been when she had first arrived in London three months previously, it was just that her work was not proving the all-consuming distraction it was supposed to be.

At first it had been fairly easy. There had been things she needed for the apartment; she had introduced herself and her project to the librarians; she had figured out the best route for getting to the library on the tube. "I just won't think about him," she would announce to herself as she set off each morning to spend a day burrowing through letters and documents, gleaning little snippets of information from her reading, enough to convince herself she was making progress. She had been befriended by Alex, another graduate student who was working on some interminable project about French exiles during the Napoleonic Wars, and the two young women would take tea breaks together in the library cafeteria. The evenings were harder, but she'd signed up for yoga classes at a local studio to postpone the moment when she had to go home, heat up some macaroni and cheese in the apartment's kitchenette, walk around the neighbourhood a few times to clear her head, treat herself to a glossy magazine and a chocolate bar from the shop at the corner and then take to her bed. At least she could always sleep—long, deep, dreamless sleeps from which she awakened feeling dopey and dull.

So, she had plodded on, unhappy, lonely, yet progressing as she felt she ought. But it was November now; the little snippets did not seem to be adding up to anything while the evening walks were cold, dark and rainy. And then that week, on the Monday morning after an empty weekend, just as she was lying in bed telling herself she really would get up and out in good time for once, her neighbour had walked past her door going back upstairs. He must have forgotten something on his way to work and returned to retrieve it, but the very sound of his footsteps coming toward her had destroyed all her good intentions.

He was a shy, oversized and lumbering young man, who worked in some IT department somewhere and usually progressed heavily down the stairs from the third floor early each morning, serving as Shay's alarm clock as he passed by her door. Her cramped apartment was on the second floor of what had once been a modest single-family home. Their landlady lived on the ground floor, in the so-called garden flat that backed onto a small, dank yard.

It was an arrangement rather similar to the one Shay had enjoyed in her last Toronto apartment. She had lived on the third floor of an old house near the university. The sun had shone through her bedroom window there, just as it was shining that day in London; she had not bothered to lower the blind the night before, and a few weak rays reached her white duvet cover, awakening memories of lying in bed under fresh sheets in the daytime, and then the footstep on the stair . . . For the tiniest second, she actually thought it was him. She was back in Toronto; she had left the side door open so he could slip down the alleyway and into the house without hanging about or ringing doorbells. He was climbing the back stairs, the ones that led to the apartments on the second and third floors. She was waiting at the top. In a minute he would be in her arms.

In Shay's admittedly limited experience, there were two very different kinds of loneliness. The first was the low, abstract ache she had often felt in her first years away from home, that undefined sense there was something more than this and that definite conviction it would be provided by a boyfriend, if only she could find one to her liking. The last one, an exotic creature who she had thought was a poet but turned out to be more interested in dope than in her, had taught her that there are worse things than being alone. After she ended that relationship, Shay had sunk back rather thankfully into the first kind of loneliness.

And then there was missing someone. And that was altogether different. It was sharp and fierce, it was a loss with a face and a name. It was a conviction there would never be another love like the one she had experienced in those afternoons, when he had whispered her name and kissed her eyelids. There would never be another who saw her so fully and came to her so completely, apparently needing her as much as she needed him. Even if she could find her way beyond this immediate grief, life without him seemed to offer only a dreary kind of compromise.

And so, she had spent the rest of that Monday morning in bed, and in the afternoon only managed a trip to Sainsbury's to buy frozen cheesecake and tandoori chips. Tuesday had been slightly better. This time, she had bought fresh vegetables and a chicken breast for dinner and wandered into a branch of Waterstones, where she convinced herself she could justify the purchase of a heavily illustrated cookbook dedicated to impracticably lavish Victorian recipes. Now here it was Wednesday. Ten a.m., according to the clock radio. She realized she was hungry. Time to eat some toast, get dressed, walk to the tube and get back to work.

Shay got off the bed, picked some clothes off the floor and put them on. In the kitchenette, she filled the kettle and popped bread in the toaster; once her meagre breakfast was ready, she put it on the messy table in the living room, plopped herself down and, looking for distraction, pulled a pamphlet toward her from the pile of scattered papers.

It was a thing she had discovered the previous week when she had ventured out to the Dickens Museum. After weeks at the library reading through Dickens' letters, or what little remained of them, the side trip to Bloomsbury felt like a distraction that could at least be considered work, although when she got there the museum only made her feel more sad. It was located in a house in Doughty Street where the writer had lived for a grand total of two years, but it was the only one of his houses left standing in contemporary London. His residency dated to the happy, early years of his marriage; the museum seemed full of sorrowful reminders of fleeting halcyon days, and Shay was in the kind of mood to find parallels to her own situation at every turn.

She unenthusiastically toured the small rooms restored to the period, noting which pieces of furniture had actually belonged to Dickens himself. It was a month before Christmas and the whole place was already done up with wreaths and mistletoe and yards of red ribbon, which annoyed Shay all the more as she peered around the decorations into display cases stuffed with old letters, pens and the writer's toiletries. Before she left the museum, she ventured idly into the gift shop. She wouldn't dare buy him anything as corny as a Dickens coffee mug and besides, they had agreed, no communication. But perhaps she would find something to send home to her mother, some nice bit of English paraphernalia she could package off before Christmas. She picked up Dickens T-shirts and Dickens mousepads and put them down again before finally turning to the large selection of books, various editions of everything the author ever wrote.

Sandwiched among all the eight-hundred-page novels, she spotted the thinnest little pamphlet with staples holding its slender spine together. She picked it up just because it seemed oddly out of place. It appeared to be a cookbook written by somebody with the unlikely name of Lady Maria Clutterbuck and titled *What Shall We Have for Dinner?*

Shay skimmed its few pages and found she had discovered a historical oddity: it was a book of menus, suggestions for meal planning for groups as small as two and as large as twenty. It paired turbot with shrimp sauce and fried oysters with a shoulder of mutton; it suggested serving sole, a filet of beef and pigeon pie to a party of six or seven; it called for such exotic dishes as minced collops, lark pie and lamb's head, and suggested finishing meals with sweet omelettes, jam pudding or toasted cheese. It seemed a fabulous insight into Victorian life, but it contained only a tiny handful of recipes, an odd selection of desserts and meats with scant instructions and fewer measurements. Who needed a book to tell you that you might serve apple pudding after a mutton stew, and how was one supposed to cook from this little text? Who had thought it was a good idea to publish it?

The back cover explained that Maria Clutterbuck was merely a comic pseudonym for Catherine Dickens, the writer's wife of twenty-two years and mother of his ten children. Catherine Dickens had thought this menu book a useful tool for the Victorian housewife, or perhaps Dickens himself had thought so, since it had been issued by his own publisher.

Shay purchased the pamphlet for only £3; she brought it home and that weekend, in between her crying jags, began contemplating Catherine's menus. Was the Swiss pudding a sweet reminder of Dickens family holidays on the continent? Was a pigeon pie a foolproof way to cheer a difficult husband? Did a nice dish of toasted cheese provide some comfort in the dwindling years of a marriage? Shay bought the much more expensive cookbook she had found at Waterstones when she discovered that it contained recipes for many of the dishes Catherine mentioned.

Now sitting at the breakfast table and reading through the little book again, she felt something stir inside her breast, a current running through her brain that she hadn't felt for months. It was excitement, a desire to know more. She had departed for England agreeing with her supervisor that her subject was the appearance of Ellen Ternan in Dickens' fiction; she had spent hours poring over letters seeking references to how his writing progressed in the years of his affair. She saw Ellen in only the vaguest outlines in her mind's eye, a pretty blonde in a big crinoline, but now a full-blown picture came to her of the writer's wife, the stout lady with the brown ringlets, the fleshy face and the dull eye, sitting there in the morning room of the big house planning the evening's menu, calling in the housekeeper or perhaps marching down to the kitchen to consult the cook herself and decide once and for all what was to be served for dinner.

Shay pushed aside her empty plate and reached for the kettle to pour more water over her tea bag. Could she possibly change topics? Shay's supervisor, cross-appointed from the Women's Studies program back in Toronto, was an old-fashioned feminist with a frighteningly good grasp on the works of Virginia Woolf. Shay wasn't sure how she'd react to her decision to abandon the mysterious Ellen Ternan in favour of the culinary talents of Catherine Dickens.

Of course, she was not Shay's original supervisor because she couldn't keep working with the original one. Not after that day of bright sunshine and churning emotions when her professor—she still had trouble thinking of him as Al—had reached across the desk and placed his hand on top of hers.

Shay shook herself, cast aside the pamphlet, got up from the table and walked downstairs, where she knocked at her landlady's door.

"Mrs. Brown," she asked as the woman appeared in a floral housecoat, "I don't suppose you have a pudding basin you could lend me? I've decided to make a charlotte russe."

It's not what I expected." Bob Stanek's tone is not so much disappointed as it is threatening. He leans back. His big body is expansively arrayed behind an oversized wooden desk with a large leather pad to protect its highly polished surface. It's an antique desk, or at least made to look so, and it's unnaturally tidy—the only things sitting on the pad are one of those old-fashioned pen sets with the pens jutting out of silly little metal holders as though they still needed to be dipped in ink and a glossy white laptop with its lid closed. It strikes me as all wrong. He should either have a battered desk covered in stacks of paper and dictionaries that threaten to bury a clunky beige computer, like some veteran newsman of old, or the pristine laptop should be perched on something all sleek and modern to indicate he is a man of the new media moment. This awkward combination only makes him look like someone who is trying to ride two horses simultaneously, which

I suppose he is. Anyway, it looks pretentious and makes me doubt whether he actually does any work. Perhaps his assistant, the frosty lady who has summoned me to this meeting, tidies up all the paper for him every evening. "Not what I expected at all," he repeats.

"What did you expect?" I ask, trying to sound nothing more than pleasantly inquisitive.

"Well, you said nineteenth century, and Dickens as a character, and that's all fine. That's a good idea, but I don't see why you have to concentrate on his personal life."

"But what is there except personal life? Personal life, emotional life, is what novels are about."

"Well, there are all his books, his literary achievements."

"Yes, but there is no point writing a fictional story about his literary achievements. It wouldn't be interesting. I mean, you can write a novel about somebody's career, I suppose, or their political struggle, or something, but only if you talk about their emotional relationship to it. I mean, I'm not writing a biography of Dickens. Nor really of Ellen Ternan."

"Then what are you doing?"

"Well, I suppose I am trying to imagine what it would be like to be her, to be the mistress of the great man."

Stanek puffs up a bit. I don't suppose he ever imagines what it might be like to be somebody else. He looks like the type who just concentrates on being himself and getting what that self wants. "But you don't make him sound like a great man. He is about to use his fame and power to seduce a woman more than twenty years younger than him. You make him sound horrible."

"I don't think he was horrible. I think he was human."

"Of course he was human. What matters are his books. He was a great writer."

"Yes, a great writer. But not a very good man. I find that interesting, don't you?"

"I don't think it's fair to use his personal life to disparage his—"

"But I'm not disparaging anything. I don't think we can demand that artists be more moral than the rest of us. But I also think their spouses and their children and their lovers are allowed to require as decent behaviour of them as of anyone else. I don't think you're allowed to say, 'Well, I am a great writer so fuck your feelings, fuck your morality.'"

Stanek bristles at the expletive. He is, I realize, unrelentingly old-fashioned. It's the glossy laptop that is pretentious, not the pen set. I don't care if I am offending him though; I'm warming to my subject.

"Dickens wanted freedom to write and he wanted freedom to love Nelly, and if that hurt his family he didn't care much. Or at least not enough to stop the hurt. He did respect morality though, the morality of his day, and that was what trapped him in the end. He was able to ditch his wife, but he never made an honest woman of Nelly."

"Well, lots of men have kept mistresses."

"Yes and it's obvious what's in it for the big guy, but what's in it for the young women?" I am sounding emotional now. "I want to know how she does it."

There's a pause. He seems embarrassed.

"And that is what you are going to write about next?"

"Yes, that sort of thing."

"Well, perhaps we should just stop the project where we are, then. We can pay you the rest of the fee but you can stop writing. I'll be honest with you. We haven't really seen the readership numbers I was hoping for and I am not sure your direction does credit to *The Telegram* . . ."

I feel fear creeping up on me. What am I going to write if I'm not writing the serial? I haven't been able to imagine any other stories for months. Dickens and Nelly, at least I know how it has to turn out. I've been having fun filling in the blanks, amusing myself. But of course, I want readers too. And I want Al to read it. I interrupt Stanek.

"No, no. Bob. Please." I smile, keeping my tone light-hearted. I want to sound like his equal, the famed author condescending to write for him, not some cowed underling. "I think perhaps we need to hear from Dickens. I wonder if that might satisfy some of your reservations?"

"It would seem more fair. Give the guy his say."

"Yes, more fair. It may take a bit of space . . ."

"What do you mean?"

"Well, what I've got planned next is a little longer and I'll need a bit more space in the paper."

"You don't ask for much, do you?" Stanek seems pleased by my boldness; he's a bully and I've stood up to him. "Okay. Talk to Jonathan. If he can't accommodate you in print, he can just throw it up online."

He rises to dismiss me but then hesitates, as though he suspects I've pulled a fast one on him. "What will Dickens say then?"

"I'll deliver it to Jonathan as soon as I can. You'll find out next week."

The Dickens Bicentenary Serial
An interlude

"What do you like to read, my dear?"

"Oh. The other day I was reading, that is to say, I was rereading *Oliver Twist* . . ."

"No, no, I was not asking you to flatter me. What do you read besides me? Tennyson?"

"Oh, yes. Tennyson. And *Robinson Crusoe*. And—"

"*Robinson Crusoe*? A capital story. I devoured it when I was a boy. And the Brothers Grimm, of course."

"Of course."

"Did you ever read *The Arabian Nights* when you were a girl?"

"No, I don't believe—"

"How I loved those tales. My father had a copy. There was a small room at the top of our house in Chatham where he kept his books. Not a library by any stretch, a box room, to tell the truth of it. I had little proper schooling; a few years in a dame's school, nothing more. But my father thought every gentleman should own books. I suppose later, in London, when he fell on hard times and I was sent out to work, all those books must have been sold to pay the debt collector who was forever at our door."

"But how sad to have given up the books. When I was a girl we travelled so much we never really had the space to keep any in the first place."

"Ah, the life of the travelling player. Our life became rather itinerant too once we left Chatham, but in that first home, the tiny attic room was my palace. I would sneak upstairs when I was supposed to be minding my younger sisters and spend many an hour with Grimm or *The Arabian Nights*. I was fascinated by the story of King Shahriyar, who marries a different bride every night and then dispatches her to his executioners the next morning . . ."

"He killed every wife?"

"Yes, so that no woman could ever betray him."

"After only one night?"

"Well, it's a fairy story, my dear. He killed every bride until Scheherazade volunteered to be his wife."

"Who was Scheherazade?"

"Why, she's the narrator of the tales. But she's no ordinary narrator. She has her own story. She was the daughter of the King's vizier and a princess of Samarkand, and she told Shahriyar such wondrous tales each night he had to keep her alive. My favourite was of the Prince of Persia, who escapes bandits and discovers a beautiful maiden trapped in a cave by an evil genie."

"An evil genie?"

"Yes. Shall I tell you the story of the genie? I love telling it. There are different versions; let me see . . . Once upon a time . . . they don't actually start like that, the Arabian tales, but the situation seems to call for it. So, once upon a time, there lived a King of Persia. He was a wise and benevolent monarch who ruled his family as he did his people, with firmness, prudence and foresight, and he had assured that his eldest son and heir received a most thorough education. The King had brought to his court many a learned man to instruct the young Prince, and these tutors unveiled to their pupil the mysteries of mathematics, geometry and astronomy and taught him to speak five languages. The Prince, as handsome as he was capable, played several musical instruments, sang with a voice that his music master envied and was schooled in the art of rhetoric by the King's ministers themselves. So learned were his disputations that word of his intellect and grace spread beyond the borders of Persia to Hind, which is what you and I would call India, where his father's friend and ally, the King of Hind, heard such flattering tales of the Prince that he sent messengers to Persia inviting the young paragon to come and share his many talents with his royal court.

"The King of Persia was happy to let his son make the journey for he believed that travel could only serve to further elevate the Prince's fine mind and bold spirit. And too, the King was not insensible of the need to find the

Prince a royal bride. Believing that the young man should make his own selection—something that thus far the Prince had shown no inclination to do from among the many beautiful ladies of high and noble birth who frequented his father's court—the monarch secretly hoped the young man might fall in love with one of the King of Hind's three daughters, which would in turn further strengthen the friendship between their two lands.

"Providing for education, politics and affairs of the heart, the King's plan was well conceived, but it suffered from what was to prove a fateful weakness: the Persian Prince's route to the kingdom of Hind would force him to cross hostile lands in a country called Gandahara. The king of this land was the fiercest enemy of the King of Persia and taught his people to hate anyone or anything Persian. At the very least the Prince would require protection on his long travel east. Not wanting to give the bellicose Gandaharans any cause for making war, the King of Persia was reluctant to send one of his impressive armies to accompany his son on his travels. Instead, he determined that the Prince should travel incognito with only five horsemen to protect him on his way, counting on a light guard that could move with alacrity to ward off any troubles that the Prince might encounter."

"That sounds inadvisable."

"Yes, clever girl. It was inadvisable. But if every king always behaved sensibly, we storytellers would be a sorry lot. So, as you've guessed, as the Prince crossed

Gandahara, a band of robbers fell upon his party. Not wishing to identify himself as a hated Persian, the Prince called out, 'Hold. We are messengers travelling to the King of Hind. Royal recompense will be yours if you spare our lives and our purses.'

"But the answer came back 'Hind! Why, the King of Hind is almost as hated in these lands as the King of Persia.' And with that the wild band descended on the small party, swiftly dispatched the five guards, stole their horses and saddlebags, stripped the Prince of his clothes and his purse and left him for dead.

"Abandoned in an unknown land without friend or companion, the Prince wondered how he could possibly survive. As the night grew colder and the wind stronger, he was forced . . . perhaps here your storyteller will just skip ahead . . ."

"No, no I want to hear it all."

"Yes, of course. All of it, but *The Arabian Nights* can sometimes be a little gruesome, I'm afraid. So, yes, eventually the Prince crept up to the bloodied corpses of his murdered guards and stole away with a burnoose to protect himself from the cold. The next morning, parched and half frozen, he crept back to their bodies to empty their pockets of the few dates they might have hidden there and whatever water or wine he could find in the skins they had slung over their shoulders.

"Thinking he must now surely be nearer to his destination than to his home, he journeyed onward on foot and,

the next morning, chilled and stiff, he sighted a sparkling
city on the horizon. The Prince was desperately hungry and
hoped he might find food there, but he approached with
caution least he still find himself in the land of the vicious
Gandaharans. He entered the city alongside many vendors
and farmers and passed easily in their midst through the
main gates. He followed them toward the centre of the city
and, as they pressed on, hung back, considering how he
should proceed. It was then he saw a little tailor, sitting
sewing outside his shop. He performed a salam and the
man courteously returned the greeting. 'Tell me, my good
man, what city do I find myself in?' the Prince asked.

"'Why, stranger, everyone knows this is the city of
Takshashila,' the tailor replied.

"'And in what land is Takshashila?' the Prince asked,
hoping that he now found himself in Hind.

"'Why, stranger, everyone knows we are in the land
of Gandahara,' the tailor, increasingly puzzled, replied.
'What land do you come from?'

"The Prince, not wishing to identify himself as a
Persian and knowing not what else he might say, only
mumbled, 'I come from far away.'

"'Stranger,' said the tailor gently, for he was a kind
man and saw the young man before him was tired and
hungry, 'come into my shop so that I may offer you a cup
of mint tea.'

"Once inside the shop, he said to the Prince in a low
voice: 'Be careful, stranger. I think perhaps from your

accent and your odd dress that you come here from Persia, and you must know you are in a hostile land.'

"Disarmed by the man's sympathetic tone, the Prince confessed all. 'I am not merely Persian, I am the Prince of Persia, travelling to the land of Hind to visit its King. But I have been set upon by bandits, lost my men, my horses, my rations and my purse, and I know not how I am to continue.'

"'The King of Persia!' declared the tailor. 'Why, the King of Gandahara hates him more than anyone in the world. You need to quickly disguise yourself if you want to survive here. I can give you food and drink, and I can sell you some clothes that will make you less conspicuous in these parts, but how will you pay me for them if you have lost your purse?'

"'I can work,' replied the Prince. 'I have many talents. I am particularly known for my disputations. Should you require a petition to be presented or a legal argument to be made, I can be the most convincing advocate for your cause.'

"'I am a peaceable man. I have no need for disputations or petitions,' the tailor replied.

"'I am also a renowned linguist. Perhaps you have documents written in foreign languages that you need translated into your native tongue,' said the Prince.

"'I am a quiet man,' replied the tailor. 'I have never travelled outside this city and have no need of foreign tongues.'

"'I am also an accomplished musician. Perhaps I could teach you to play the tar?'

"'I have no use for music,' the tailor answered.

"'I know,' said the Prince, grasping finally at his one branch of learning that might be of use to a humble tailor. 'I have studied mathematics. Perhaps I can do your account books for you.'

"'I have the abacus for that,' replied the tailor.'"

"So in the end, his learning is no use at all. He might just as well have had a year or two at a dame school."

"My dear, you are teasing me. These are extraordinary circumstances the Prince finds himself in. He will have need of his learning again; you'll see. Shall I continue?"

"Oh, yes, please do."

"So the tailor suggests he find work as a woodcutter. 'Here on the steppes firewood is always in short supply, and the woodcutters travel far to the forests to the north to bring us what we need. My cousin is a woodcutter; I can lend you clothes and he can give you an axe and tomorrow you can go into the woods and earn the money to pay us back and feed yourself.'

"The Prince felt a wave of sorrow swamp his tired body. Was he, so full of learning, so bold of purpose, so graceful of posture, to put his back to the axe and keep no company but trees? Where was a father or friend who might know his worth and restore his dignity? Alas, he was alone in a strange land, so he resigned himself to accepting the kindly tailor's offer.

"And so the noble Prince of Persia set out the next day to become a lowly woodcutter. He worked long and hard in the forests to the north, first paying the tailor for food and clothing and the tailor's cousin for the axe, then carefully saving the few coins he made from selling the wood that he brought back each day to the city. He hoped in time to buy a new horse and continue on his journey, but he found the money was barely sufficient to do much more than pay his saviour for his bread and board.

"One day, after a few months of this labour, he had ventured deeper into the forest in hopes of finding stouter trees that would fetch a better price back in Takshashila and so hasten the day when he could leave. He picked a good thick one and swung his axe at its very base. A loud metallic clang reverberated through the forest. Clearing dead leaves and dirt away from the roots, the Prince discovered that his axe blade had hit a sturdy brass ring hidden in the ground beside the tree. He tugged at the ring and found it was attached to a heavy stone. By dint of tugging and pulling, he managed to shift the stone and slowly manoeuvre it to one side, and there was a hole large enough that a man might fit himself in it. When the Prince crouched down and peered into it, he saw that he had discovered a passageway with a stairway leading deep into the earth. Descending the stairs the Prince found himself in a lushly furnished chamber hung all about with drapery in a damask cloth of red and gold. Soft divans upholstered in yellow and purple velvet invited one to linger, and underneath the sea of cushions that covered the floor one could glimpse multicoloured Turkey carpets made from the finest silk thread. As the Prince took in this luxurious scene, stunned to find such quarters hidden away in a cave in the depths of the dark forest, a voice spoke to him. It was a female voice, light and delicate and expressing mainly puzzlement at the sound of a visitor arriving in the room.

"'Is that you, my lord?' it asked. The Prince looked about him, wondering for a moment where the owner of this sweet voice might be, when he realized the sound came from behind a richly carved ebony screen in one corner. He stepped forward and, not knowing how to answer but knowing himself to be a lord, he replied boldly, 'Yes. It is I.'

"At that a figure emerged from behind the screen and said with a peevishness more charming than grating—and certainly quiet forgivable since the lady in question was confronted with a complete stranger in the midst of her boudoir: 'No. It most certainly is not. Who are you?'

"At first all the Prince could do was to admire a beauty that left him with a certain breathlessness he had never experienced on meeting any of the many noble ladies at his father's court. This creature's figure was slim but shapely, wrapped in a silken robe; her jet-black hair fell to her waist; her skin was as white as porcelain and her lips were as pink as rose petals. But her dark brown eyes flashed warningly at the Prince."

"Porcelain and rose petals? She sounds like a heroine in a lady's magazine."

"Very well. Snowflakes and rhubarb then. 'I,' said the Prince, 'am the Prince of Persia.'

"'Then why,' she demanded quite reasonably, 'are you dressed like a woodcutter?'"

"She sounds a rather sensible sort."

"Rather like you, my dear. Imminently sensible and exquisitely beautiful. Shall I continue now?"

"Please do."

"The Prince looked down at his dirty work clothes. Confronted by this wondrous room and this wonderful lady, he had quite forgotten his own situation. 'Well,' he replied, putting down the rough log carrier he bore on his back, 'it really is an extraordinary story. Would you like to hear it?'

"The lady thought for a bit. 'I find myself unoccupied at the moment. You may sit down there'—she pointed at the divan farthest from her—'and tell me your story.'

"So, the Prince began to relate the story of his journey, his escape from the bandits, his arrival in Takshashila and his rescue by the kind tailor who sent him to work as a woodcutter. So skilled an orator was the Prince and so engrossed was the lady by the story that with each subsequent chapter she moved closer and closer to the teller so that, by the time the Prince was relating his discovery of her cave, she sat but inches away from him gazing into his face.

"'Oh,' she said finally, 'that is indeed the most remarkable tale.'

"'Now you must tell me your story,' the Prince said. 'How does such a beautiful lady come to be living in a cave under the ground?'

"At that, the lady gave a little gasp and a tear came into her eye.

"'Why, good lady, what is wrong?' asked the Prince.

"'I am also of royal blood,' she said, wiping away the tear. 'I am the Princess of Samarkand, and for five long years I have been held a prisoner here.'"

"I thought Scheherazade was the Princess of Samarkand."

"It's one of those places with many princesses."

"And so the Princess of Samarkand began to relate her own story, but since the Prince rather than the Princess is our chief concern here, you will excuse me if I give you only a summary of her tale."

"I just want to know how she came to be living in the cave."

"Yes, of course. I am getting to that. Goodness, you are an impatient little thing. Yes, so, the Princess had been travelling with her attendants in the forests near her home, gathering wild strawberries or some other lady-like activity, when one member of the party disturbed some shrubs, causing a mighty genie to appear. The genie rose before them, terrifyingly large, frightened all her attendants away and left her standing there at his mercy. He picked her up and carried her miles through the forest on his giant legs until he brought her to this cave, where he has kept her prisoner ever since. For nine days the genie is nowhere to be seen, off doing some mysterious and demonic business the nature of which we would not even want to guess, but on the tenth day, he comes to the Princess and spends the night at her side. That day he had just left when the Prince arrived.

"'So,' said the beautiful Princess with a shy smile, 'you are safe here for nine days and may stay with me.'

"'No,' said the Prince, horrified at such an unmaidenly suggestion. 'I will not stay, but I will take you with me. Come, we will mount the stairs and journey through the forest and somehow find a way to return to our fathers and our lands.'"

"Quite the proper thing to do, I expect. Imagine attending the pleasure of such a wicked creature!"

"Unthinkable. Nonetheless, it was the Princess's plight. Now, where was I? You have me all tangled. Oh yes, she rejects his plan because, says the Princess, sadly, 'I think you will find the stairs are no longer there.'

"The Prince turned to where he had come through the tunnel into her rich chamber and indeed there was now only an impenetrable stone wall at the spot he had entered.

"'The wall only parts when the genie comes to visit,' she explained. 'It shuts again as soon as he leaves. You must somehow have slipped down the stairs before the rock closed them off again.'

"'Have you never tried to run up behind him when he leaves?' the Prince could not help asking."

"That's clever of him. He's got a point there."

"Yes, it's all that learning, you see. At that suggestion, however, the Princess looked even more pained: 'The genie is an angry master. He has threatened me with the most gruesome fate if I ever try to follow him out of the chamber,' she said. 'As long as I obey him, he brings me books to read and delicacies to eat, thread for my sewing and jewels to wear. If I crave a pomegranate to eat or need oil for my hair, I have only to call him and he will come.'

"'How do you call him?' the Prince asked.

"The Princess led him over to a corner of the chamber farthest from the stone where he had entered and showed him an inscription carved into the wall in some ancient script that even the Prince, erudite though he was, could not read.

"'I have only to touch these words and the genie will appear,' she said.

"'Then let us call him and I will battle him until he releases you,' the Prince said, reaching out his hand toward the inscription.

"'No,' the Princess shrieked in horror, grabbing his arm to pull it away from the wall. 'You will never be able to conquer a jinn; his body is the size of two men and his magic is too powerful for any mortal to fight.'

"'Better to fight honourably than to live a captive soul,' cried the Prince, thinking as much of his own enslavement to woodcutting as of the Princess's sad plight. And so saying, he reached out with his other arm and touched the magic inscription.

"Instantly a roaring sound filled the air and plumes of smoke billowed into the room. Rocks crashed away from the wall where the Prince had first entered and gradually the wall itself fell apart. Into the room stepped a creature who was, just as the Princess had warned, the height of two men, with a bare chest the size of a table-top and legs as thick as tree trunks. 'You have called me back, my Princess. What can your jiin provide?' But as he said these words, he caught sight of the Prince and now bellowed out, 'Who is this?'

"'I am a lowly woodcutter who stumbled into this cave,' the Prince replied.

"'Liar,' cried the genie. 'You are her lover.' And he turned now on the Princess. 'You harlot! You have hidden him here even while I visited. Have I not provided you with everything a woman could ever need or want, given you jewels and entertainment, fed you delicacies and pro-tected you from harm, and yet you have betrayed me with this common man.'

"He pounced on the Prince, displaying the agility of a cat despite his huge size, and seized him up in his mas-sive hands.

"'I will kill you, you foul human, but first I will tor-ture her until she confesses her crime and I will make you watch as she suffers.' He set down the Prince, who might have been tempted to bolt up the open staircase were it not that the monster now took hold of the Princess, whose piteous cries filled the Prince's heart with dread. Looking

144

about in desperation for some way in which he could stop the genie, he spied the axe that he had set down when he was telling the Princess his story. He grabbed it up, took a wide swing and plunged it into the genie's leg."

"Oh, that's it. That's the way. He'll get him now."

"Not as easy as that, my dear. The genie gave a cry of pain but the Prince saw that his mighty blow had barely scratched the creature's leg. Nonetheless, as the genie roared in anger, he put down the Princess so that he could stop the Prince, who darted out of his grasp and ducked behind the largest of the divans. The thought occurred to him, with what little mental capacity he had that was not devoted to his immediate survival, that if the mighty genie had to struggle so clumsily to determine how he might hold on to both his captives simultaneously, then whatever powers this monster possessed, those of the intellect were not among them. So, as the genie plunged forward and was about to rip the piece of furniture out of his path, the Prince stood up from behind it and cried loudly, 'Hold, oh great and mighty genie. In the name of Allah, I promise you the lady has not been unfaithful to you. I am only a lowly woodcutter who ventured down the stairs to this chamber in error and would never dare to meddle with a power as large as yours. You could kill me and torture the lady until she expires too, but then you would have lost the thing you most prize.'

"The genie stared at him now. 'Then I will just kill you,' he said and he started forward.

"'No doubt you can do that in an instant, oh powerful one, for the strength of a genie is legendary,' said the Prince. 'Is it true you can also change shapes at will?'

"'I can double my size like this,' replied the genie, beginning to swell toward the ceiling of the chamber as his body grew in every direction.

"'Be careful, great one, you will break the roof and burst out of this cave,' the Prince warned, and the genie, like a deflating balloon, returned again to his already monstrous size.

"'You can make yourself huge, but I don't suppose you can make yourself small,' said the Prince. 'I wonder how you can possibly fit down the opening at the top of the stairs.'

"'I can make myself any size or shape I care to,' boasted the genie. 'I have made myself as light as a feather and flown over the world on a breeze; I have made myself twice the size of this room and strode across continents.'

"'Really. As light as a feather? I find that difficult to believe,' said the Prince. Then, pointing to an ornate box with a lid of inlaid pearl that sat at the end of one divan, he continued, 'I mean, a lowly human like me could crawl into a space as small as that chest over there and hide himself from a great genie like you, but I doubt a great genie could hide himself from me.'

"'Of course I can make myself that small. Just watch.' And at that he began to shrink down to the size of a child and slip inside the chest.

"'Quick, sit on it,' cried the Prince to the Princess as he ran for his rope, wrapped it several times around the chest and tied it with the tightest of knots. Inside, the genie fumed at his captors but could not unknot his own limbs enough to swell his body back to his regular size.

"'Run,' cried the Prince as he grasped the Princess by the hand and led her toward the opening in the stone wall. So, they ran up the stairs, through the forest and back to the tailor's shop in Takshashila. The next day, they set out to sell a few of the Princess's many jewels so they could pay the kind tailor, buy horses and start the journey for Persia.

"By the time they arrived back in the Prince's kingdom, he had secured a promise of marriage from the Princess, and his father, the King, was overjoyed not only to be reunited with his son who had been missing for many months but also to welcome his prospective bride, even if she was not one of the five beautiful daughters of the King of Hind."

"You said three before."

"Did I? No, I think he had five daughters. At any rate, the King of Persia was just as happy to see his court allied with that of Samarkand, and following the solemn ceremony and lavish feast that marked their marriage, the happy couple made a triumphant visit to her kingdom to meet her long-lost family. And what do you think happened next?"

"They lived happily ever after."

"How dare you?" Al looks up from the Saturday paper. He is so calm and smooth a personality, so rarely angry, that for a second I don't realize he is serious and mistake his tone for ironic awe.

"You like it?" I ask but before I have even finished the words I know I've got it wrong. It was a risky play; I wanted to woo Stanek and Jonathan and *The Telegram* readers; I was convinced by my own cleverness and conveniently ignored where I got my clever idea. Al quickly slaps me down.

"I think it's appallingly presumptuous."

"But you all complained it was just about Ellen Ternan. I decided to let Dickens get a word in," I say, but it now sounds unconvincing even to my own ears.

"I'll leave others to judge your talent for pastiche. It's the story he tells . . ."

"'The Second Dervish's Tale.'"

"It's one thing to do Dickens. You studied him before

you quit; he's still one of the most popular writers in the language. I can't pretend to own him, although I do think you are treading in pretty well-worn territory here . . ."

"But you own *The Thousand and One Nights*? Is that it?" I sound angry.

"No, but I am the leading, the only, scholar who has really traced the influence of *The Nights* on Dickens." Al's assessment of his scholarship is perfectly accurate, but when he puffs himself up like this I always remember my mother saying in her acerbic way, "If you are really good, you don't need to boast."

"That's my stuff," Al continues. "You're stealing from me."

Part of me knows he's right and that I should acknowledge it now and make peace, but intellectual sparring comes far more easily to both of us. "Come on. I may be using your research as a jumping-off point but you didn't just stay up to midnight two nights in a row trying to write a retelling of 'The Second Dervish's Tale' in the style of *The Pickwick Papers*."

"Oh, is that what you were doing? Well, the point you are making is mine."

"So, your work inspires me. Imitation is the sincerest form of flattery." Flattery, this is where I should have started, before publication. Last week, after my six-month checkup. I got the all-clear. Al and I went out to dinner to celebrate; he smiled at me in his old way. Things were looking good and now I've blown it.

"You've got your bestsellers, for Christ's sake. That's your turf. Why do you have to come poaching on mine?"

My anger, tamped down to get by, returns to me in full force. "You are always sneering at my books. You think they're just romance novels. And here, when I'm doing something more literary . . . " Lost in my own sense of grievance now, I'm surprised when he comes right back at me: "This is so like you. It's always about the needs of your story, never mine."

Al has hit at the heart of something there. I stumble towards the table where he sits and grope for a chair, collapsing into it. He starts up towards me, anxiety instantly subduing him.

"Are you okay?" He touches my back. "You're not well enough to be working yet. I hate to see you exhausting yourself."

His concern somehow infuriates me more; I am tired of his pity and worry; they are no replacement for passion.

"That's not true. You just hate to see me working."

"What are you yelling about, Mummy?"

Anahita has come into the kitchen. She sounds more inquisitive than alarmed, but she has heard us. We are trying so hard to give the girls stability after all that has happened, to let them trust in their home and their parents again.

"Oh, nothing, sweetie. Daddy and I were just arguing about Dickens."

"Charles Chickens," Anahita replies. "Stupid old Charles Chickens. Can I have some hot chocolate?"

She is easily distracted by the prospect of her hot drink, but as I stick the mug in the microwave I am fighting back tears. Al grabs his tablet off the kitchen table and removes himself upstairs to his office, shutting the door behind him. He doesn't come out until lunch, which he eats in silence before preparing to depart with the girls for a birthday party. I dress them up in their new velveteen pants and frilly blouses, press colourfully wrapped packages for the birthday girl into their hands, shut the door and start to cry. I had wanted Al to like the serial, to understand that writing was part of getting better. I wanted to be somebody other than a patient; I wanted to be me, the old me he used to love. In my convenient fantasy, the serial was going to draw us together again, revive our mutual interest in literature, make daily life about something more than getting by without a fight. But with "The Second Dervish's Tale" I had only got his attention by treading on his toes. I had misjudged my audience again.

I want to phone Becky, seek solace and rehash the rights and wrongs of the situation, but I know she won't welcome the call. Becky does casseroles, she does babysitting, she does hand-holding, but she has made it very clear that she doesn't do marriage counselling any more.

———

It was a breach in our friendship that happened before Al returned to the house. I was well launched into one of my regular phone calls with Becky, asking for the umpteenth time how anyone who had so wanted children would jeopardize his relationship with his precious daughters by betraying their mother and gambling that some babe twenty years his junior was going to stick by him beyond next year when Becky said something that brought me up short.

"I guess he wasn't happy."

"What do you mean? How could he not be happy? He had everything he said he wanted, me, the house, the girls, the big job. A week before he told me about the affair, we had been talking about finally making a trip to Iran."

"Just because people have the things they want doesn't mean they are happy. Maybe he wasn't happy with you. People drift apart sometimes."

"We had a date night every week. We still had sex."

"It's not really about sex. It's about being connected or something. We're all so busy, you know, with the kids and work. Maybe something got lost in the shuffle. Anyway, he seems to have found something he was missing."

"Oh, he has, has he?"

I was angry again, angry at Al, angry at Becky, although I knew what she was saying was half true. At least after the girls were born. We had made the un- spoken, incremental pact of parents with young children: we will love each other a little less so that we can love them more. Love is only infinite in stories; in real life, there are only so many hours in the day.

"Do you really believe that?" I continued haughtily.

"Well, I think there are two sides to—"

"And which one are you on?"

"I don't want to take sides, Sharon. David and I want to remain friends with both of you. I don't want to do he said, she said."

"Great. Thanks. Okay. What do you want to talk about then?"

"What did we used to talk about? Our jobs. The kids. Our mothers."

"Our husbands."

"Yeah, but, I don't know, the environment. Municipal politics. The ballet. We used to talk about lots of stuff and now all we ever talk about is Al and the blessed student."

"Yeah."

"So let's just try talking about something else, okay?"

"Nice weather we've been having lately."

The next time I called her it was to tell her that I had cancer.

The Dickens Bicentenary Serial: Chapter 8
London. June 2, 1859

"It is a beautiful house. The gas may require a few improvements, but the plumbing is new and the garden is very pleasant. What I propose is this . . ." said Charles, tracing lines on the tablecloth with his dinner knife like a general laying out his battle plans. Nelly associated this business-like voice mainly with the ordering of carriages or meals in restaurants. Indeed, he had begun that day's lunch at Verrey's, an establishment that he compared favourably with restaurants in Paris, by ordering the fish and the veal for all three of them in a rather similar tone, but it was not one she heard from him often. Mainly, their conversations tended to take a bantering note with a good deal of idle flattery on both sides. He indulged her opinions on art and even asked her to read his manu-scripts—she remembered the thrill she had felt when he had first said to her, almost shyly, "Perhaps you could look this over?"—but they never discussed politics, and after the disasters of the previous year, he kept her well clear of both his professional engagements and his domestic affairs. He organized outings and meals with efficiency and discretion, but she had certainly never heard him unfold a scheme as complex as this one.

"Nelly cannot hold the property until she is twenty-one, so I would buy it in Maria's and Fanny's names, on the understanding her sisters would then sign it over to her next year," he continued. "The lease would be hers and hers alone, with no conditions attached. It has eighty years to run: she would be housed for life, or she could dispose of it at any time if she so chose."

"A very generous idea, Mr. Dickens," Mrs. Ternan murmured over her coffee cup.

Charles had found a house just off Mornington Crescent, a large house by his description, three storeys with room for all of them, and he was proposing to buy it for them. He addressed his remarks primarily to Mrs. Ternan but he kept looking over at Nelly to gauge her reaction. She said nothing.

"The house"—and here his tone faltered as he turned to her directly—"I ask nothing in return, Nelly. It would be yours no matter what happened, no matter what happened to me or to you."

She met his eyes but still said nothing. He pressed on, more desperate and now simply ignoring her mother's presence, and said, "I am not your equal . . ."

She raised a half-mocking eyebrow at him.

"I mean, I cannot offer you my hand, the way I would wish, but I offer you my heart . . ."

His heart—and a house in Mornington Crescent. Was it what she wanted? Was it enough?

She was thinking it over later that evening when her mother put their tea on the table. Maria and Fanny were appearing together in a revue at the Haymarket that night, and after lunch in the best restaurant in Regent Street, Nelly and her mother were eating tinned sprats on toast. They ate in silence for a while, but the food was soon finished, and as Mrs. Ternan pushed aside her plate, she spoke her mind.

"The time has come to make a decision, Nelly. This friendship cannot continue in this manner forever. If you ever wish to marry and have children of your own, you must refuse him and we will make our own way. I have always provided for you and your sisters. Fanny and Maria have good opportunities ahead; so do you."

Nelly made a small moue. None of them were playing leading roles. Fanny, once renowned as a child prodigy, had been unable to establish much of an adult stage career. Her Italian music lessons had fuelled her love of grand opera without providing her much opportunity to sing it and she hated the sentimental songs of the kind she was performing that night. She talked about taking in students instead. Nelly and Maria, meanwhile, were

always being asked to play minor roles in the most grotesque farces. Maria had spent the previous month learning how to land on her back in such a way that her
crinoline would fly up over her head, affording the gentlemen in the audience a nice view of her bloomers.

"We will always find work," her mother insisted.
"We have always managed somehow and we will continue to do so. If, on the other hand, you want his company and you want this house . . . well, I think you know
what goes with the house."

Yes, the time had come. Some might say she had
played him very nicely; she suspected that was what a few
of his friends thought, his male friends, of course. The
ladies did not know her. It had been almost two years now,
two years since her appearance alongside him on stage in
Manchester; two years since their misunderstanding in
Doncaster, and theirs remained, whatever the gossips
might say, an innocent friendship. She thought back with
amusement on her own naïveté; she had thought him a
lovely new family friend bringing wonderful opportunities
to herself perhaps, but mainly to Fanny and Maria. And
he had proven such a friend: taking them on walks and
picnics, putting in a word with theatre managers for all
three of them, paying for Fanny's music lessons in Italy
and keeping a fatherly eye out for her and Maria when her
mother and Fanny left for the continent. But he was neither a father nor a brother, and if she had been naive in
those first months, she could no longer pretend that she

did not know what she had read in his face that day at Conisbrough Castle. Perhaps they were right; perhaps she had played him these past two years.

But her compliments, her laughter, her jokes—they came naturally to her. She had grown to like him, to enjoy his company. She could not deny, however, her secret fantasy that a handsome young man with a good income would show up some day soon.

"Do you hear me, Nelly? I would never force you one way or another. If you do not wish to live in his house, the house he will buy for you with certain expectations . . ."

"He said it would be mine no matter what . . ."

"That is generous of him. He is offering you the house no matter what happens in the future, but I think it would be silly of you to think that he offers you the house with no expectations for the present. If you don't want that life, we will refuse him and we will support ourselves, and I will hope that some day you and Fanny and Maria will all marry and that I will be a grandmother."

"And if I do want it?"

"Do you love him, Nelly?"

How could one not love him? He was funny, he was generous, he was quick and smart, full of life and jokes and stories. He made her feel glorious, elevated above the grimy streets, the cramped cottage and the gas-lit theatres, as though all life were just a day at the races, a golden bracelet or cakes for tea. On stage she had but glimpses of her own power, she had never taken a lead role and it was only on that odd occasion when the audience laughed at one of her lines or applauded her exit that she had the slightest whiff of that elation that comes from winning over a crowd. With him, she knew it every time they met; every time, he got that particular look in his eye and she knew that she, and only she, was the cause of it.

But still, that was how his love for her made her feel. What of her love for him? Yes, he was funny, generous, quick, smart, full of jokes and stories . . . and handsome too, she supposed, handsome for an old man. She liked the way the flesh crinkled around his eyes and yet, she knew that was not what she felt when she watched Mr. Birk play Romeo and she knew that when she imagined the young man with a good income his face looked more like Mr. Birk's than Mr. Dickens'. She sensed vaguely there was a difference between loving his love for her and loving him. But it was an abstract thing, hard to discern as long as he had no rival. It wasn't as though Mr. Birk had ever paid her the slightest attention; her imaginary young man was precisely that. She would turn twenty-one next spring; she couldn't afford to wait much longer and she saw that her power in this instance was unique. No audience seemed to believe she was so special; no other man had ever appeared so moved. This must be her destiny. She felt its pull.

"Tell him to buy the house in Mornington Crescent. Tell him that I understand."

found the lump the way everyone does: in the shower. I was just raising one arm above my head to wash an armpit when the hand holding the soap brushed against something. I stopped, put down the soap and felt my left breast. There was something there, something hard buried deep down. I puzzled for a moment. I had once had a big cyst on my neck, but it was softer and closer to the surface than this. You could sort of push it around, but this thing resisted. What could it possibly be? It took me a few seconds before the reality dawned.

When I was younger, we were all told to examine our breasts every month, lie down on the bed and paw about a bit, right up into the armpit. I was always forgetting to do it and then one day the doctors all changed their minds and decided self-examination mainly produced false alarms and I gratefully abandoned my erratic practice of it. Breast cancer seemed a very distant and unlikely prospect. It was the proverbial something that happened to somebody else. My mother's friends mainly: well-groomed post-menopausal women who had their mastectomies quickly and quietly and reappeared in a few months as though nothing had happened. "Shirley has breast cancer," my mother would sigh into the phone one winter and then the next summer there Shirley would be, a gracious, grey-haired grandmother apparently unchanged by the disease. The younger women were unknown to me, those tragic bald figures for whose benefit someone was always organizing a run or a bike ride, that unlikely acquaintance of Becky's who had found the lump when she was breastfeeding and died before the child was three. As a healthy person, I gave them barely a second thought, they were outliers, the wildly unlucky ones. I am an active woman in her late thirties and the mother of twin girls whom I delivered in ten hours without a C-section. I have no family history of cancer; I drink lightly, a few glasses of wine here and there, and eat well. Not too much red meat. I've never smoked. I go to a cardio class twice a week and I do Pilates. This was not happening to me.

So, I proceeded to my doctor's office and from there, a few days later, to the mammogram machine in a state of calm denial. This would all go away. I could not, as a newly single mother, be suffering from cancer. There had been far too much pain and drama in my life in the past year; it seemed statistically impossible there could be more. Al had been gone five months. We were just starting to establish new routines. The girls had only recently stopped crying at night and accepted it was every other weekend at Daddy's new apartment and Wednesdays for pizza after school. We could not possibly be so unlucky as to add cancer treatment or, worse yet, unsuccessful cancer treatment to this mix. I would not indulge in disaster scenarios. I let the technician squeeze my breast between the glass plates of the mammogram machine the way I let the massage therapist work on the knots in my lower back, with a kind of gracious mental absence that suggests I am rather above mundane things like pain.

"Sorry. Is that okay?"

"No problem."

"We usually try to go easy the first time but in your case we do need to make sure we have a good image."

My case? Oh, I suppose she means because I am not here for a routine checkup.

"No problem. You have to do your job."

"Okay. Deep breath and stay still."

The technician stepped behind a screen; there was a whirring sound, and then she came back and started the whole process again from a different angle. She did both breasts. Might as well, I suppose.

Rather to my surprise, the doctor's office phoned within a few days with an appointment for a biopsy the following week. I was still doing my ladylike denial thing when I went to get the results a fortnight later. I felt I was there under false pretenses: the good doctor should not have been wasting her time on me; there were sick people who needed her attention.

She had always been a motherly sort but there was no way to sugar-coat what she had to tell me: there was a significant cancerous tumour. A surgeon would need to remove the breast. An oncologist would tell me what came next, radiation possibly, chemotherapy for certain, probably a drug regimen after that. The treatment might force me into menopause several years early. She gave me a fistful of pamphlets and said her office would phone in the next few days with an appointment to meet the surgeon.

"We don't want to delay," she said. "I know it's a lot to take in. You'll need help. You'll be off work for a while and you'll want to warn the girls that you won't be well. Is Al here with you today?"

I waited a week, then two; then, ten days before the surgery date, I finally phoned him and told him the truth.

He listened without interrupting but barely paused before he spoke.

"I'm coming home."

He showed up a few hours later, walking through the front door with a gym bag and enfolding me in a hug. It was the first time he had touched me in almost nine months. We sat and had a cup of tea in the kitchen and I told him what I knew so far and cried and said I was terrified for the girls. It was after about an hour of this, when I realized it was almost time to go and pick them up from school, that I told him he'd better go.

"I'll stay," he said.

"You can't stay. I have to go get the girls."

"I'll wait here."

"It's not your night with them. What would we say to them?"

"That I've come home. I have a few things with me for tonight. I'll go get the rest tomorrow." I stared at him. His decisiveness was insane. "We'll need to tell them about the surgery soon. Maybe not use the C-word, eh? Do kids know what that means?"

"Al, you can't just come home all of a sudden. You can't return for a bit and then go away again." He loved his children so much but could be completely clueless as to their needs.

"You and the girls need me."

"But what happens when the treatment is over? What happens when I get better?"

"I guess we'll just have to see."

And there began several days of negotiation as to the terms of his return. I didn't let him stay that night but we agreed on a family meeting that weekend; it was like a repetition of the one six months before when we sat the girls down and told them he was leaving. But this time they cheered. I don't think they really heard the part about the cancer; all they knew was that Daddy was coming home.

He moved back in to the house that Sunday night, bringing a few suitcases of belongings. It seemed ridiculous to make him sleep in the basement so he moved back into our bedroom too. A week later, on the night before my mastectomy, we turned instinctively to each other in bed. It was the last time I ever felt a man's touch on my left breast.

"Do you have any mutton?"

"We have lamb, miss. Nice spring lamb."

"Yes, I know. It's always called lamb, but I wonder, would any of it really be mutton?"

"Certainly not, miss." The man behind the butcher counter looked offended at Shay's question. "I have fresh spring lamb today, not more than six months old, arrived from Wales this morning. Mutton is the meat of an adult sheep."

"And you don't have any?"

"There's no call for it any more. I have to order it in special."

"Does it taste any different? I'm making a recipe from an old cookbook and it calls for mutton."

"It takes a good bit of stewing and it's gamier, stronger flavour. Some people like it. I can order it in." The butcher's tone softened as soon as he realized he was not being accused of passing off old mutton as young lamb.

"No, unfortunately, I'm cooking it tonight. I guess I'll take the lamb. I need enough for six."

"Have the New Zealand, from the freezer," he said, gesturing in that direction. "It's always older and it'll have a bit more of that flavour you're looking for. Cheaper too."

Shay purchased her New Zealand lamb and moved on to the greengrocer feeling rather important and highly competent, an adult woman discussing the difference between lamb and mutton with the butcher and selecting the freshest bit of sole at the fishmonger's. She usually just bought all her food at Sainsbury's but this was a special occasion and she wanted to reproduce the traditional housewife's morning progress from shop to shop. She wondered if Catherine had done her own shopping and supposed not. Catherine must have had several servants from the earliest years of her marriage; Dickens had published his first novel, *The Pickwick Papers*, to much acclaim and steady sales during the year of their engagement. Still, she was clearly a careful housekeeper; her book might include menus for grand dinner parties and explain how to make coffee for thirty people but it also gave instructions for making stock from a neck of mutton and began with family menus for two or three persons that offered giblet soup, pork cutlets and rice pudding for supper. The book suggested she was both a generous hostess and a frugal housewife, a woman accustomed to plenty but not wasteful of it. There was something both cozy and responsible about her suggested meals; the menus spoke of her easy confidence in her situation, her unshakeable faith in being a wife.

Shay had always assumed she would be a wife, feeding a family and keeping house, no matter what profession she pursued. It was surely just a matter of time before the right candidate came along. People got married; that's what people did. So when, still single, she first began graduate school, she also assumed that her inspiring supervisor, blessed in every aspect of life, must be happily married too. She imagined him living in a nice house with his charming wife and adorable babies; she thought he would give any promising student the same attention, the same smile he gave her, all the while secretly hoping that somehow this was different. And then there was the day of the hand, its pressure firm, the gesture unmistakable. Another day there were a few elliptical remarks about happiness; then there was a kiss.

And then there was the affair. Six months of ecstasy and heartbreak in equal measures: the furtive daytime encounters at her apartment; quick, short emails cramped by their consciousness that he, her supervisor, was compromising his position and, when they abandoned caution, long, emotional emails flowing from desperation and honesty. Or at least a seeming honesty. A truth of the heart. She knew he wasn't happy at home. Why else would he be lying in her arms at three o'clock on a winter afternoon?

He told her stories of his childhood and youth but said nothing of his wife. His family had escaped Tehran just after the revolution. He was barely a teenager when they had arrived in Montreal with suitcases full of carpets so that his father could set up a branch of his grandfather's business. But his father was really a poet and a scholar; he spoke Farsi, Arabic, French and English. They should have been ideal Canadian immigrants—they had the money; they had the languages—but the man himself was cramped and unhappy in business and seemed to wither in the cold climate, mumbling away in an increasingly heavy accent in whatever language he was speaking. Meanwhile, Al's mother, once a docile Iranian housewife who made meat-balls and watered the plants, became hard, pushy, as deter-mined to never miss a language class as she was frantic they would not be cheated in this new place. She was falsely nostalgic too, plastering the fridge with newspaper clippings about the Pahlavi family, sighing over the Shah's death and their sad exile, as though she had completely forgotten the repression and the pocket-lining of the old regime that her husband had so bemoaned. There were arguments: bitter words between a father and a mother who had once been the benign rulers of a childhood para-dise. There was pain here, and it moved Shay to tears.

Al and his sister knew their role was to fix things. His sister did an excellent job of it. She married a Syrian-Canadian whose mother went to the same Orthodox church as theirs; she and her new husband took over the rug business on Crescent Street. She had babies. But Al, well, Al had problems doing what was needed, what was required. Yes, it was a sad story, but frighteningly, titillatingly, that was rather the point. Al had many lovers before her who had heard this tale; he had been feverishly sexually active as a student even as the girls all worried about birth control and the transmission of AIDS. And then, married, he had been chronically unfaithful to his wife. Somehow, lovers plugged the hole, compensated for the loss. But Shay was the one, the special one, she would save him. He had told her his Persian name. Arsalan, the lion. It had been shortened to Sal in a Montreal schoolyard. And then just Al. That worked well in Toronto. But to her, he could become Arsalan once more.

And so he left, and for a few glorious months it seemed true. Shay felt she had won, had graduated to a real life. He quickly found a small apartment. She quietly found a new supervisor. Occasionally, they would eat together in restaurants or walk in a street holding hands.

And yet part of him always seemed absent, preoccupied, and then one day he simply announced this had to stop. He needed to go home. He gave no explanation and when she begged said only, "Please, don't."

She wept for three months, all but vomited from anxiety every time she ran into him in the hallways of the department, and finally bought a plane ticket for London to get some research done. Finding Ellen Ternan in the library, however, was an all but impossible task: to

preserve his secrets, Dickens had burnt all of his correspondence soon after he separated from Catherine and
had asked friends to do the same with his letters to them.
Then Shay had discovered Catherine's menu book.
Catherine was not secret nor invisible and here was her
hand. Rabbit pie. Cock-a-leekie. Eve's pudding.

Her new supervisor, Vivian the Virginia Woolf scholar,
had not been particularly pleased at the proposed change
of topic when Shay had first got up the nerve to email her
an outline of her idea back in January. They had emailed
to and fro for a bit and finally Vivian had said she would
try to find a culinary historian to co-supervise. It was
March now, and Shay had yet to hear back.

Vivian seemed cool, cynical and unimpressed, whether
by her specifically or by the world in general, Shay wasn't
quite sure. She missed Al's enthusiastic encouragement,
his passion. She wanted to know what Al would think of
her new topic. She was sure he would be more interested
than Vivian. She had ached to send just one small email,
but they had promised each other when she left for
London that would be the end of communication. And
she had broken that promise at least twice the previous
fall, not to mention sending him a Christmas message.
So, she sat tight and didn't tell him what Vivian had said,
even though she had been shaken by her new supervisor's
first response to her idea: "I gather you would rather

study for the role of wife than that of mistress," she had written. The "for" must have been a typo, Shay told herself. Vivian had just meant you'd rather study the role of the wife than that of the mistress. She and Al had kept the relationship very quiet. Even when Al had left home and found his own place, she had held on to her apartment. Nobody in the department knew they were together, and Vivian spent all her time over in Women's Studies anyway. Al had arranged things with the chair of the department and to explain the need for the change to Vivian, Shay had simply said at their first meeting that she and Professor Soleymani could not entirely agree on the direction of her research. She suspected Vivian thought he'd harassed her and she dearly wanted to defend him, but Al had only laughed and discouraged her from discussing it with Vivian at all.

"Stick to the research, kiddo," had been his advice. So, for now she was sticking with Vivian, waiting for a culinary historian and occasionally dropping into the library to see what she could find of Catherine's letters. And she was planning a dinner party.

Sole with lobster sauce. Saddle of lamb with potatoes, mashed and browned. Asparagus. Charlotte russe. Toasted cheese. Shay ran down her shopping list: she needed to find a can of lobster bisque somewhere and Sainsbury's had not obliged. She dropped her groceries at the flat and set out again in the opposite direction, happily determined she would get what she needed to make her dinner a success. As she walked briskly along, she began talking to Al in her head, explaining Catherine's menu. New Zealand lamb because it tasted the most like mutton, a savoury course after the dessert and, yes, she had mastered the trick of unmoulding a charlotte russe.

The best thing about life in Mornington Crescent could not be mentioned.

Like many acting families, the Ternans were a nomadic tribe and Nelly had lived her first eighteen years in a succession of rented rooms above High Street shops, boarding houses in lesser neighbourhoods and the cheaper station hotels. Washing was performed in a basin in the room with hot water provided by the landlady or her over-worked maid, who placed a jug outside a tenant's door in the morning. In the evening, the day's ration of water had long since cooled. A bath was a weekly event Nelly shared with her mother and sisters, with the water heated on the kitchen fires and hauled upstairs, lukewarm by the time she got her turn. The other facilities were outdoors at the back of the garden and often shared by several houses. As a girl, Nelly could not make up her mind which was worse, to line up with strangers to use the cold and stinking privy or to relieve herself in the warmth and privacy of their room but endure leers and taunts when she went out to empty the chamber pot. Bold Maria could sometimes be convinced to do it for her in exchange for her weekly ration of sweets.

At least at Park Cottage, they only had to share the privy with one neighbour, but the space between it and the house, which could hardly be dignified with the word *garden*, was a short one, and often the cess pit made its presence known, leaving Mrs. Ternan and the neighbour arguing over whose turn it was to pay the shilling required to get a man around to empty it.

In the better houses in those years, there was an upstairs water closet or at least a pipe into which maids might empty the contents of their masters' commodes and chamber pots and sluice them down with water from a jug. Most of these facilities were connected to a cess pit outdoors or even under the house, and smells wafted back up the plumbing. The most geographically privileged were now hooked up to the new London sewers that had been built after the Great Stink of 1858: that burning-hot summer was marked in Nelly's memory by the pain, confusion and excitement of Charles's letter to the press but the rest of the world remembered only the smell of the Thames awash in sewage.

Just around the corner from the elegant terraces of Mornington Crescent proper, the house in Ampthill Square was recently built and boasted the latest improvements, including a water closet where the occupant could use a built-in commode and then pull a lever to open a sluice himself. If the closet emitted unpleasant smells, it paled in comparison to the privies of Nelly's youth, and she could always open a little air vent that had been strategically cut into the outer wall. In her new home, Nelly rejoiced in a warm and private toilet.

It was located in a small alcove on the second floor, up a few short steps off the main staircase and across from the largest bedroom in the house. This was her room—it was the first time in her life she had not shared with her sisters—and there was also, right next door to it, a large bathroom fitted with a metal tub and permanent washstand. She did share the bathroom with her mother and sisters whenever they were in residence, but she was, from the start, acknowledged in her family as the lady of the house and for her alone the maid could be required to haul the hot water upstairs and fill the metal tub every day of the week if she so chose. Her mother and sisters would still make do with a Monday bath night but Nelly might now luxuriate daily. She often took a warm bath on a cold, lonely evening, or would enjoy a long, perfumed soak in the morning if she knew Charles was coming to visit that afternoon.

Growing up in the theatre, she was not ignorant in the ways of the world and, in theory, was aware there might be a high price to pay for her new relations with Charles. In the two years before he had purchased the house for her, he had often visited her with her family at Park Cottage, escorted her home from the theatres where she worked, walked with her on the heath, dined with her in restaurants and waged a quiet but relentless campaign to do these things with her alone. Mrs. Ternan's defences were increasingly overwhelmed and when he offered to pay for Fanny's Italian music lessons, her mother went abroad with an eldest daughter whose virtue was perhaps more easily protected and at less steep a price than her youngest's was proving to be. Nelly and Maria, now both working at a theatre where Mr. Dickens knew the manager, looked after each other in new lodgings he had helpfully found for them near Oxford Street, but Maria could hardly be expected to chaperone her younger sister all the time nor protect her from their great benefactor. In those months, Charles's attentions became increasingly ardent, although Nelly still permitted him only the occasional kiss. It was not until the day they toured the newly purchased house that he first took Nelly in his arms. And it was in the large second-floor bedroom, one afternoon when her mother and Maria were out shopping, that she gave herself to him.

Once established as a possibility, Charles panted for these encounters; on an afternoon when her relations had tactfully removed themselves, he would arrive at the house in a state of agitation and, barely into the drawing room, he would begin by taking her hand, then swing her arm to and fro with a boyish guile and soon tug her toward the stairs and so up to the bedroom. Afterwards he was calm and expansive, full of confident plans for the future. Nelly, on the other hand, felt mainly confused; she did not dislike his embraces but nor did she long for them. Parts of the process were pleasant enough; other aspects were occasionally painful. Mainly, she found their relations messy, especially in the aftermath.

It was another woman at the theatre, a character actress named Jeanie now well into her thirties, who, when Nelly quietly mentioned her forthcoming retirement from the stage at the tender age of twenty, had advised her how she might best take precautions.

"Oh, you're off with your Mr. Dickens, are you?" Jeanie had asked when Nelly let slip that their current engagement would be her last. Surprised at the name, Nelly looked at her with what she was a good-enough actress to know was an air of blank incomprehension. The progression of her friendship with Mr. Dickens was her secret, the protective cloak in which she could wrap herself if another actor upstaged her with an improvised bit of business or a gentleman the worse for drink whistled at her from the boxes. Sometimes at home, if her mother and sisters were out, she would gaze at herself in the one looking glass, hug herself tight and think, "He loves me, only me. He can't do without me." If he was beloved of the world, she was beloved of him and she clung to that as a delicious, invisible secret. She rarely discussed the nature of their friendship with her family and never mentioned his name to anyone else. Jeanie, who might certainly have noticed Mr. Dickens in a box or at the stage door, made their friendship sound unremarkable and very real. The idea was new to Nelly, dangerous, worrying but exciting too.

"You needn't look like that," Jeanie said. "I can't say I blame you going off with him. You'll be living the life. You'll be having his babies before you know it."

At this, Nelly recoiled. The prospect of bearing children was a vague and distant possibility that she in no way associated with Charles.

"I certainly hope not," she said, now replacing blank incomprehension with injured pride.

"No offence meant, love, but if you give him what he wants, and it's all men want, well, babies follow."

Nelly simply stared at her, and Jeanie misinterpreted her silence.

"Did your mother not tell you that?"

"Oh, yes, I know that . . ."

"You'll need to take precautions if you don't want babies."

"Precautions? Are there precautions . . ." Nelly ventured.

"Oh yes, there are precautions. How do you think Sam and I managed it after Mary was born? We couldn't possibly have toured with two children. I suppose your mother did it with three, right enough. Your mother is a powerful woman, Nelly. Stronger than many of us. I could not have led the life she has."

So, Jeanie explained to Nelly what was required. She was to go to a certain apothecary's shop, wait until the female assistant was ready to serve her and express concern about hygiene. She might even discreetly mention there was a smell she disliked. She would be provided with a special bag and a special powder.

"It's quite easy," Jeanie assured her. "You just flush it all out of you every time."

And so, the large bathroom in Mornington Crescent was also the place that Nelly carefully syringed and washed herself after every visit from Charles.

Over the months, they gradually established a pattern; now that they had the house, he was increasingly cautious about being seen alone with her in public, inviting Mrs. Ternan to join them to eat at Verrey's or attend a play at Covent Garden, but he spent long afternoons and evenings alone with her in Mornington Crescent several days a week. While Mrs. Ternan joined Maria as she toured the provinces or returned to visit Fanny on her second sojourn in Italy, Charles and Nelly had the house to themselves. They would read to each other; she would play the piano and sing for him; he would bring instalments of his latest novel for her to read before publication. In those years, he was producing *Great Expectations* and she took a certain pride not only in discussing the development of his characters and catching every typographical error in the page proofs but also in having inspired the idea of a grand

and hopeless passion in the first place. Not that Charles's passion was hopeless any longer. Inevitably, after reading and editing, they would make their way upstairs.

She came to enjoy their relations more, to find something if not ecstatic at least comforting in their union. She settled into this new existence, savouring its luxuries while still always vaguely assuming that marriage and motherhood were distant things that would happen to her one day with some other man after this phase of her youth was past. If she privately wished Catherine Dickens dead and buried, so that she might marry Charles, she certainly never told him; it was too faint and ill conceived a thought to even articulate completely to herself. She saw herself as so entirely different from that lady who had knocked over the umbrella stand in her mother's vestibule, she could hardly imagine taking her place. And so, she never mentioned his wife's name to him, and their secret life together seemed happy enough, until the day Nelly had to admit to herself, as she sat in her warm and comfortable closet staring at her spotless white undergarment, that her monthly visitor was now three weeks late.

During my treatment, I became intimately acquainted with the tile on the bathroom floor. It was a light grey with a darker grey fleck that I had always thought tastefully unobtrusive and a nice backdrop for the blue towels, but up close it began to look like static on an old black-and-white television and it made my head ache. Within weeks of starting chemo, I decided if I lived the first thing I would do was renovate the bathroom.

Many days the anti-nausea drugs worked and I was left feeling slightly queasy until I managed to get some breakfast down. Other days, they were not enough and I would wake at dawn in that awful will-she-or-won't-she state that left me sitting beside the toilet bowl just in case. If things settled a bit, I would try to choke down some toast to still my stomach but it would often come back up again. Things improved as the day wore on and I found, as I had when I was pregnant, that the queasiness could be kept at bay by the continual nibbling of dry crackers.

It was a new kind of morning sickness; the horrible irony of cancer was that it kept reminding me of child-bearing, the removal of the tumour and the treatment to ensure it never returned a grotesque reversal of the growing of life inside me. The surgery to remove my left breast was the first time I had spent the night in hospital since delivering the twins. Besides the pain kept at a dull throb by the drugs, the wound left me unable to lift my arm above my head so I had to hunt out all the big, floaty button-front blouses and pyjama tops I had worn when I was nursing.

Soon after the arrival of the twins, I had realized my long dirty-blond hair was simply a nuisance and got the hairdresser to cut it into a tidy bob that I had grown out again when the twins turned four and life seemed, for a time, to settle down. On the advice of the cancer clinic, I once again cut my hair in preparation for losing it all. Goli cried when I came home with it short, although the worst was yet to come. It came out in handfuls, leaving unattractive clumps of straw-coloured fuzz all over my head until it disappeared altogether, along with my eye-brows and lashes. We had warned the girls that I would lose my hair; we had told them I was sick and that Daddy had come home to help look after me and would stay until I was better. After that? "We'll see," we said, not wanting to promise something we could not deliver. In my experience, children usually think "We'll see" means yes, perhaps because it often does. "Can we have ice cream after school?" "We'll see." "Am I getting a Barbie for Christmas?" "We'll see." "Daddy will stay, though, won't he, when you get better?" "We'll see." "You will get better soon, won't you, Mummy?"

Even the Internet is tactfully quiet on the prognosis for triple-negative—tamoxifen is of no use against it—and the oncologist certainly wouldn't speculate; she just said the cancer was "aggressive." Thinking of our neighbour's defence of her obnoxious dog, I said, "Don't you mean assertive?" but she only responded to the joke with a tired, gentle smile. It wasn't encouraging.

Al and I simply put aside our differences to get through the days, and he set to it uncomplainingly, cooking meals, washing laundry and fetching and carrying when I felt too sick or simply too exhausted, doing more housework than he had ever done before. He actually seemed pleased to be able to help and I found that the sight of him spreading peanut butter on toast for Goli or finding Anahita's lost shoe comforted me deeply. They could manage. They would manage.

Well-meaning friends kept bringing over casseroles and containers of soup but I never knew, from one day to the next, what I would be able to stomach. During pregnancy, once the initial morning sickness passed, my body would announce to me what I needed to eat, the mythic cravings of the expectant mother. Green salad, a voice in my head would trumpet. Or red meat. I found it both amusing and reassuring. At least my body knew what was required. Now it mainly told me what I mustn't eat. As the children and Al dug in, the parmesan crust on the noodle casserole started my stomach churning. The smell of chicken soup could send me running for the bathroom.

Al hovered, coaxing me to eat, plying me with delicacy after delicacy. "Pizza, you always love pizza. Let me order some." "I can fry up a steak, tons of protein." "Yogurt. It will settle your stomach."

He hovered on the bad nights too, worried, uncertain as to what he could possibly do. Standing at the bathroom door in the half light of dawn wearing only a pair of boxer shorts, he was a benign and enduring presence more sensed than seen as my mind concentrated on every lurch or every lull in the battle ruling my innards and my focus narrowed to the grey-fleck tile. It was how he had been present in the delivery room too, mopping my brow and holding my hand and there, as the pain had so gloriously exploded into two new lives and finally subsided; it had seemed the most exquisitely intimate and loving way to be with someone else. But now, as I vomited up bile, water and what little remained of the previous night's dinner, I thought to myself this was not a smart way to welcome home an errant husband.

"Will your uncle be visiting again soon, madame?"

"Quite soon, I expect," Nelly replied in her best French as she slipped the change and the stamps into the folds of her pardessus and turned to leave the post office.

She walked slowly home by way of the beach with Foxie, the fox terrier Mrs. Ternan had acquired on her return from Italy, running along beside her. It was March but there was no sign of spring yet and a cold wind was driving whitecaps onto the shore. As Nelly tightened her shawl around the bulging buttons of her pardessus, she considered the postmistress's question. Her French was really not good enough to assess the tone in which she made her inquiry. Was it an innocent passing of the time of day or a bit of malicious insinuation? Nelly could not tell, and if she could not discern another's tone, no more did she suppose she was able to affect the polite snub she would have managed with a few well-chosen words in English.

Most people in Wimereux seemed ready to believe that she was the young and delicate wife of an Indian army officer, unable to tolerate the heat of the subcontinent and so quietly awaiting his return in a French fishing village with only her mother for company. Charles had made a joke of it, saying the French were so convinced of the superiority of their land, it would never occur to the citizens of Wimereux to question why Mme Lawless would not prefer the equally mild winter and equally pretty beach at Eastbourne. He visited from time to time, when he could get away from his magazine work in London and his family in Kent. The boat train from Charing Cross to Folkestone and so to Boulogne arrived in the space of a morning; the carriage ride from Boulogne to Wimereux was less than an hour. In case of an emergency, a telegram could summon Charles by the following day, as he had pointed out when he had picked the seaside village for a stay of some months. But there were no emergencies, only little questions, blandly evasive answers and Nelly's ever-loosening stays.

She found at first she had merely to loosen her corset and wear her pardessus over her skirt to mask the thickening at her waist. Then she had discovered that if she hitched her crinoline higher, she could hide her belly beneath it. Still, her condition was increasingly obvious and had to be laid at the door of the absent colonial officer. Of course,

Madame would not want to suffer her first confinement in a hot climate thousands of miles from home. That explained her presence all winter in the rented villa on the edge of town. Perhaps the citizens of Wimereux guessed that the English ladies' status was not as stated; perhaps they guessed at the role, if not the true identity, of the older gentleman who joined them from time to time; perhaps they gossiped with the villa's serving girl about how the ladies filled their days, but they seemed happy to accept what they might know to be a polite fiction. Charles insisted the French were much more humane in their judgment of a woman's reputation, but Nelly felt there was no point trying their hospitality by flaunting her condition. She stayed very close to home and, as she proceeded along the cold beach, decided that would be her last trip to the post office before she left for Paris.

They had agreed she would remove herself to the city when her confinement approached. Charles had rented an apartment there and found a good doctor; Nelly had already travelled into town twice to see him. He was blandly encouraging about the state of her pregnancy and told her to rest. She might have been happier in Paris all along, shopping, walking in the parks, going to the theatre, but neither she nor Charles felt they could risk placing her there for a long stay. The city was, after all, filled with English tourists who might ask questions of a compatriot or, worse yet, might recognize both her and her condition. Some had linked their names together at the time of his separation and the sight of a pregnant Nelly was certain to create a scandal.

Despite his determination that no one who knew him should know of her condition, Charles kept promising that the baby would change everything—when he wasn't promising that the baby would change nothing. On the one hand, he declared he would now regularize their situation, and on the other, he swore his eternal, unchanging devotion. He promised they would find somewhere to live together as the family they would be, perhaps in France, perhaps in Mornington Crescent.

One day he would suggest they would defy convention; that any prude who dared to criticize had never loved; that his love for her was too large, too grand a thing to possibly be wrong. They would live in London and weather the storm.

Hearing him, Nelly would briefly imagine herself as a kind of Mrs. Dickens, a different Mrs. Dickens, a new one but still one who would preside over a big house with many children, the babies who were testament to his love.

But other days, more common days if not perhaps more sensible ones, he would suggest they move to some village like Wimereux permanently and live there quietly. He would write and she would raise their baby, who would grow up with superb dramatic talents that she— he was sure it was a she—would practise equally well in English or French. The father of only two much adored daughters but seven disappointing sons, Charles seemed to want and expect a girl, although he did sometimes wonder out loud if it would not be quite the thing to finally have a son with sound parentage on both sides.

Nelly was also convinced things would change, and had been from the first evening when, sitting quietly by their French fireside with her mother a few days after they had arrived in Wimereux, she had felt the baby move. She was wearing the loose house dress she now favoured in the evenings, finding other garments too constricting by day's end, and was sitting in a deep chair that let her lean back comfortably and prop her book on one of its low arms.

"Oh," she had gasped as she was startled from her reading by a sudden flutter deep inside her. Her mother looked up from her tatting and smiled.

"Did the baby move?"

Nelly nodded, amazed.

"Most remarkable feeling. Nothing else like it. You were quiet enough but Fanny and Maria used to dance the jig inside me every evening."

She laughed at Nelly's expression. "You'll get used to it," she said.

She did get used to it, and at first, she thought she liked it. Here was a life palpably growing inside her and that made her life palpable too. Until then, she had seen herself playing a role—"I am the beautiful young actress who has attracted the attention of the greatest living author," she would think as she admired the way a shawl draped around her slim shoulders or a gold locket sat at her neck—but she perceived the real Nelly faintly, as someone yet to be born. She was some future creature awaiting a handsome husband and darling babies; she would emerge, soon, after this particular bit of play-acting was at an end. The baby's movements excited her, as though that new stage of life were now approaching.

Still, she had always recognized, if only in a sleepless hour or lonely moment, that her play-acting had repercussions; that to be adored by Charles was satisfying but that it was also slowly, stealthily closing the door on any other life, that she could not be that other Mrs. Dickens and that, worse yet, there might never be another, different Nelly. And as the baby's movements grew stronger day by day, they finally dragged those thoughts into the light, forcing her to see the here and now for what it was: the handsome husband, whosever face he wore, was a fantasy and this darling would be born a bastard.

Charles had promised her day and night that he would take care of her. And he did take care of her. He had selected the apartment in Paris and was certain she would find it both comfortable and charming. He had discussed her treatment with the doctor, who came with the highest recommendations. She was promised chloroform. The next village, the second village, had been selected and several larger properties there duly inspected and considered. There she could live sedately as a married

English lady with a new baby . . . perhaps recently wid-owed . . . no, no, married to the gentleman who came to visit, well, the gentleman who lived there with her, when his business did not require him to cross the Channel. All that was required was a final decision and a letter to the house agent and this new life would be set in motion. Charles loved to plan things, she had learned, and all of his plans for her next few months were now in place.

And yet, that March morning, a full week before he was to come for her and Mrs. Ternan in a carriage that would take them to the train station in Boulogne, Nelly got home from her walk along the beach feeling decid-edly odd. By night, she was experiencing repeated cramp-ing in her belly: it seemed that the darling baby had not heard of her illustrious father's well-laid plans.

"Koofteh, koofteh!" the girls cry with delight as we push open the front door on the way home from the park that Sunday. It's early April, cold but light again in the afternoons; I've dragged myself away from my computer and we've been out breaking the ice on mud puddles and trying to fly a kite while Al cooks our Easter dinner. On our return, the house feels wonderfully warm and is filled with the unmistakable scent of saffron. Apparently, he is making koofteh berenji, his mother's particularly aromatic version of Persian meatballs. It's a time-consuming dish full of fresh herbs and exotic spices that have to be bought at an Iranian grocer all the way up in North York, which now explains where Al had disappeared to the day before. "You'll have to do the kite thing tomorrow," I tell Al on my way into the kitchen. "I can't run fast enough to get it launched." I peek into the pot on the stove and take a whiff. "Mmm. How did you figure out the recipe?" He rarely cooks, although he did become a master of the microwave in those hard months the previous year. More recently, I've returned to my role as the family chef, albeit with much-reduced ambitions. Al smiles slyly and raises his eyebrows before giving up the pretense of some secret culinary knowledge: "I called my mother."

The dish proves as good as hers and then we eat panettone that I've bought at the supermarket and, after the meal, when the twins have run upstairs to play, we tidy the kitchen together.

"Thank you for making meatballs for the girls," I say. "It was a treat."

It's not long after our fight over my retelling of "The Second Dervish's Tale." I am on my best behaviour, trying to remember to be grateful and polite. The division of labour this Easter has been carefully negotiated; Al said I couldn't spend all weekend at my computer. I said if I was going to be hiding chocolate eggs and going to the park, I couldn't cook dinner too, and he has outdone himself there.

"You don't need to thank me. They're my children too, you know."

"Yeah, I know. It's just nice to see you doing things for them. It's reassuring."

There was a pause.

"I'll always look after them," he eventually replies. "If . . . whatever . . . whatever happens." That's a promise he has made many times since his return. Whatever happens he will look after our girls.

"What if what happens is that I stay better."

"That would be good."

"But if the crisis is over . . . I mean, are you staying forever?" It is an issue we've dodged around; as I've emerged from chemo our old routines have reasserted themselves without much discussion, which I find either comforting or depressing, depending on whether that means sharing breakfast with Al or picking up his socks.

"I'm not planning on going anywhere," he replies. Then he adds. "But I'm not interested in going backwards; I'm not interested in the marriage I left. I want something else."

Dismay creeps over me. I wonder if I can ever satisfy him.

"Okay," I say lightly. "What's that?"

"I just need more of you, that's all."

"Sure." What else can I say? I can hardly refuse. "More. You got it."

Al nods. He seems content for the moment and simply offers: "And I'll try to cook more often. And tomorrow I'll fly the kite with the girls."

He looks at me, waiting now for my side of the bargain.

"I'll try to work less," I say without any enthusiasm.

"It's not the work that's the problem; it's that it makes you tired and distracted."

"I kind of like that. I can use distraction at the moment."

"You need to pay attention to the girls."

"I do pay attention to the girls." But what he is really asking is that I pay more attention to him; fair enough, I guess. It's been more than six months since I finished treatment. "Al . . . " I take a breath and try to think straight about it, to find the words. "When you have been through what I have, it strips you bare. I'm empty. I can't love the girls properly and I can't love you again unless I can somehow be myself. Working is part of that. Writing gives me . . . well, I guess it gives me a sense of mastery. It makes me strong."

"Yes," he says slowly. "I can see that."

It's true. One of the reasons I want Al to like the serial is because I like it so much. I like the way it demands a healthy capacity for work, giving the days shape and purpose. After mapping out a general structure and preparing the first few instalments before *The Telegram* started publishing, I quickly fell behind and I am now writing and filing each instalment the week of publication. I have ever-increasing respect for Dickens' power of invention; while in the midst of a novel, he must have been writing twenty thousand words a week. I calculate that his output, about twenty novels written between the ages of twenty-four and fifty-eight, averages out at two thousand words for every single day of his life. And that doesn't include the plays and the magazine articles. My measly two or three thousand a week is hard enough and serial composition certainly doesn't leave much room for rethinking the plot.

Nonetheless, *The Telegram* is increasingly pleased with the results. Stanek and Jonathan seem to have got over their squeamishness about sullying Dickens' reputation—Stanek actually sent me an email calling *The Thousand and One Nights* interlude intriguing—and the paper has started promoting each instalment on the newspaper boxes. The Thursday after the holiday, on the way into the cleaner's with an armload of Al's shirts, I spot the box and see the card on the outside with big red letters blaring: CHARLES DICKENS' SECRET LOVE CHILD!! In smaller type, it promises "The Dickens Bicentenary Serial continues this Saturday. Only in *The Telegram*."

I laugh out loud at the audacity of it, but seeing it on his way home at the newsstand in the subway, Al is unimpressed.

"Exploiting Dickens like he was some cheap Hollywood celebrity."

"It wasn't my idea," I protest, although Jonathan had sent me an email the night before, informing me that *The Telegram*'s defiantly retrograde print-only idea appears finally to be working: newsstand sales were up seven thousand copies the previous weekend, online discussion got five thousand hits, which was considered remarkable for a holiday, and Stanek wants to pump up the marketing campaign. "Bring on the long-lost heirs!" writes Jonathan.

"The paper has decided to promote the serial in a good old-fashioned tabloid tradition," I say to Al, stoutly defending it. "I think it's perfect."

"I thought everyone at *The Telegram* was all huffy about the Ellen Ternan angle."

"They were. But I gave them an illegitimate child and now they seem to love it. They may be hypocrites, but it feels like progress to me."

The Dickens Bicentenary Serial: Chapter 11
Paris. June 9, 1865

Charles discreetly lifted a finger and, without a word on either side, the waiter was instantly at their table, ready to replenish Nelly's coffee cup. Even the breakfast room at Le Meurice was luxuriously quiet, with thick rugs, silk curtains and well-trained waiters muffling the sounds of a guest rustling a newspaper or a silver spoon knocking a chafing dish. Their daring stay in adjoining rooms had been superbly indulgent and far too short.

The glorious week in Paris was Charles's idea. They walked the new boulevards and dined at the Café Anglais and visited the dressmakers and even ventured one evening into a café in Montmartre. They could not stay in the apartment where Nelly had given birth—it, if not its painful memories, had been given up long since—so instead they basked in the rare luxury of a grand hotel. It was a last hurrah before they settled into their new, quiet life back in England. Well, quiet for Nelly at least.

She did not suppose Charles really wanted a quiet life; he just wanted a private one, at least as far as she was concerned. They had agreed she would let out the house in Mornington Crescent; Fanny, who had been using it during her absence, would find rooms in town and Nelly would move to Slough, a Buckinghamshire village but twenty miles from Paddington. It would be a kind of a cross between Wimereux and Paris, a place small enough they could live incognito but close enough to the train lines and the city that Charles could spend the day at his desk and still drop by for dinner before returning to Kent by bedtime. After all his big dreams of a defiant establishment in Mornington Crescent where Nelly would reign over a house full of children, servants and dogs, it was a compromise. Nelly was learning that life was full of compromises.

But Slough was yet to come and in Paris that week there were no compromises, just poached salmon and roast guinea fowl and chocolate éclairs washed down with champagne, and paintings and theatres and dress fittings and trips to the jeweller's. It was a week of pleasure and fantasy. It hovered, it glimmered, it enveloped and then it was over. And the truth was, of course, that no feather bed or French pastry could erase what had come before it.

The cramps that day in Wimereux had proved to be a false labour—thankfully, or so Nelly thought at the time. In the end perhaps it would have made no difference where the baby was born. At any rate, by the time Charles arrived from London the next afternoon, Nelly was resting comfortably and seemed no longer to be in any danger of delivering a baby in a French seaside town with only her mother and the country doctor as attendants. Charles telegrammed to and fro with the Paris doctor, and after a week without any further pain, the men agreed that Nelly could proceed, in the company of a good nurse hired in Boulogne, by train to Paris. So, with strict instructions to the coachmen not to jostle his passengers, Nelly, Charles and her mother took a sedate ride into Boulogne, where they met the nurse at the train station in time to catch the smooth-running afternoon express.

Nelly still had, by the doctor's calculations, a good month before the baby would arrive, and now that the anxious day in Wimereux and the danger of travel were past, she was looking forward to some time in Paris with Charles no matter how little her condition would permit her to venture much beyond the apartment. At least there would be luscious food and amusing company. It would be a decided improvement over the winter in Wimereux, with the lonely beach and the servant girl's overcooked meat.

But that Paris sojourn was not to be. Perhaps hastened by the vibration of the train, she went into labour two days after their arrival, a few hours after Charles had departed for London, where he had a reading to deliver. The process proved short—Nelly's mother kept repeating enviously, perhaps in an attempt to cheer Nelly, that not

one of her three deliveries had lasted as little as six hours—
but brutal. Nelly had never known such pain and, in that
moment at least, hoped she never would again: hours of
increasingly intense cramping developed into pains that
felt as though she were being kicked in the middle from
the inside out, which gave way to the feeling her innards
were being ripped apart. She begged for chloroform but
apparently the doctor had misled Charles with regards to
his support for or familiarity with its use, for he simply
cried, "Mais non, madame!" whenever she called out for
it. As Charles was neither in the apartment nor in the city,
there was no one who could argue with the man about
the services he had agreed to provide. She began to feel the
baby was some kind of monster inside her and desperately
wanted it out, with not even a passing maternal care for
the fate of the creature that would emerge.

The creature that did finally emerge was small. Too
small, the doctor said, shaking his head and washing his
hands. He departed soon after, leaving Nelly in the care
of a nurse, who, try as she might to instruct the mother
and coax the child, could not get the baby to suckle at the
breast. Two days later, the nurse was desperately feeding the poor thing by means of smearing goat's milk on
her finger when the doctor returned and called in a wet
nurse. The girl, a buxom peasant from Brittany who
spoke nothing that could be recognized as French, had a
lot more luck teaching the baby to suck and, by the time
Charles arrived the same afternoon, the immediate crisis

was past and Nelly could sit up in bed in a pretty lace nightdress to present him with his eighth son, a tiny thing wrapped in a white cambric cloth.

Once the baby was stable enough to travel, they removed themselves to the second village. With dredging of the harbour at Dover and improvements to the schedules of the ferries, Charles was increasingly using the Dover–Calais route rather than the slightly longer crossing between Boulogne and the naturally deep harbour at Folkestone. He had chosen for them a small town called Audruicq, just inland to the southeast of Calais, calculating it was far enough north of Wimereux that locals from the two places were unlikely to be comparing notes about the young English lady living in their midst. He helped Mrs. Ternan settle Nelly, the baby and a second wet nurse in a cozy farmhouse on the edge of the town, larger and less draughty than their little seaside villa in Wimereux, and departed for London.

At first things went well: the wet nurse's milk seemed to agree with the baby, who ate hungrily and began to grow; Nelly, her own milk now dry, slowly felt her body return to its former shape and became comfortable changing and dressing her son. She was happy to go for little walks down the country lanes carrying him in her arms until a proper perambulator could be shipped over from London. The wet nurse showed her how to make a sling out of a shawl so she could strap the child to her like a peasant woman while Mrs. Ternan followed beside her with Foxie. At six weeks, the baby appeared to be a healthy if undersized specimen and, as the weather grew warmer, Nelly would sit out with him on a blanket in a meadow behind the house, laying him on his back and dangling ribbons or rattles above his head to amuse him. After the anxiety of her pregnancy and pain of her delivery, she began to relax and as she relaxed she began to love her baby with his tiny little fingers and light grey eyes.

At eight weeks, as April gave way to May and the weather grew warmer, he caught an unseasonable cold. Nelly and the wet nurse were up all night with him two nights in a row, trying to clear his nose with warm compresses and quiet his crying. The third night he slept better; the fourth, they put him down as usual in the bassinet across the hall from Nelly with the wet nurse on a cot at his side. Nelly was finally able to enjoy an uninterrupted night's sleep but was roused at dawn by the nurse's cries.

"I can't wake him, madame. I can't wake him," she called as she came across the hall carrying his limp little body to an uncomprehending Nelly.

"But he needs his rest, nurse," she said fuzzily, pulling herself up to sitting. "More important to rest than to feed, don't you think?"

"No, madame, no . . ." the nurse replied, sobbing now as she handed Nelly the baby. Nelly took the lifeless child in her arms, looking down at him in disbelief.

The dead baby's father arrived in Audruicq that evening, fell at Nelly's feet and wept. She knew he had suffered such losses before. She had heard others speak of his sister-in-law Mary, dead from a mysterious attack at seventeen; once, he had mentioned baby Dora, his ninth child, a creature too good for this life, lost to the other at eight months. Rather than inuring him to the world's sorrows, it seemed to her that those deaths must have taught him how to cry. She, on the other hand, found herself tearless and numb.

Ever since Charles had courted her at Conisbrough, her whole life seemed to be unfolding as though it were happening to someone else. The day a gold bracelet had been delivered to Park Cottage, the time they had first walked alone on the heath, the lunch where he had proposed the purchase of Mornington Crescent, the busy weeks preparing the new house, each was full of excitement, nerves and elation, the kind of sensation that makes you feel you should pinch yourself to check this is actually happening. Occasionally, during her years settled in Mornington Crescent or the previous weeks in the meadow with the baby, she did experience the calmer but pleasant sensation that she was herself, a rather ordinary person leading a rather nice but quite real life, instead of playing a character in a melodrama. And then something would happen to sever the connection and she would return to her play-acting. Charles, with his relentless drive and his ready charm, seemed to demand it, propelling her life forward from one glorious role to another. At first the times between, when he wasn't there, were her other life, the life he had lifted her from, empty days in the cramped quarters at Park Cottage or disappointing nights back-stage at the Haymarket waiting to make her entrance and say her few lines. More recently, however, she had to recognize that the hard winter in Wimereux was the direct result of the bedroom in Mornington Crescent. She had always loved pretending: dressing up to go on stage and donning the role of the mysterious mistress or the inspirational muse had mainly seemed fun. Now, play-acting the mourning mother was a lot easier than actually feeling the pain, and the baby's death became misty. She would have babies someday, many babies, just not today.

They buried this one in the local churchyard with only his given name, Thomas, the same as her father's, on the little headstone. His middle name was Nelly's middle name, Lawless; Charles had registered his birth in Paris and Nelly had never asked what surname he had decided to give the child.

She recognized that her baby, whether a Dickens or not, would have bonded his parents together irrevocably, making her yet more dependent on Charles but also giving him a lasting reason to provide for her, whatever the vagaries of love. A living child would have made her life more secure, yet closed off any other life. She had thought that, for better or worse, she had walked through a door, and yet here she found herself standing on a threshold once again. She paused there but for a moment. The truth was, her renewed childlessness did not make her feel any more independent; she might hesitate to move forward but she was certain she could not move back. She felt adrift and there was only one anchor close at hand. In a fog of pain and confusion, she clung to him desperately when, three weeks later, he returned to Audruicq for a final time. They packed up their belongings, she gratefully costumed herself once more for the role of his companion and they headed for Le Meurice.

"You aren't wearing that, are you?" asked Mrs. Ternan as she joined them at the breakfast table that final morning and caught sight of Nelly in the beautiful pale blue silk day dress purchased at Worth's that week and hurriedly adjusted to perfectly fit Nelly's newly slim figure. "You'll spoil it, darling. Trains are so dirty." She spread her napkin across her lap and smiled at the waiter now offering her the pot of well-steeped English tea that she always preferred to the French habit of coffee in the morning. "Goodness, it will be pleasant to be in London again."

B efore I had children, life was about finding a cab if I was running late, or making sure there was always a bottle of champagne in the house, just in case. Or keeping my calves, shins and ankles in a permanent state of such smooth hairlessness that I could go bare-legged at the first sign of warm weather.

Of course, life was not about that. Life was about my career, my relationship with Al, my friends and family, Becky, David, my mother back in Halifax. Those were the important things, the things I would have listed for you if you had asked.

But the fabric of life is really the little things, the trivial tasks, annoyances and pleasures running about in one's head. If we could hear other people's thoughts the street would surely be a cacophony of the insignificant. "There is that woman from yoga who always wears purple." "God, this light is slow." "I should never have taken the extra hot sauce." When I am in the early stages of writing a book, that kind of chorus is sometimes replaced by thoughts about characters: "Would Gwen really steal Amanda's paper for the Austen conference? Why not just vote against her presidency?" At a certain point the characters' dilemmas would seem realer than the world around me and I would find myself asking Al to repeat himself because I had not heard what he said. "Next Saturday? Are we free next Saturday? What if Jack finds Amanda's laptop but thinks it must be Gwen's?" But once the girls were born life was about pink mittens and bits of rejected food wrapped in tissue, sitting at the bottom of my purse, and remembering the pediatrician's appointment was on Wednesday. And I liked that better. The girls seemed real to me, realer than my characters, realer than Al and me, more pressing in their needs and so more important in the scheme of things. How could one worry about the plot of Chapter 2 or the professional complaints of a work-weary husband when the girls needed to bake cookies for school or the wrench that would remove a set of training wheels had gone missing? Finding socks, applying bandages, reading stories—life now was supposed to be trivial, whether joyously or annoyingly so. Cooking meals for tired and hungry children or playing a board game in which there can only be one gleeful winner were all-consuming tasks but might easily end in tears. I loved buying their clothes, rubber boots, sun hats, warm leggings, pink in size 2 for Goli, orange in size 4 for Anahita, because it was done for them but without them, their absence making the heart fonder, allowing me to triumphantly parade my self-less motherhood through the mall without fear of contradiction from a complaining child. Yet still, the best days were the ones when the craft project worked, nobody whined on the bike ride or everybody agreed the new library book was a really good story. Life was about these things, and the joyous chorus in my head moved sweetly from "I need to remember to buy some plasticine" to "I bet if I added spinach they would never notice" while glancing down at my legs on the way to the daycare, I would see that stray hairs were growing on my kneecaps.

That was the worst thing about being sick. I felt divided against myself every moment of every day. Thoughts about the minutiae of illness, pain and mortality began to crowd out everything else. "My head is scratchy. My left armpit aches. Did I remember to take the pill for stomach acid? Oh, I feel queasy. I need some crackers. I am thirsty. I want to lie down. I can't sleep. My right armpit aches. Maybe I have a tumour in the other breast. Maybe it's growing inside me right now and I won't last till Christmas."

"Mummy. Where's my hair bow? My purple hair bow. Mummy, I can't go to school without it. I can't find it. I looked. Mummy, are you crying?"

Yes, I was crying, and in truth I was not crying because I didn't have the energy to find a hair bow. I didn't care about the hair bow. I was crying because my right armpit ached and I just wanted my child to go away. And that afternoon, I would be crying because that morning I wanted my child to go away.

Last autumn, after I finished chemo and was gradually regaining my strength, I took to walking in Mount Pleasant, in the cemetery. Sometimes, on the weekends these days, when I want to get the next instalment mapped out in my head and can't find any peace in the house, I leave the girls with Al and go up there again. Like so many big cities now, Toronto seems painfully short on the green space its burgeoning population craves, and the place where old Toronto buried its dead—all those McGregors, Pitfields and Llewelyns—is now mainly used as a bike route, running path and dog-walking park. On a sunny spring day, the place is bustling with activity.

God knows what it would cost to erect an actual monument here, and only a small number of people still do. Mainly, you see lots of little plaques marking the entombment of mere ashes, small, tidy and unobtrusive memorials to moms and dads who shuffled off politely in their eighties and nineties without making much show of it at all. But occasionally someone springs for a big new monument to mark a conventional grave, a memorial to some fresh tragedy, an untimely end or sometimes just a very wealthy one, a marker that draws attention to itself. Grave diggers come out when nobody is looking and dig their six-foot hole; relatives gather, a coffin is lowered; fresh earth is piled on top and then, some months later, you'll be wandering through the cemetery and notice this new and startling addition, some mighty reminder that this is not just a park, not just a piece of forgotten history, but a place of death, current death, real and raw.

This Sunday, to plan something a bit new for the serial, get another voice well registered in my mind, I am walking what I think is my regular route through Mount Pleasant when I come across one of these new eruptions, a huge wall of polished red granite with a whole family of names freshly inscribed. I stop, caught halfway between horror and voyeurism. Can some entire family have been wiped out by a car accident or house fire? The first two names, a man and a woman, were born in the 1970s, almost middle-aged now, parents of the names below, born two years previously. Three names, all born on the same date, babies, triplets. I start doing the math. One died within a week of birth. A second died at two months, like some Victorian babe. They must have been premature. Multiple births are often dangerously early. I was lucky to carry Goli and Anahita right to term; even twins have the habit of arriving too soon.

I keep staring at the grave. What happened to the third triplet? There is the same birth date but no death. I puzzle over it briefly before I realize the obvious: the third triplet survived. So did the parents; their names don't carry death dates either. The parents of this little family, with its one surviving child, have carved all their names on their dead babies' tombstone as though all they are doing is waiting for their turn. I am shocked by the bleakness of their grief, the irredeemable gesture of this grave. Will they spend their entire lives like this, all three of them, just waiting to join the pair they lost? Will the need to bake cookies or remove training wheels never take over, never fill the gap? Out buying one pair of rain boots in the mall, will the child's mother never, for a moment, forget that she should have been shopping for three pairs?

If I die, Al might marry his student. It's not like it hasn't occurred to me. I hate the thought of it, of her winning, taking over my house, sleeping in my bed, but I suppose better to have someone mothering my daughters, someone keeping their father happy. Better they should not always live with the shadow of the dear departed hanging over them, better their lives should move on.

I shake myself mentally and walk away from the monument, drawing deep breaths of cold spring air into my lungs. I feel healthy. I am full of life.

The Dickens Bicentenary Serial
Mrs. Dickens at Park Cottage—Round Two

Have you ever been to America, Mrs. Ternan? Oh. Really. Fancy that. Touring the theatres, I imagine. Long before your daughters were born, of course. Such a trip would have been impossible with young children.

What a pity your two eldest girls could not be here today. Oh, but I understand, their work must come first and so lovely for you they have followed you in to the theatre. No sugar, thank you, but a slice of lemon would be lovely. Yes, I believe I will, thank you: I am always partial to a bit of seed cake. Why this is all very pleasant. Such a cozy room and how pretty it looks in the sunshine.

And in what year did you visit America, Mrs. Ternan? Why, just a few years before us. We went over in '42. It was a remarkable experience, like nothing I have lived before or since, although I cannot say I would wish to repeat it.

We'd been married only a few years and I was by then

the mother of four. Walter still had a wet nurse; Charley, our eldest, was about to turn five, and the girls were two and three. Our babies. Goodness how we loved them, a cozy little family. I didn't want to go, I have to say. As a mother yourself, you'll understand that I could not imagine leaving children so young, for such a time. We calculated we would be gone four months and in the end it was six. When Mr. Dickens first proposed it, I refused to consider it. It was the only occasion I can ever remember where I contradicted him outright. I probably do not need to tell you that Mr. Dickens does not like to be contradicted.

But I don't think I was being stubborn or selfish. I understood the benefit of the tour. He needed to meet his American readers, and talk to American publishers. Perhaps stop the fiends from simply copying the British editions without ever paying. He thought if he could just show himself in the flesh on the other side of the Atlantic, so that he was not simply a distant name but a real man, it would both reward his readers and perhaps shame the thieving publishers, to whom we must have lost thousands of pounds. Besides, he was fascinated by the Republic and so wanted to see if its liberties truly provided happiness for its citizens. He needed to meet Americans and he wanted to see America.

Yes, it made sense for him to go, but I felt my place was with the children. When Mr. Dickens first proposed the trip I wondered if they would even remember their father after an absence of such a length. He always adores the babies and I cannot imagine little ones could have a fonder father but when he sets his mind to something he will never give way until he has seen it through. He was determined to go, and so the children and my scruples in their regard were merely obstacles to him. He insisted he needed me at his side and pointed out the children could be well taken care of by others. Of course, they had their nanny and in the end both our families happily took charge of them, and our friends the Macreadys too.

You know Mr. Macready professionally, I imagine. It was he who persuaded me to go in the end—or rather Mr. Dickens had him persuade me. He thought I would be more susceptible to the arguments of a disinterested friend. I felt so torn between my two duties: Did you ever suffer those moments where your husband seemed to pull you away from your children? Mr. Macready has, of course, remarkable rhetorical skills, as many an audience can attest, and he set about persuading me with all his powers. He convinced me that he and Mrs. Macready, who had borne many children herself, would love ours like their own. Finally, Mr. Macready convinced me that my first duty was to Mr. Dickens—or at least that the larger mistake was not to meet his needs.

We set off in January and the Atlantic storms were ferocious that winter. Did you cross in a steamer? Ours was one of the first and they were reputed to be much faster than sail, but in the end the boat was so subject to the weather, it took longer and was, of course, much less comfortable. The cabins are so horribly cramped. I remember Mr. Dickens' face when we first entered our state room at Liverpool and he realized he would have to live in such quarters for the next ten days. Imagine if someone had told him that it would be three weeks before we saw land again! I tried to make the best of it, tucking things in every corner, and told Mr. Dickens we must pretend we were living in a doll's house, but it is hard to feel cozy when you are as sick as we were. We spent most of the voyage in our bunks, calling out to our maker.

We were greatly relieved to finally arrive in Boston and what a welcome we received. There were cheering crowds at the dock and outside our hotel; there were banquets in our honour. Mr. Dickens used to say that we were treated like royalty, and that I played the staunch Albert to his monarch. Indeed, I don't think I have ever smiled and waved so much nor shaken so many hands. At first, it was most gratifying, but the crowds and the demands on his person rapidly began to wear him down, and he increasingly missed the comforts of home, which did put him out of sorts.

We met many congenial people in Boston, writers and scholars, and Mr. Dickens hired a secretary there, the good Mr. Putnam. We depended heavily on him because I simply could not keep up with the correspondence. Mr. Dickens was soon dictating dozens of letters a day. Requests for meetings. Invitations to parties. One person wrote repeatedly asking if Mr. Dickens might not spare a shirt as a souvenir! When we travelled south to New York and Philadelphia, Mr. Putnam came with us, and we were thankful we had him, for beyond Boston we found the crowds more pressing and the people less congenial.

The worst of it were the bores. We would go to a banquet and be pursued by men with wild schemes or ladies suffering from literary ambitions. My job was to keep them at bay, to change subjects, miss hints and ignore conversational demands. I would come away with promises of manuscripts, blueprints and business proposals that would all follow us to our next destination, but the more we were assaulted, the more I repelled. I became quite good at it, and Mr. Putnam and Mr. Dickens would laugh about it and ask how could we possibly sail through the day without Mrs. Dickens at the helm.

If the crowds in the cities were exhausting, so too were the roads in the country. We proceeded by land and by river boat through Ohio and Kentucky and travelled as far west as Missouri. I have never seen countryside like it, so wild in parts and so grand in others. I don't imagine you went West, Mrs. Ternan. The prairie is a sight to be seen, like a mighty mountain laid on its side.

Well, that is the view from the coach at least, but inside the coach, it was another matter altogether. How we bounced, how we shook. We were bruised all over by day's end. I did not complain, taking the view that every new inconvenience was an adventure to be discovered or a joke to laugh over at day's end. Anything was better than seasickness. Mr. Dickens always praised my vigour and calm; he would call me his intrepid companion.

The most remarkable part of our voyage was surely the sight of the falls at Niagara. Did you see the falls during your trip, Mrs. Ternan? The spectacle is almost spiritual, didn't you think? And the sound, both deafening and yet somehow soothing. Mr. Dickens was so impressed he thought the water spoke to him. He said he heard the voice of Mary, my sister, calling to him as she did the day she died. Our grief was still very fresh in those days; it had only been four years. She was but seventeen and had come to help us with the baby when Charley was born. She suffered some kind of attack one afternoon and died the following day. Mr. Dickens was quite overcome by hearing her voice at Niagara and wept that night in our room telling me about it. I comforted him as best I could under our restricted circumstances.

We recovered ourselves and made for Toronto, a dismal city with muddy streets, although the citizens were much more polite than those in America and did not press themselves on Mr. Dickens in the same way. We liked Montreal far better, and Mr. Dickens had a grand time there organizing theatricals with a local regiment. His theatrical projects always improve his spirits and put his energies to good use, and the excitement helped somewhat compensate for that which he had so missed during our long voyage. Mr. Dickens has always been a most affectionate husband and I hope I have been an affectionate wife, but our voyage would have been impossible had I been with child during that period. Over the years, Mr. Dickens has never enjoyed the restrictions my confinements imposed on him, but during the months before our departure for America he swore himself to chastity with some fervour because he knew how necessary that was if I were to accompany him. Once there, however, the intensity of his motivation dwindled just as his enthusiasm for America flagged. He grew more and more disillusioned with the state of the Republic, finding Americans grasping and uncouth; meanwhile, he grew more and more discontented with the state of our relations. It was all I could do to hold him off until that last month when we felt we might safely resume marital life in all its fullness.

After a big farewell banquet in New York, we returned by sail—no more steam for us!—and thankfully this time the voyage took only the promised ten days. We landed in Liverpool one morning and made for London at once. How we had missed the children! Of course, there had been letters to and fro; their uncle and the Macreadys had regularly reassured us the children were happy and well, but it was not until I saw their faces that I realized what a burden of anxiety I had carried for six months in their regard. We coddled them and kissed them for days and in a few weeks all was right again in our little family.

It remained our little family for some time, however. It was almost two years after that Frank was born; there's almost four years' difference between him and Walter. I was becoming increasingly alarmed, I must confess, that our American gap had put an end to a growing family, that somehow my capacity for motherhood had been diminished by our unnatural abstinence in those months. You can imagine my joy when I first guessed that my fifth was finally on its way.

"There's a mistake here."

"Really?"

It's Jonathan on the phone. I have sent over the latest instalment for his Wednesday deadline. He, typically, is calling Friday with his changes.

"I get that it's Catherine Dickens speaking. Very clever. But she's eating cake . . ."

"Yes."

"But before, what's her name, Mrs. Ternan, was offering her store-bought biscuits. Remember the bit about biscuits from Fortnum and Mason's."

"Yes, I do."

"And she took sugar in her tea."

"Yes, no biscuits, two lumps of sugar, all three of Mrs. Ternan's daughters were present and it was a rainy day."

"So, she went a second time?"

"I doubt it. We don't even really know if she went once. This is all speculative."

"Speculative?"

"Yes, I am writing fiction, after all. So this is a different version, a different piece of speculation about what might have happened if Mrs. Dickens came to call."

"The readers won't understand that. If they notice at all, they'll think it's a mistake."

"Maybe they're smarter than you think."

I argue the point with Jonathan, who finally agrees to the inconsistencies if he's allowed to put his own headline on the piece. "Mrs. Dickens, Take Two, or something like that."

On Saturday, Al is much more appreciative.

"I like the seed cake and the slice of lemon," he says, looking up from the paper. "Nice touch."

"Thanks."

"So we are going to hear from the wife?"

"Yeah, I thought it was about time."

"Is she going to issue warnings? 'Let me tell you now, dear, before it's too late, he snores.'"

I laugh. It's the first time Al has appeared anything but irritated by the serial.

He goes back to his reading and finishes a few minutes later.

"How did you figure out the abstinence thing?"

"Just by charting the gaps between her pregnancies."

"Clever you. Who would have imagined someone with ten kids practised any form of birth control."

"Ten pregnancies, and at least two miscarriages,

in fifteen years. And then he dumped her for a younger woman."

The minute I say it I wish I could take it back. I can't keep beating Al with that stick. But he seems unperturbed.

"If only they had the pill," he says, folding up the paper.

The Dickens Bicentenary Serial: Chapter 12
Slough, Buckinghamshire. September 13, 1865

"Have I done enough?"

"No, miss. You keep eating them."

"I love fresh peas. I don't know why we bother cooking them."

Nelly was sitting at the kitchen table shelling peas awkwardly with one hand and popping many of them into her mouth while Jane smeared suet on a leg of lamb she was preparing for the oven.

"I imagine Mr. Dickens likes his lamb a little pink?"

"I have no idea." Nelly paused, puzzled by her own answer. "Is that an odd thing not to know?"

"No matter, miss. I'll cook it nice and rare so that if he's late, it won't be overcooked."

"And if he's early?"

"Well, then he will just have to wait a bit."

"Maybe if you overcooked it and turned the peas to mush, he would take me to a nice restaurant in the city."

"Or maybe he will just send another one of his baskets." Jane laughed. Nelly liked her new servant's boldness. In the theatre, the Ternans had grown up with a merry band of actors, managers and dressers who did not make large distinctions between the classes. Nelly felt a rather familiar camaraderie with Jane.

"Maybe he will. And," she added a little bitterly, "I will just stay home in Slough."

"Slough must be dull for you after Paris, miss."

"I don't mean to disparage your home, Jane, but everything is dull after Paris." There was a little pause and then, as though to soften the thought, Nelly added, "I didn't live in Paris that long, though. Mainly I lived in the countryside in France and I didn't like that much either."

"They all speak French, I imagine."

"That didn't bother me. I knew some French and it improved while I was there. I just felt homesick, that was all. I missed my sisters."

"You were lonely, miss."

"Yes. I was. Do you like dogs, Jane?"

"Oh yes, miss. I love dogs."

"Good. That's settled then. I am going to get a dog."

"What kind of dog were you thinking, miss? My father has a lovely bulldog. People think they are fighters but he's the sweetest creature. Of course, you'd want something smaller."

"Why something smaller?"

"Well, with your hand, miss. You wouldn't want a big dog tugging at the lead."

"No. I suppose not. I'll get a small dog."

Nelly's right hand had not healed properly since the railway accident. Charles had made an appointment for her with a surgeon in London, who said she had severed a nerve and that she would probably never regain full use of it. Jane was under instructions never to let her lift anything for herself, although Nelly wondered if this was not a case of closing the stable door after the horse had bolted. She suspected she had done the real damage after the accident, tugging at Charles's bag with her cut hand, thereby saving several chapters of *Our Mutual Friend* but permanently injuring herself. She could not fully close her palm now. Pincer movements were difficult, so it was sometimes hard for her to pick up an egg without breaking it or to retrieve a dropped earring; fine work that required both hands, such as sewing, was impossible and her handwriting was still a bit wobbly, but she could just manage the piano and was determined not to lose that. A little music, if she were alone in the evening, was a comfort to her. Other things, like combing her hair or shelling peas, she was learning to do with her left. Charles, meanwhile, had taken to referring to her as the patient and routinely sent over baskets of delicacies as though she were convalescing.

———

Three hours later, Nelly and Charles were sitting at the table both poking listlessly at their food in a lengthening silence. The lamb was dry and only edible if covered with lashings of gravy while the roast potatoes, appealingly crispy an hour previously, had gone soft. Charles had arrived late and flustered because he had missed his usual train; by then the meat had sat so long in the oven it was all but ruined and Nelly had eaten enough raw peas she really did not feel like much dinner.

"Did you finish number seventeen?" she asked finally, after searching about for some topic of conversation.

"No." He poked at his food with his fork but didn't eat. "I can't find my way to it."

"Don't you need it ready by tomorrow? I was going to read it through tonight."

"Yes. Well, I'll be late." He gave up on the food, pushing aside his plate, and slumping back in his chair.

"Doesn't the printer—"

"Damn the printer."

She made no reply but rose from her chair, gathered up their plates and approached the door that separated the parlour where they ate from the kitchen behind it. She had to balance the plates against her body with her right arm to turn the knob with her left; it was an awkward business and took her a moment but Charles did not look up from the table. She put the plates down and scraped their uneaten food into the scrap bucket, trying to hide the lamb under the vegetable peelings so as not to give offence to Jane. She transferred the plates into the sink, where the servant, who had left the meal in the oven and retired to her room before Charles arrived, would wash them the next day. There was a bowl of stewed fruit and a pitcher of custard waiting on the kitchen table, so she stuck her head back into the dining room. Charles had still not moved and was staring blankly at the floor.

"Will you have some fruit and custard?"

He did not reply at first but looked up when she repeated herself.

"No. No, thank you."

"You haven't had much to eat."

He examined his shoe and then knocked it against the table leg but said nothing.

"Would you not like something else to eat?"

He kept staring at the floor.

"Charles . . ." Her voice held a small note of warning.

"Oh." He looked up finally. "Umm. I'll have some cheese."

When she returned with the block of cheddar Jane had left in the pantry, he was now leant over the table, shifting bits of cutlery to and fro. He cut a slab of cheese for himself and turned to her.

"I'm not good company tonight."

She did not try to contradict him.

"No one can be expected to be good company every night of his life."

"No, but I wasn't good company last week either, as I recall."

"No, you weren't." He had been equally morose on both occasions he had visited the week before, but she had felt more energetic herself and had teased him out of his mood those nights, entertaining him at the piano. Tonight, she waited; she was annoyed by his behaviour and refused to be the one who threw him a lifeline and pulled him out of the water yet again. She had seen his dark moods before, in the years on Mornington Crescent when he despaired over the future of his sons, lamented his daughter Katey's hasty marriage, worried over a particular chapter or railed against a publisher, but they had grown markedly worse in recent months. For a moment she felt nothing but recalcitrant and bloody minded, her own anger washing over her. They sat there for a bit before she relented.

"Do you still dwell on the accident?" she asked.

He nodded and swallowed as though choking down emotion before he could speak.

"The noises. I hear those appalling noises . . . I think I will be fine; I get to Paddington, all chipper. I sit in my carriage saying last week's fuss was an aberration; there is nothing to it, little more than a quarter of an hour. Half an hour and I will be in your arms; what is a quarter-hour's journey in exchange for an evening of bliss?"

He smiled at her winningly but she made no response to the flowery compliment; their dinner had hardly seemed blissful.

"And then . . ." she prompted him.

"And then the whistle blows, the train starts to move. At first we shunt our way slowly out of London and that's all right, but when we gather speed I can feel the fear rising in me. And when the carriage shakes or leans around a bend, my memories take over. I hear the screeching, and the people crying . . ."

"Yes. It was horrible," Nelly said with almost perfunctory sympathy. "I found my trip to town to see the doctor quite difficult."

"Afterwards, it makes it difficult to write," he continued. "It crowds out the stories. It is as though my brain is still too busy with it to invent other dramas."

"I don't forget it either," she replied without malice, turning over her right hand to show her scarred palm.

"No. No, of course you don't, my dear." He reached for her hand, but she had withdrawn it under the table.

She felt the accident had become for them a convenient fiction. Of course, it had happened and it had been horrific, traumatizing and unforgettable. Yes, it was now difficult to even make the twenty-minute ride into Paddington. She knew that he went to and from the city in a state of high anxiety; the occasional time she took the train, she sat there clutching the arm of the seat and starting at the slightest lurch or unusual sound. She knew she was in trouble if she started to see a swath of blue silk in her mind's eye; she would hang on with her eyes closed, breathing deeply and just waiting until it was over. She preferred her mother and sisters to come and see her in her new home at Slough rather than going to them: Maria was married now and living with her husband in Oxford, but Nelly had yet to visit them there. Still, it was not the memory of the accident that was the cause of silences between her and Charles, and she doubted it was the accident that made it difficult for him to write. It was the memory of the moments afterwards that afflicted them, whether they said so or not. He had failed her, and she supposed that he knew it, and she supposed that he also knew she found it difficult to forgive. They did not speak of any of this but let the accident stand as a kind of code for the trap in which they found themselves.

"I'm sorry, my dear. Let's have some music. That will cheer us both."

She dutifully took her place at the piano and sang for him for a bit, an Italian aria or two that Fanny used to sing, the English folk songs that he preferred. Gradually, once again, his humour returned to him and he began to entertain her with tales from the magazine office, where a sub-editor had mislaid proofs and found them again under a colleague's bacon sandwich, and from Gad's Hill, where the gardener had severed a water pipe and created a gusher in the middle of the lawn, mundane disasters all told for the greatest comic effect. She laughed despite herself but when he took her hand and swung her arm in his old way, saying teasingly, "Shall we to bed, milady?" she dropped her hand away.

"I think I will stay down here and read for a bit."

"Nelly . . ."

"The light is better here. I want to finish my book."

"But you were supposed to proofread for me tonight."

"You said you hadn't finished number seventeen."

"No, I haven't," he said grudgingly. "I just meant, well, you can't have been planning to read your book . . ."

"No. I wasn't but now I want to."

He stood there staring at her for a long moment; she looked unblinkingly back with no visible emotion, standing there as apparently unmoved as she had stood a few months before on the embankment at Staplehurst.

"I am sorry," he said finally. "I am truly sorry."

It wouldn't do, love. It just isn't big enough. Not now that you've got the Royal Doulton."

Shay nodded in agreement and looked dispiritedly down at the card table onto which she was trying to squeeze six place settings. She had pulled it out into her living room and placed it in front of the couch, where two of her guests would have to perch on extra cushions to reach the table height; the remaining four would have chairs on the other side of the table and at each end, but the truth was there really wasn't room for two place settings on the sides of the square table. A pair of the large Royal Doulton dinner plates that Mrs. Brown kept for special occasions could just fit side by side on the tabletop but they left almost no room for the cutlery, let alone the flowers Shay was planning for the centre.

"I've got another like it down in the shed," Mrs. Brown volunteered. "You could put the two tables side by side, throw the cover over the top and nobody would be the wiser."

"Oh, Mrs. Brown . . ."

"You'll have to clean it off, mind, and I am not lugging it up those stairs."

"No, of course not. I can manage it, no problem."

Shay waited while Mrs. Brown accumulated the necessary energy to negotiate the stairs and followed her out into the small back garden to the shed. She was feeling rather guilt-stricken about all Mrs. Brown's contributions toward her dinner, which included the pudding basin, the Royal Doulton china, the tablecloth, two extra chairs and now the table itself. The flat came furnished with basic kitchen utensils, china and cutlery and there seemed no good reason to demand the inventory to accommodate six dinner guests and the making of charlotte russe. Mrs. Brown's growing list of initially grudging offers reminded Shay of the old fairytale about the two soldiers who trick the hungry villagers into sharing their firewood, their pot and finally their vegetables to help the strangers make a miraculous stone soup. Perhaps it was a story about a con; maybe it was a moral about hospitality. The problem with Mrs. Brown's generosity was that Shay increasingly felt that it would only be polite to invite her landlady to dinner and she had neither enough lamb nor enough space to accommodate a seventh guest. And, if she were honest with herself, she did not feel Mrs. Brown was quite the type of person who would mix well with the group she had assembled for her dinner party.

Shay had few friends in London, so the guest list had proved a challenge. She had started with her desire to re-create one of Catherine's dinners and once that had taken hold, the power of the idea had proved strong enough to overcome her social anxieties. First, she would invite the Clarks. The Clarks were contacts of her brother's—he did something in the City, she was a publicist for a small theatre company—who had been kind to her when she first arrived. That is, they had invited her over to their small flat on two occasions and she felt she ought to reciprocate. So, that was two guests. Then she invited her one real friend in London, her fellow researcher Alex. A cheerful young woman from Birmingham who seemed a rather unlikely personality to be spending her days in a library, Alex was perpetually single, a state she lamented with an almost gleeful self-dramatization. Shay had racked her brains to find another male guest for Alex's benefit but had finally given up and invited Fiona, the shy and rather dour assistant librarian who they both agreed needed to lighten up.

And then there was the fifth guest, Jeff. Shay had met Jeff in the park. He was her best find in London, her big hope for her stay. Her flat was in North London, and when she made the effort, which wasn't often, she could reach an entrance to Hampstead Heath in twenty minutes. So, one clear Saturday a month previously, just as the pleas-antly early English spring was starting to appear, she had been out walking on the heath, bored and disconsolate despite the day, when Jeff ran into her. Literally. He was jogging with headphones on and had run smack into her as he emerged from a walking path that led at an abrupt angle onto the main route she was taking. She all but toppled to the ground, and as she was steadying herself, he snatched the headphones off his ears and began apologizing profusely. When she finally managed to interrupt him to tell him all was okay, he heard her accent.

"Hey. Are you American too?" he asked with an enthusiasm that was so boyish it was rather appealing.

"Sorry. Canadian," Shay replied.

"That's okay. Canadians are nice too," he said. "I mean . . . I'm sure you're very nice, if you're Canadian. I mean . . ." He heard himself and started to laugh.

Jeff often laughed at himself; Shay found it a change from Al, who laughed at the world around him but, when it came to himself, seemed to believe, without the least hint of snobbery, in some sense of slight superiority conferred by his own charm, as though he was truly a blessed being whom others ought to be rather grateful to know. He floated above the world a little bit and drew you up to that plane. Shay liked that about him; she was grateful to have known him. She did not, on the other hand, feel the least elevated by the friendly Jeff, who seemed to live with both feet resolutely planted on the ground, although she was also grateful for his existence. He was an escape route, Plan B. She just needed to get over Al—she hadn't spent a morning in bed since Christmas; it had been at least a month since she'd cried—and fall in love with Jeff—he really was sweet—and go back to the States with him. (He was an MBA on a three-year posting with an American multinational that believed potential executives should have foreign experience.) They would have babies, and she would finish her dissertation, and they would live in New York and it would all be lovely, cozy and calm just like other young couples without anguished emails and tearful phone calls and promises and compromises and separations and reunions.

So, she was thinking fondly of Jeff as she carefully penned his name in black ink on a rather expensive blank business card she had purchased at a stationer's down the street from the butcher. The name cards were, of course, utterly unnecessary for a table of six, but Shay liked the idea and felt they would lend an appropriate formality to the proceedings. She had also written out her menu twice on larger cards and fiddled about trying to position it so everyone could read it without it blocking her flower arrangement, a few early tulips and a bit of baby's breath she had picked up at Sainsbury's.

By six thirty, Shay had her table ready and her food prepared. The charlotte russe that she had made that afternoon sat cooling in her minuscule fridge, all ready to be turned out of its mould later in the evening. The potatoes were cooked and mashed, and could be browned under the broiler at the last minute. The leg of lamb should start cooking as the guests arrived, she calculated, having already checked that the roasting pan could actually fit in the tiny oven, while the asparagus could be steamed in the microwave. The fish she planned to fry up as they were having their drinks; the lobster sauce could be quickly heated in a pan on the other of the stove's two burners. She was poised, ready for her guests, and feeling rather smug when she looked down at the jeans she was still wearing: the lobster bisque had spattered a bit when she opened the can. With fifteen minutes to spare, she raced into the small bedroom behind the kitchen, clawed a pair of black dress pants out of the overcrowded closet, changed her blouse and charged into the bathroom to attempt to do something about her hair. She was yielding the mascara wand when someone pounded at the door.

It was Alex.

"Your landlady let me in," she explained, bouncing through the door and plonking two bottles of sparkling wine on the few inches of bare space beside the kitchen sink. "Bubbly. The Victorians drank a lot of it, if I recall correctly."

Shay began thanking her profusely, but Alex waved it off and moved across the room to admire the table.

"Oooh. Place cards. Very posh," she said as she walked about the table, admiring it from all directions. "Greg. Liz. That's the couple, is it?"

"Yes."

"Jeff. He's the one, right? The American?"

"Yes."

"Watch Fiona doesn't nab him right from under your nose," she said and both of them giggled. "Well, I'm early. I wanted to make sure I was here to get the festivities started. Shall I pop a cork?"

They were both sipping Alex's wine when the doorbell rang downstairs.

"I'll get it, Mrs. Brown," Shay called out as she headed through the door she had left open and downstairs to the house's cramped entrance hall.

She opened the door and found Jeff standing there accompanied by a very tall, very blond young woman.

"Hi," he said cheerfully. "Hope we aren't the first. We came early because we have dinner reservations for eight."

The Dickens Bicentenary Serial: Chapter 13
Florence. November 7, 1867

Somewhere a bird was singing, a low note and then a
second higher, the pair repeated again and again. At the
very edge of consciousness, Nelly was deliciously aware
of sleep. She felt the cool sheets and the soft pillow; she
stretched out an arm across the bed. She was alone. For
some reason, that was a good thing here, an indulgence
rather than an absence. The two notes gradually grew into
a whole chorus of birdsong. A glimmer of light appeared
beneath the curtains. It was a late autumn dawn. Oh yes,
she was in Italy, in the Trollopes' villa. Today she planned
to visit the Uffizi, and later take tea in the Boboli Gardens
with Mrs. Watson, if the day were clear. She smiled at the
thought, rolled over and went back to sleep.

By three that afternoon, Nelly was wandering through the
parterre of the Boboli Gardens on the arm of Harry Watson,

an amiable young American who seemed to lack any particular direction in life beyond traipsing around Italy after his formidable mother. His conversation alternated between a discussion of Italian art and comments on the view while his eyes would stray occasionally to hers and then move quickly to his shoes. Nelly had to repress a giggle; the effect was wholly innocent and rather sweet. But by four o'clock, rather to her surprise, it was with Mrs. Watson with whom she was engaging in a tête-à-tête on the tea-house terrace while Harry went in search of a waiter.

"Where do you live in England, Miss Ternan?"

"Oh, you would not know the place; it's very quiet."

"I have spent a good deal of time in England. Do you live in the home counties?"

"Yes, just outside London. In a village."

"A village in Buckinghamshire? I think your sister mentioned Bucks. I have friends who live at Aylesbury."

"No, not in Bucks any more. I moved recently."

"Oh really, closer to the city?"

"Yes, a bit closer."

"In Berkshire, perhaps?"

"No, not Berkshire." Nelly, who was beginning to feel as though she was playing a game of hunt the thimble, relented a bit. "South of the city. At Peckham."

"Oh, Peckham. Why, you are almost in the city. Do you manage to have a garden there? The English always have such lovely gardens."

"Yes, I have a garden."

"How pleasant for you. And what kind of house is it? A cottage perhaps? English cottages are so pretty."

"Well, you might call it a cottage," Nelly replied vaguely. Her new house in Peckham was twice the size of the cottage at Slough and had a generous garden in which she could walk the dog.

"And would your home be a family legacy? Your sister told me your father died when you were just girls. Very sad for you."

"Yes, well, my father did not leave much of a legacy," Nelly replied. "At least not in real estate." She had started to spy where this conversation was headed.

"Something from your mother's family then?"

"Yes," Nelly lied definitively now. "From an aunt."

"But your sister was working as a governess before her marriage, I believe?"

Nelly grasped the implication immediately. Fanny had married her employer, the recently widowed Tom Trollope, older brother to the novelist Anthony and himself a writer living in Italy with his young daughter. If Fanny needed to work for her room and board as the Trollopes' governess, how did her younger sister have the means to live in her own house?

"It is a rather modest place we recently acquired, but it belongs to all of us," Nelly improvised. "Fanny always wanted to make her own way. She had taken music lessons here and her work with the Trollopes did prove a welcome opportunity to see more of Italy."

"I see. How admirable of her. Your sister is a powerful personality, my dear, and such a beautiful voice."

At that point they were interrupted, much to Nelly's relief, by Harry himself. She foresaw no difficulty in gently ridding herself of a love-struck American but his inquisitive mother's attempts to ascertain her suitability as a daughter-in-law were becoming conversationally difficult.

Fanny and Maria had met Mrs. Watson, a wealthy Philadelphia widow with artistic tastes, when all three were sketching in the Uffizi the previous month, and they were quite devoted to their new friend. It was easier, however, for Mrs. Trollope, recently married into a famous literary family, and her sister Mrs. Taylor, whose wealthy husband back in Oxford indulged her interest in travel and art, to become fast friends with a new acquaintance; their unmarried twenty-eight-year-old sister had to be more careful about how she described her circumstances.

"I was thinking, Miss Ternan, that if tomorrow is just as fine, we might rent a boat," Harry said after he settled himself at the table, promising tea was imminent. "I know the river seems rather dreary in Florence but I am told that if we can just row out of the city a bit, the Arno is really quite scenic. I don't imagine I could get us all the way to Pisa . . ."

"Oh, you are proposing to row yourself?" Nelly asked in some surprise, assuming that one of the boatmen on the quays would do the job.

"Yes. I'm a bit of an oarsman. Back home, on the Delaware, I row every morning."

"The Delaware River?" Nelly asked.

"Yes. Do you know it?"

"No, I've just heard of it. Fanny was born on the Delaware."

"Really? How did that come to pass?"

"My parents were visiting America and were travelling when my mother gave birth. Fanny was born on a paddle steamer."

"How romantic!" Mrs. Watson broke in. "What were your parents doing in America?"

Nelly paused. Perhaps American prejudices against the acting profession were less pronounced than those in England. Still, it was better to be judicious; if Fanny wanted to tell Mrs. Watson that her parents had been travelling players and Mrs. Ternan was retired from the stage, she would do it herself. Nelly should never have let slip the bit about the paddle streamer; Fanny would not be pleased. She had become increasingly sticky about appearances since her marriage, worrying away about who might think what about their family arrangements. It was as though she cared more for her in-laws' reputation than she ever had for her own. "We wouldn't want . . ." she had said to her sister when Nelly had first arrived but had never stipulated exactly what it was that wasn't wanted.

"Oh, my father was travelling on business," Nelly replied vaguely now.

"Have you ever been to America yourself, Miss Ternan?" Harry asked.

Nelly had been promised America, and she fairly longed for the prodigal land of teeming cities and red Indians. "Next month, I'll be in New York," she would say to herself. "By spring, I will have seen Niagara." Her nomadic instincts drew her to a new land, she wanted to follow her mother's footsteps—and others' too; she wanted to see for herself what she had so often heard described. If she could not have a distinguished writer for a husband and an Italian villa to live in like Fanny; if she could not have a wealthy businessman and a rose garden in Oxford like Maria; if she must always hide the reason for her spinsterhood and the source of her real estate, she could at least be the one who travelled to America. She would not be cheated of that honour along with all the rest.

Charles was resolute. After the heartbreak of France and the boredom of Slough, he had moved her to a larger house, with a garden for her little dog, in Peckham, a short train ride into the city. And he had promised her a trip to America. On his second American tour at least, he would enjoy the company and she the position that they both deserved. She had agreed to the trip with some trepidation but much enthusiasm and, although she did not tell him so, was no less determined in her own way. This time she would be the one he would call his intrepid companion. She would be there if he were overcome by the roar of the falls. She would be his helpmeet and mainstay. She was worthy, more worthy, more fitting.

Of course, she could not travel as his consort, but as his goddaughter instead, a young protégé to whom he wished to show the world; she would be introduced everywhere, attend all the banquets. There would always be separate rooms. All would be achieved with the utmost propriety. The Americans were a hospitable people, welcoming, happy to oblige a guest without judgment or preconception. She, however, saw the trouble: if she was named as his travelling companion in newspaper accounts of his progress and word got back to England that Mr. Dickens was accompanied by a Miss Ternan, some people might remember when and where they had heard her name before. Some Americans might even remember. They might recall there had been rumours of scandal associated with his name; that stupid letter had been published first in an American paper. He had been ill advised to write it; he was half mad at the time. It might yet come back to haunt them.

Still, Charles refused to be deprived of her company for the length of a six-month tour, and Charles was used to getting his own way. He decided he would go ahead and get the lay of the land, see what the hotels looked like, ask a few discreet questions, see if she could travel with him but only attend private functions perhaps, and he tentatively booked a passage for her on a steamer from Liverpool leaving a month after his own departure. She did not like the idea of crossing by herself; neither did he. She feared seasickness; he feared a shipboard romance. But it seemed their best chance and so now she waited for a coded telegram that would tell her "All well" and send her to claim her ticket in Liverpool.

In the meantime, Fanny and Tom had invited her to stay; Tom, who knew Charles well, was aware of Nelly's situation and less concerned with appearances than his new wife but tactfully refrained from asking his sister-in-law whether she had got any news from America. They all found it simplest if Charles's name was not mentioned and she tried to tell herself that the trip was unlikely to happen anyway. That she did not want to make the long voyage by herself and feared that some awkwardness might await on the other side of the Atlantic. It was her way of guarding against disappointment. It didn't really work, however, for as the days in Italy went by and Christmas beckoned, she grew increasingly excited and kept catching herself thinking, "Soon I shall be at sea!"

"No, I have yet to have the pleasure of seeing America," she replied. "But I hope someday I will."

"I hope so too," said Harry emphatically.

———

A few days after the walk in the Boboli Gardens, the housekeeper came into the breakfast room. "Telegramma, signora."

Fanny glanced at the envelope.

"It's for you, Nelly."

Nelly took it from the housekeeper's hand and ripped it open.

SAFE AND WELL. ALL MY LOVE, it said.

Nelly stared down at the page. "All well" meant come. "Safe and well" meant the trip was impossible and his assistant would cancel her passage.

"Bad news?" Fanny asked as she watched her sister's face.

"I wonder if I might stay for Christmas."

"Oh. It would be lovely to have you here for Christmas. You, and mother and Maria too, if we can convince her to come back. Stay as long as you like. Stay till the spring comes."

"Thank you. Spring in Italy might be very pleasant," Nelly said, swallowing her emotions.

Lying in bed that night unable to fall asleep, she mulled it over. Springtime came early in Italy and first there would be a family Christmas in the villa. It would be a safe haven. No lonely steamer passage. No awkward meeting in New York. No misunderstandings in unknown towns or difficult questions from strangers. No waiting in hotel rooms while he was out at banquets. She released her image of the roaring falls and the busy streets and replaced it with one of lemon trees in flower. In the end, she was not disappointed at all.

The girls' banner almost broke my heart. It was hand-lettered with marker in their best grade two block capitals on what appeared to be an old sheet and was hung across our front hall on two bits of green garden twine. WELCOME HOME MUMMY! CONGRATULATIONS! YOU DID IT! There hadn't been quite enough room for "congratulations" on one line so the N and the S were mashed together with the exclamation mark tucked in below.

It was late September and I had just completed my final round of chemo. Al had picked me up at the hospital in the car and we had driven to the community centre where the girls had been enrolled in an after-school program ever since I began treatment and couldn't be sure to get them at three thirty every afternoon. I waited in the car while Al went inside. I was exhausted and didn't feel like moving: the effects of chemotherapy are cumulative and I was reaching a low point by this stage. When the three of them emerged, the girls were all giggly and kept

whispering to each other. Al smiled—clearly he knew
what was up—and, as soon as he had belted both of
them into the back seat and took his place at the wheel,
announced, "So. Mummy's done treatment. Tell her congratulations." They cheered from the back seat but kept
up the silly stuff all the way home.

As I came through the door I saw what the surprise
was: the pink-and-green banner strung across the room
and a huge bouquet of yellow lilies and ornamental dai-
sies sitting on the hall table. I swallowed, bit my lip and
told them it was a lovely banner and a fabulous way to
celebrate finishing treatment and I loved them very much,
all of which was true.

"Lily helped us. It was her idea." Lily was one of the
young instructors at the community centre, a gentle soul
who was a particular pal of Goli's.

"And Daddy hung it up for us after you left this
morning. Didn't he do a good job?"

"And he bought the flowers."

"There wasn't room for *congratulations*, it's a big
word," Anahita pointed out, adding airily, "but that
doesn't matter."

"Anny thought it should say *get well soon* but I said
you're finished being sick and *welcome home* was better,"
Goli said.

"It's wonderful the way it is. Thank you, girls. Thank
you so much."

"And Daddy got a cake for dinner."

"Anny. That was supposed to be a surprise." Goli gave her sister a little shove of annoyance. Anahita, older by twenty minutes, could be bossy and Goli sometimes resented it, but when I thought about it I realized it had been months since they'd had one of their knock-down, hair-pulling brawls. There had been a lot of tears and complaints and temper tantrums when Al was gone from the house, but since I had been sick the girls always seemed sweet and quiet. Maybe Al had just been particularly successful at keeping them out of my way when I was in bad shape.

"The cake will still be a surprise because I haven't seen it yet," I reassured Goli.

The real surprise would be if I was able to eat it. During chemo I'd lost ten pounds and was continually being lectured by the nurses about keeping my strength up. Al had bought a cake at the grocery store with YEAH MUMMY! piped on it in blue icing. Sitting at the dinner table when all I longed to do was sleep, surrounded by my girls' excited and expectant faces, I thought I would cry. They just wanted life to return to normal. They wanted a healthy mother they could trust to pick them up after school and make their meals and read them stories. They shouldn't always have to be good because Mummy wasn't feeling well or quiet because Mummy was resting. Was it right to let them think that we were out of the woods?

———

I thanked them for their surprise, and I thanked Al and leant across the table and kissed him on the lips. The girls clapped delightedly: they never seemed to pay that much attention to our interactions as long as they were polite, but they must always have had their antennae out. When Al first came home, they would cheer encouragement anytime we offered each other a peck on the cheek or a hug.

"I think Mummy better get to bed now. She's had a long day," Al told them, giving me cover to retreat.

Thirty hours later, at dawn on the second day after the treatment, I was back on the bathroom floor with the toilet seat up, longing to vomit so that I could get some relief from the nausea.

Al appeared at the door, shrugging on a bathrobe and tying the belt around his waist. He seemed prepared for a long haul that night.

"It's okay. Just leave me. Go back to bed."

"I can stay, in case you need me."

"I'll be fine." I waved him away and gulped; there was a lurch in my stomach. And then I remembered Al saying those same words on his way out the door, that I would always be fine, and now I wasn't. "I'm not fine, Al," I corrected myself tearfully. "I'm not fine."

"It's okay. I'm here," he said, gently patting my back. After a bit he added, "It's nice to be needed, you know. You used to need me, when we were younger."

"Did I?"

"Yeah. This whole thing has felt like the first time in, I don't know, the first time in years that you have actually needed me."

"You make me sound like an Amazon or a rock or something. I've always needed you."

"Not really." He stretched his legs out in front of him and considered for a moment. "Not the way you used to. Not the way it was at first. I kind of missed that, I missed being useful to someone, you know, being necessary."

"You're necessary to the girls."

"It's not the same. They're children, and they're my children. I would expect them to need me. You're the only adult, except I guess my parents, who ever made me feel if I weren't there it would have mattered."

"The only one who ever needed you?" I asked. "All those women, before, when you were a student . . ."

"They needed me because they needed a fuck or they wanted to prove something to their last boyfriend or their mother or whatever. It's not the same thing. You remember that email you sent me? You told me it wasn't working for you. It wasn't working for you being without me. It was like a cry for help."

"And you came riding to the rescue."

"Yes, because you had just rescued me. You had made me necessary. Otherwise, I was invisible. But somehow you've always been able to see me."

I hadn't felt like I had been able to see him, or anybody else for that matter, for months—sickness makes you self-absorbed—but it was the kind of connection I had been at such pains to remind him of when he was trying to leave. I squeezed his arm and then leant on it to pull myself to my feet. My nausea had passed.

The Dickens Bicentenary Serial
Mrs. Dickens at Park Cottage—Round Three

Do you take any interest in mesmerism, Mrs. Ternan? No? You never fell victim to that particular fashion. It was a great passion of my husband's for some years. Oh, thank you. I am always partial to a bit of gingerbread. So good for the digestion, I do think.

Magnetism, they used to call it, submitting a subject to magnetic powers. My husband was quite convinced of his own magnetic powers in the early years of our marriage. He could easily put myself or my sister into a trance. He would do it to entertain our guests, although they say the practice has therapeutic benefits. Dr. Elliotson was certainly convinced it had medical applications, but in our house, it really began as a parlour trick.

Dr. Elliotson was our family doctor. Lovely man. He had become convinced that mesmerism could help those with nervous complaints and he regularly gave demonstrations and lectures on the subject. When he noted

Mr. Dickens had an interest, he suggested he try his hand at it, showed him how it was done, the most effective gestures for achieving the trance state, and how to rouse the patient once he was finished. Mr. Dickens began practising on me and Georgina and seemed to master it right away.

Oh, it's an odd sensation but not unpleasant. Your eyes are closed; you can hear people's voices but as if they are very far away. The sensation is, well, very lazy, comfortable. You feel unworried and rather warm. A bit like being at the seaside on a nice summer day and closing your eyes but not actually falling asleep.

Well, I wouldn't really call it obey. I would respond to his voice and certainly do as he said. But I wouldn't jump out a window on his command or run into the street in my petticoats. That kind of thing is nonsense, put out by people who want to discredit it, I imagine. It is not really about actions anyway; it is more about a state of the mind. I would think what he suggested I think or feel what he said to feel. You know, he would say you will stop worrying about your mother's health or you will feel more charitably toward, I don't know, some friend of his I didn't like or something of that nature. And when I came out of the trance I would be very calm and feel much more kindly disposed to the person or less unsettled about my mother.

We thought it was all good fun but then Mr. Dickens found a subject with more serious worries to address. It was in Genoa. It must be at least ten years ago now, fifteen perhaps. We often travelled on the continent for lengthy periods in those years, taking houses in Italy for some months. That time, we had been in Genoa hardly a week, I think, when we met the de la Rues. M. de la Rue was Swiss, I believe, a banker, a prosperous man, very proper in the way Europeans are, always immaculately dressed and very formal in his manners. He would kiss my hand most gallantly whenever we met. His wife was English, so naturally we were friendly, the way one is meeting a compatriot in foreign parts. They had a beautiful apartment at the top of a grand old palazzo and they showed us around the city, acting as the most generous hosts and guides.

I must say that to an outsider Mme de la Rue appeared quite healthy; she was an amiable person, a good conversationalist in company, although very quiet at some other times, a pretty woman only a few years older than myself, but M. de la Rue soon confided in my husband that she was very ill, plagued not only by burning headaches but also by the worst anxieties and fits that came over her, especially at night, as well as terrible nightmares that disturbed her sleep. By day she could remain calm but as soon as the sun set she became increasingly fearful of what state she might find herself in as sleep approached, to the point where she did not wish to go to bed at all and then suffered terrible exhaustion as a result. As we came to know her better, I did notice she also suffered attacks during the day. On one occasion when we were lunching she clutched the side of her face. She cried out to her husband that she could not stand the pain, as though this were not the first occurrence of such an attack. It passed in a moment and we tried to resume our lunch; he explained that she was a martyr to tic douloureux, and the attacks could sometimes be triggered by the motion of the jaw while eating.

Mr. Dickens said, "Imagine living a life where one would fear to eat during the day and sleep at night for the pain both might bring!" Mr. Dickens quickly suggested Dr. Elliotson be consulted, for his magnetic treatments had particular success with just this kind of nervous complaint. M. de la Rue thought they might travel to England to consult Dr. Elliotson. I don't know if they ever did in the end—we have fallen out of touch with them in the intervening years—but in the meantime, Mr. Dickens suggested he might attempt to mesmerize Mme de la Rue himself. I believe their initial agreement was that he would make some trial so that M. de la Rue might see how the process worked and whether his wife was susceptible or not. Some people, you know, are not the least susceptible and will sit there staring at the mesmerist quite perplexed as to what it is they should be experiencing for they feel nothing at all. Mr. Dickens once tried to mesmerize our coachman to no effect whatsoever. The young man kept turning his head about, all the time his eyes were shut, saying, "Have you started, Mr. Dickens?" Mr. Dickens was not very amused.

At any rate, Mme de la Rue was highly susceptible. From the beginning, she made an excellent patient.

Mr. Dickens was delighted; at least, I could see he was delighted. One did not like to express it in exactly those terms to M. de la Rue, since his wife was so ill. Mr. Dickens indicated he was pleased that he could be of assistance, and both husband and wife were hopeful that mesmerism might show results and very grateful to Mr. Dickens. In her sessions with my husband, Mme de la Rue would have visions. Now, I have been placed in a mesmerized trance on many occasions and I have to tell you, Mrs. Ternan, that I do not see visions. Clearly, Mme de la Rue was a much more suggestible creature than I am for she saw all kinds of things while in a trance, dream-like places, land-scapes and such, peopled by friends or members of her own family. But especially she repeatedly saw some fear-ful character that Mr. Dickens called her bad phantom. Some sort of ghost or devil who hovered about at the edge of view; it sounded to me just like a bad dream, the way you sense a wicked presence in a dream but can't really say on waking who or what it was.

Mr. Dickens became fascinated by this bad phantom to the point where I believed he put Mme de la Rue into trances in the hope of glimpsing the creature himself, somehow conjuring it up or perceiving it through her descriptions. Apparently, her dreams seemed entirely real to her; he said she shook in terror when she described the phantom. You must understand, Mrs. Ternan, that by this point I was no longer present for these experiments. Mr. Dickens felt Mme de la Rue was more likely to trust him and fall into a trance if they were alone together, so I don't really know how this phantom manifested itself or what form her reaction took beyond what Mr. Dickens told me and her husband. Mr. Dickens now said he wanted to exorcise this evil figure from her mind and so he began to mesmerize her almost daily.

She became increasingly dependent on their sessions and would cling to Mr. Dickens whenever we met, hanging on his sleeve and telling him how clever he was and how grateful she was. When they were not together, they would exchange regular notes and letters about her mental state and, I have to say, Mr. Dickens seemed to rely on their regular communication as much as Mme de la Rue did. She did seem to improve. Perhaps any woman would have felt better given an important man's undivided attention. At any rate, she was calmer both during the day and at night, and as well as repeatedly expressing her gratitude to Mr. Dickens, she would thank me most touchingly for sparing him and allowing him to devote so much time to her cure. That was always the word she used, *allowing*. I have to say I might have laughed at such language had I been in a happier frame of mind. I don't know how your marriage operated, Mrs. Ternan, perhaps being an actor your husband was a more liberal sort, but in my experience one does not allow or disallow a husband to do anything. A husband does what he wishes, what he thinks best or what pleases him, and there is little point arguing about it.

However, I did think Mr. Dickens' attentions to her were becoming unseemly and that he was motivated as much by his own appetite for her pitiful reactions as by any desire to cure her. Even though he was not a doctor, he liked having a patient. He often called her that, the patient. At any rate, I gently suggested that, now she was improved, we must make a planned sightseeing trip to Rome, which we had delayed for some time. Mr. Dickens agreed we would leave soon but would not specify a date. And then Mme de la Rue, with an uncanny knack for timing, took a turn for the worse, and M. de la Rue called Mr. Dickens to her side one night, sending a messenger to our villa to wake us from our sleep.

At this point, I had to remonstrate. Mr. Dickens was not, I repeated to him, a doctor. What would people think of a man attending another man's wife in the middle of the night? Surely I would not be alone in considering such a thing beyond the bounds of propriety, no matter how desperate the cause or how deeply desired the cure. I know Emile de la Rue was none too happy either; he agreed with me that the situation might easily be misconstrued. He said as much to me one day by way of an apology, and I think he felt increasingly uncomfortable that it fell to another man to help his wife out of her troubles. Mr. Dickens accused me of jealousy, that I feared being displaced by Mme de la Rue, and said I did not understand how his artistic temperament gave him an inquisitive mind and required him to make such experiments. Of course,

I am not an artist, Mrs. Ternan, but I think I am as inquisitive as the next person; I am not without an education. One can study a subject without becoming enthralled, and I do not think that my concerns and my requirements at the time were unreasonable; surely I was owed more delicate behaviour. I had discovered by then that I was expecting our Alfred, my sixth, and, of course, we were not at home in England, so I expect I was feeling a little vulnerable. Perhaps Mr. Dickens was right, that I just wanted his attention for myself; that might explain what I did next.

It was a little ruse, Mrs. Ternan, just a small one, and I believed at the time that it worked rather well. After that difficult night, I insisted we depart for Rome immediately, saying no matter how much we might wish to help the de la Rues, we had given them enough of our time already and could not completely rearrange our travels for them. If we wanted to see more of Italy before we were due to return to Genoa and collect the children for our return to England, we needed to make our trip. Let M. de la Rue take his wife to Dr. Elliotson if she seemed to profit so much from mesmerism. So, at my insistence, we left for Rome that week, but only after Mr. Dickens and Mme de la Rue had agreed that he would attempt to magnetize her remotely at eleven o'clock each morning by means of both parties concentrating their thoughts deeply on each other at that precise moment.

We set off for Rome by coach one morning with Mr. Dickens checking his pocket watch from time to time to make sure he would keep this mental appointment. I looked out the window and admired the scenery; it is a beautiful road from Genoa to Rome, along the coast with views of the ocean much of the way. Mr. Dickens often sits silent for long periods on a journey, or at home for that matter, thinking, pondering his writing or his ideas, so there would be nothing unusual about him not speaking to me while we travelled and I would know never to interrupt him under those circumstances. I would not dare speak unless he spoke first. I am sure you would agree, Mrs. Ternan, that a great artist requires a certain deference that a wife might not show an ordinary husband.

So, on this occasion, I was silent as always, but did pay close attention to the time; I had a small watch secreted in the work bag I had with me—needlework is all but impossible on a coach, don't you find? But I do sometimes manage some simple tatting. So, when eleven o'clock arrived, and Mr. Dickens continued to sit silently, I knew he was now attempting to mesmerize Mme de la Rue. I have no idea if his long-distance mesmerism worked—later Mr. Dickens always claimed it did—but I gradually gave way to a trance myself. Or, at least, I let him suppose that was what was happening as I slumped against the side of the coach and began to murmur his name in my supposedly magnetized state. It took some moments for Mr. Dickens to realize what had happened; at first, he tried simply to shake me, assuming I had fallen asleep, but I did not wake and now called out his name more forcefully and more desperately than before. He soon realized that, whatever was happening back in Genoa, he had succeeded in mesmerizing his own wife, seated at his side. And when he made that realization, he very gently and very properly brought me back to myself.

The de la Rues followed us to Rome not long after, and Mr. Dickens did several more sessions with Mme de la Rue, but eventually we continued on our tour of Italy and then returned to Genoa to take the children home to England. The following year, when we travelled to the continent, I insisted we go no farther south than France, and on this occasion Mr. Dickens took full consideration of my wishes. Eventually we fell out of touch with the de la Rues. To this day, Mr. Dickens maintains I was unnecessarily jealous of her, but privately I felt it was perfectly natural to be alarmed by the connection and take steps to sever it.

His experiments with mesmerism ceased soon after that. I suppose you could say he fell out of love with the practice. At any rate, we found other parlour games to amuse ourselves and our guests, and my husband threw himself into amateur theatricals.

I wonder at myself for talking on at you all this time, Mrs. Ternan, but I suppose the story I am telling you is something of a warning. My husband has abandoned mesmerism but he remains a magnetic personality who likes to have his way. Mme de la Rue was not the first woman to fall under his sway. People very seldom say no to my husband; I certainly can't. Why else would I be here today?

"So, remind me again. Do we know if this meeting with the Ternans really took place?" Al has actually picked the paper up off the porch and spread it out on the dining room table to give himself more space to read. The girls are upstairs, supposedly dressing for ballet.

"Ana. Goli. We have to leave in fifteen minutes," I call to them before I answer. "Katey Dickens' account says she came upon her mother crying and Catherine explained that Dickens had told her she had to pay a call on Mrs. Ternan. Katey told her not to, but she didn't say whether her mother followed that advice. Some assume Catherine didn't go; others think she did what she always did—"

"And obeyed her horrible husband."

"Her magnetic and charming husband."

"Well, she certainly dealt with Mme de la Rue. You make her sound wily."

"Everyone always describes Catherine as a doormat, fat and tired and depressed after all those babies, and

266

always compliant. But she must have found some ways to resist him, just occasionally to have her own way."

His cellphone, sitting on the table beside him, rings. He picks it up.

"Hello . . . Sure . . . Yeah, okay. Four then."

He seems in a hurry to get off the phone.

"Who was that?"

"Just David."

"What did he want?"

"We're scheduling a squash game for this afternoon."

"But they're coming over tonight. I'm doing something special for Becky's birthday." Since I had been feeling better, we had actually managed to reinstate our family parties and that night was our turn. For months, Becky had helped with shopping, cooking and baby-sitting; I wanted to surprise her with a cake, make her the centre of attention for a change.

"Yeah. I guess I had forgotten that. Well, that doesn't stop us from playing squash."

"But if your game is at four, they're supposed to come over at five. We're starting early."

"Okay, well, maybe David and I will be a bit late."

"Was that really David on the phone?"

There's a pause as Al digests what I'm asking.

"I've told you it's over."

"Actually, I think you just said it doesn't matter. And I shouldn't worry."

"It doesn't matter because it's over."

"Okay." I wait a bit. "Where is she?"

"She's transferred out of the department. I think she has a new boyfriend somewhere."

"So, what happened? Who broke it off in the end?"

"Nothing happened. It was kind of mutual. This just took priority." He gestured around the dining room and kitchen beyond it. "I guess my way of looking at it changed."

"How so?"

"I realized . . . Clearly, it wasn't fair to make her wait . . ."

"Just on the off chance I might die?" I ask with a smile.

"No. Until you were better, obviously. But it didn't feel . . . I mean, she's young. I guess what was going on here made me more aware of the age difference between us."

"She doesn't understand cancer?"

"Well, she's afraid of it. She was afraid of the situation. She was kind of panicky and that wasn't particularly helpful."

"What did she have to fear?"

"Getting blamed for breaking up a marriage, and somehow that would be much worse if you were sick. I don't know, maybe she just couldn't deal with the spectre of death or something. I mean, it's real grown-up stuff we've been going through."

"And why should she have to deal with it?" I agreed. "I think that's the problem with May–December relationships. You're out of sync on so many issues. When they start, he's the wise, sexy older man, she is the sweet young thing. He's forty-five to her twenty-five or whatever. She wants a glamorous adult life, career, family, the things the wife has. He wants youth, so they think they want each other. But they're at cross-purposes. He wants to be young and she wants to be old, or at least older. She wants to stop living in a basement apartment. He wishes his knees didn't creak whenever he bends down."

"My knees don't creak . . ."

"No, it's your back you need to look out for. Anyway, I think a big age difference can come back to haunt a relationship later on."

He smiles at me gently. "Yes, I'm sure you're right."

I reach over and kiss him. "Trust me. She'd have got bored and wanted you to go clubbing Saturday nights."

"I would have wound up in a retirement home supporting an aging trophy wife," he replies. "Yeah. I suppose if they had lived today, Dickens would have just divorced Catherine and Nelly would have been a trophy wife. Much less drama all round."

The cellphone rings again and Al picks it up.

"Yeah. Sharon just pointed that out too. Shall we try for three then?"

The Dickens Bicentenary Serial: Chapter 14
Manchester. March 11, 1869

Mr. Wiggins was a master—superbly skilled and completely thorough, equipped with all the tools of the trade, yet possessing a genius for improvisation, patient but demanding, exacting of himself but forgiving of others. Nelly had known his kind before; you depended on them absolutely. The dresser who could somehow change a twenty-year-old into an old man with a dash of greasepaint or fix a badly torn hem during the interval; the character actor who could understudy every role in Shakespeare. Or, in Mr. Wiggins' case, the gas man who could create any number of dramatic effects by careful adjustment of the valves.

He was busy setting up when they arrived at the Free Trade Hall that afternoon, muttering to himself as he darted to and fro about the stage experimenting with the jets.

"All satisfactory, Wiggins?" Charles called out from the back of the hall.

"No, Mr. Dickens, not satisfactory in the least, but I'll fix it. How do you do, Miss Ternan? I trust you had a smooth trip to Manchester."

"Very well, Mr. Wiggins. The trip was perfectly agreeable, thank you."

In truth, the trip was nerve-racking, as it was one of those rare occasions when they travelled together by rail. Both had become more or less accustomed to taking a train alone or with other companions—Charles made the short trip from Gad's Hill to his office or over to Peckham all the time; Nelly went shopping in town from time to time— although an unexpected jolt or sudden braking was still enough to leave either of them clutching the armrest. However, when they sat together, alone once more in a first-class carriage, they were reminded more forcefully of the accident four years previously and both found themselves squeezing the other's hand and counting the minutes until they would arrive. Nelly was attending as much of this reading tour as they could manage, but usually she only ventured out to venues in or around London, meeting him there. He had wanted them to travel together to Manchester for sentimental reasons: it was the hall where they had performed together in *The Frozen Deep* twelve years before. She had made an early start from Peckham, changed trains at Victoria and headed to St. Pancras, where she simply met him in the carriage on the Manchester express. Once they arrived in Manchester, he left their compartment ahead of her carrying only a grip, leaving her to find a porter and make her own way to the Mitre, where they registered separately for their separate rooms. They washed up and met in the lobby at three, proceeding to the hall where Mr. Wiggins was still fussing with the position of the jets.

She followed Charles to the front of the auditorium, where he fairly leapt up the few short steps to join Wiggins on the stage. Nelly always noticed that he was invigorated by the prospect of a reading, an effect that could be counted on to last until he took his bow; in the dressing room afterwards he would be exhausted.

"The red, Wiggins. Is it the right red? I thought it looked a little faded in London."

"I bought a new medium today, Mr. Dickens. Had the devil of a time finding the right fabric here, but I think it will do the trick."

"Good, good. We want it nice and bloody."

"Sure enough, Mr. Dickens. Should be good and bloody tonight if I can just get the jets operating properly. The supply seems erratic."

"Erratic. That will never do. Well, we will leave you to it. Just a quick word backstage and we'll go to dinner," he said, holding out a hand to Nelly to help her up the steps.

And so, they were back in a theatre. Wiggins would spend the afternoon fiddling with the gas supply and Charles would spend it prowling backstage, discussing details with his manager, Mr. Dolby, eating dinner abnormally early and drinking precisely two glasses of water one hour before the curtain would rise.

He entered the hall that evening to thunderous applause; he had been getting rave reviews from Aberdeen to Plymouth on what was being billed as a farewell tour. He stood at a lectern against the simple backdrop of a deep purple cloth. No more paraphernalia was needed to set the scene. The dramatic tones of the reader—and the impressive effects produced by Mr. Wiggins—would do the rest. The gas man began by bathing the whole stage in a warm yellow light, a jovial hue that flattered the reader's complexion and made the audience comfortable. It depended on a perfectly even row of footlights all set to a medium flame with a pale yellow fabric mounted in the cylinders in front of them, as well as the same colour on the winglights that illuminated the sides of the scene. Mr. Dickens began with a reading from *The Pickwick Papers*, the passage where Sam Weller gives evidence in the suit that Mr. Pickwick's landlady has brought against him for breach of promise. It was always well received, and as usual that night it had the audience laughing themselves silly. Charles was a good-enough performer he never gave in to the temptation to laugh at his own material; he was as fully in control as ever, except that Nelly could not help but notice he was having some problem pronouncing the word *Pickwick*. It kept coming out *Pigwig*. He also, when rendering Sam's comic habit of confusing Vs and Ws, often confused the two letters himself so that the joke was somewhat obscured.

It was hard to say if the audience noticed any of this, since they were already laughing at every word the reader spoke and Charles seemed unaware of his mistakes. At the interval, Nelly rose quietly from her aisle seat in the third row and slipped out a side door. She walked a short piece along an alleyway that ran the length of the building and knocked quietly at the stage door. The watchman opened the door to her, tipped his hat and let her in. In his dressing room, Charles was as ebullient as he always was in the midst of performance, entirely involved in the minute details of gratifying laughter or an annoying cougher in the front row as he sipped a small brandy, the only refreshment he took during the performance. She had come to realize that he drew his sustenance from the audience itself: "They loved the Pickwick, Nelly. Just loved it," he said joyously as she entered. He did not mention that the title had seemed to trouble his tongue but moments before and she did not point out his mistake to him. She sat with him until the five-minute call and then returned to her seat.

After the interval, he was to perform the passage from *Oliver Twist* in which the thieving Bill Sikes becomes convinced that the prostitute Nancy has betrayed him to the police and brutally murders her. A scene of graphic violence without redeeming sentiment until Sikes himself is killed, it had been a bold choice for a public reading and Charles had tried it out on colleagues in London before he dared perform it on tour. The professional consensus had been that its emotional pitch took his public reading to a more exalted level and he was encouraged to go forward with it. It had proved a spine-chilling success with audiences but Nelly thought the violent emotions of the passage were increasingly unhealthy for him. He felt every part as though he himself were experiencing a character's lovesick longings, bitter shame or murderous rage. In this case, he built himself to such a fever pitch with Nancy's murder that Nelly could see him shaking as he read. As she witnessed his fevered condition night after night, she had urged him to reconsider the length of the tour or at least cut that passage from his repertoire, but he vowed it was now so renowned that to drop it would be tantamount to abandoning the stage altogether. She had begged, she had pleaded, but to no avail, and as she sat in the audience waiting for the second act to begin she had to recognize that he could not imagine living a life without his public.

As he stepped on stage again, he seemed in perfect control, however, untroubled by the slips that had plagued his reading earlier. By the time he reached Nancy's murder, he was in full cry, building as chillingly as ever toward the violent act. As Sikes began his battery, Wiggins, on cue and to gasps from the audience, pulled the wire that spun the cylinders into a new position and now washed the scene in a ghastly blood red with purple hues coming in from the winglights. The new fabric he had found in Manchester had done the trick. The effect was startling, but the deep red light made it almost impossible to make out anything but the vague outline of the reader's face.

It was always contorted by this point in the drama, but while the audience gasped and cried, Nelly still peered anxiously through the odd, unpleasant dimness trying to see what effect the reading was having on the reader that night. Wiggins pulled his magic wire again and the red gave way to an eerie blue as the murderous Sikes found himself pursued by visions of Nancy's ghost. Now Nelly could see that contortions rippled across Charles's face. Still his voice did not falter and he built unrelentingly to the crescendo as the desperate Sikes falls from a rooftop and inadvertently hangs himself in a dangling rope. The audience cheered. Then, in the postscript intended to give an overwrought audience some breathing room before they would break into thunderous applause and finally leave the theatre, Wiggins switched back on his gentle yellow light and Nelly saw the truth. Charles stood there exhausted, soaked in sweat, his face ashen. Most alarming of all, his left eyelid twitched without ceasing.

She rose from her seat and rushed out into the alleyway as the audience broke into applause. They screamed for more, but he never gave an encore. Nelly ran to the stage door and pounded on it, pushing past the watchman and running now toward the wings, where Mr. Dolby stood with a towel waiting to receive the reader as he left the stage. She elbowed the manager aside, and as Charles staggered toward her, she caught him in her arms. It was no embrace; he collapsed, dragging her to the floor with the weight of his stricken body.

"Big death-bed scene next? We should get the final promo ready for next weekend if you're wrapping up."

"Not quite," I say, annoyed at his presumption, even if Jonathan now seems, like Al, to be enthusiastic about the serial. "We said June 9. I have three more instalments to file."

"Right. Okay. And you'll want to tell us what happens after he goes. Left Nelly with enough money she never had to work again, while Catherine Dickens died soon after a lonely recluse. I checked Wikipedia."

I bite back a withering retort. Becky always says I am too hard on people. I sometimes think the novelist is my better self, interested, understanding, wanting to know more. If Jonathan were one of my characters, I would be seeking out the wellspring of his weakness, puzzling out the working-class background in the middle-class newsroom; the tough-guy father who wanted him to be an engineer, whatever it was that makes him both so convinced he has to cover for something and so laughably bad at doing so. The novelist would want to find the true person underneath all that, but in real life, I don't have much of a talent for hiding my contempt.

"Catherine Dickens received condolences from the Queen and lived another seven years after his death, visited regularly by her children and grandchildren. I think she was probably happier as a publicly acknowledged widow than as a publicly shunned wife. Nelly was left £1000 and the house in Mornington Crescent. Not enough to live on, so there's speculation there was also some kind of insurance policy or annuity. She married and had two children and ran a school in Margate with her husband, so she did have to work. She was never rich. Dickens did have an awful lot of dependants to take care of."

"Okay. Well, I don't care much about Catherine then; just finish up with Nelly."

That evening I tell Al about the conversation. The girls have bolted down dinner and rushed off to play, leaving us at the table finishing a glass of wine.

"Poor Catherine. She was a very social person and had artistic interests and hobbies. If he hadn't beaten her down like that, she would have probably matured into a happy matriarch when she finally got a break from child-bearing."

"Do you think she regretted having all those children?"

"No. I don't think so. Why would she? Victorian women were proud of their big families. I think she truly loved her children. And Dickens barely let her see them after the separation. Imagine being parted from them like that . . . The youngest was six." I choke up and can barely get those last few words out. Ana and Goli are seven now; they'll be eight in July. I bite my lip and blink back tears. "I don't want to be separated from the girls."

"You are not going to die, Sharon."

"We are all going to die. It's whether I will live long enough to see my children to adulthood." I look down and fiddle with the stem of my wineglass. Al waits. "When they first told me it was cancer, all I could think about was the girls. I was completely panicked. How would they survive without me? I thought they would be traumatized by it, their lives would be ruined. I remember Anahita crying for me one of the first times I left her at daycare. 'Where's Mummy going?' It was heartbreaking. I thought of them crying like that for me all the time, no mother to make cheese sandwiches . . ."

"I can make cheese sandwiches."

"You know what I mean. No one to braid their hair, or find their socks. No one to cook Goli's eggs the way she likes them or to talk Ana down when she's in a temper."

"Sharon." Al puts a hand over mine. "We've been over this. I promise you I'll take care of them whatever happens. I'm not incompetent."

"I know you aren't incompetent. That's what I'm trying to say. I started to accept it, I guess. I began thinking, Well, they would survive. They would learn to do without me; they would rely on you and it would be okay. The living go on, and gradually they forget the dead. They have to." I tell him about the grave at Mount Pleasant. "People should not be like that, I don't think people are like that. I think they recover from huge losses, and making dinner and getting homework done begins to fill in the gaps. You can't spend all your life grieving, no matter how large the loss. Anyway, once I stopped worrying so much about the girls, I started to think about myself. About non-existence. I had to ask myself if I minded . . ."

"Minded dying?"

"I don't want to be in pain . . . Chemo was bad enough."

"They'd give you morphine . . ."

"I don't mean that. I don't mean I would rather die than be in pain or be sick. I mean, it's dying I am afraid of, not death. I mean, afterwards, what's to be afraid of? Unless you believe in hell or something. If it's just non-existence, and that's what I've always believed. We never took the girls to church or anything. So, you aren't there any more to resent the fact you aren't there any more . . ."

"So you don't care if you're gone?"

"God, I care, of course, I care. I like life and I want

to keep living it. I love you, I love the girls and I want to stay with you. I don't want to miss anything, but if I have to, well . . . I guess all I mean is that I'm not afraid of what happens next."

S hay sat on the couch contemplating the bare surface of the two card tables and the ruins of Plan B. Her friends were long gone; Mrs. Brown, a last-minute addition to the guest list, had stayed afterwards to help clean up but once the Royal Doulton was safely back downstairs, they had agreed the table from the shed and the extra chairs could be returned to their proper places in the morning.

Despite Jeff and his unexpected companion the party had been a success, Shay thought. Alex had instantly grasped the situation when Shay had appeared in the apartment doorway with two guests and a pleading expression on her face. Alex had plied the new arrivals with sparkling wine and interrogated them on their nationalities, professions, and educational backgrounds—Philippa was English and worked in Jeff's office—and soon gleaned that Jeff had snagged an eight o'clock table at Bibendum.

Clearly, he was trying to impress somebody and it

wasn't Shay. Meanwhile, Shay hurriedly swept the name cards away but could do nothing about the table itself.

"Oh, sorry. Is this a dinner party?" Jeff asked as he noticed her bustling about. "I thought it was just a party party." Shay tried her best effort at a relaxed smile, waved dismissively at her carefully laid table and said, "Yes, yes. An any kind of party. We are just expecting a few people for dinner a bit later."

Thankfully, this proved true as Fiona didn't arrive until seven thirty while Greg and Liz Clark showed up at twenty to eight filled with apologies about a late baby-sitter just as Jeff and Philippa were heading for the door. Glad to see the last of Jeff and relieved the party could now revert to plan, Shay belatedly put the lamb in the oven and turned to the fish. Looking at the six perfect pieces of sole she had selected, she had a moment of inspiration. Why not? "Do you think I should just pop down and ask Mrs. Brown to join us?" she whispered to Alex, who was standing at her elbow in the kitchen.

"Won't she have eaten already?" Alex asked.

"Baked beans on toast at five, I imagine." Reminding herself that the best parties were spontaneous, Shay headed quickly downstairs and tapped lightly on Mrs. Brown's door; her landlady must have been sitting very nearby for she opened it instantaneously.

"Everything going nicely, love?" Mrs. Brown asked.

"Yes. Everything's good, but we did have a guest drop out."

"Oh. That young man, was it? I didn't like the look of that girl he had with him," Mrs. Brown said, lowering her voice as though the offending couple might still be within earshot. "Overdressed, I thought."

"Or under," Shay said, and they both laughed. "I was just wondering if you would like to join us? I realize you've probably already had tea, but you've been such a help and I would love you to at least try everything . . ." Shay was fumbling her belated invitation but Mrs. Brown did not seem to mind in the least.

"I'd be honoured," she said as she removed the apron she was wearing, turned to a small mirror hanging in her entranceway and patted her hair, and then happily followed Shay upstairs.

There, Alex quickly commandeered her and introduced her round while Shay started cooking her fish and heating her lobster sauce. When it was ready, the guests took whatever places seemed convenient, oohing and aahing over the menu cards that Shay now pulled out from the bookshelf where she had hidden them when Jeff and his date had showed up. They listened enthusiastically to Shay's explanations of the dinner, enjoyed a very rare leg of lamb, applauded the charlotte russe that had emerged perfectly from its mould, and finally recalled the various tables at which they had been served a savoury at the end of a meal, a practice that needed to be revived, they all agreed.

Mrs. Brown regaled them with her mother's tales of wartime rationing, trying to make cakes without eggs and living off Spam hash, and even Fiona warmed up and got the giggles at the idea of the Victorians using gelatin made from cod bladders to set their fruit jelly or eating sweetened macaroni as a dessert.

They all appeared interested by Shay's research and agreed that when they thought of a Dickensian dinner it was only Christmas pudding and a goose or something of that nature. Shay had expanded their horizons, gathering around her a convivial group entirely comfortable with a party that included only one man and four single women, one of whom was at least seventy, and all in perfect agreement that this was a splendid dinner. Shay's nerves and embarrassment evaporated and she again felt the rush of excitement over her culinary discoveries that had inspired her menu planning in the first place.

They only finished eating at eleven, by which point the Clarks had to hurry home to the babysitter. Fiona left soon after, and Alex and Mrs. Brown and Shay chatted for a bit and then set to cleaning up, agreeing that the party, for which all three now took credit, had been a huge success.

By midnight, that left an overstimulated Shay sitting alone in a tidy apartment with time to think. Even now that the awkward moment was well past and the rest of her plans had gone smoothly, the willowy Philippa in her short skirt had left a nasty little kernel of nervousness and disappointment in the bottom of Shay's gut. She had misread Jeff; she had assumed he was an easy catch; there for the taking if she wanted him. Perhaps he had sensed her condescension and just wanted to prove others desired him too; perhaps Philippa was just window-dressing. Or perhaps not. She would ask Alex on Monday, or phone her tomorrow. Alex always knew these things.

Still, on reflection, she didn't think she had the necessary enthusiasm to take another stab at Jeff. She wanted love, not game-playing. She wanted an adult, not a boy. She wanted that feeling of falling into another person, trusting his instincts, his fidelity, his embrace. She looked at her watch. 12:25. It was only 7:25 in Toronto. It was spring but still cool in the evenings. Shay pulled on a light jacket, flipping her dirty-blond hair over the collar and speculating nastily whether Philippa's straw-coloured tresses were just a dye job. She slipped down the stairs and out the front door as quietly as she could. The Internet café that she relied on was about a ten-minute walk away, down a main street that would still be full of pedestrians. It stayed open until two most nights. She had had occasion to discover this on a previous instance where she had broken their moratorium on communications.

The place was all but empty when she arrived; she took one of the screens as far removed from the counter as possible and logged on to her email. She supposed she could have written pages, but she didn't really have much to say. "This isn't working for me. Is it working for you?"

A l did respond to my email that night in 2003, and I stopped worrying about Catherine Dickens and Victorian cuisine and went back to Toronto. He finally left his wife, his first wife, Soraya, a Lebanese Canadian whom I think he married mainly to please his parents, and we planned our small wedding the minute the divorce was final. I dropped out of grad school, wrote a novel about Jane Austen to amuse myself and published it under my full first name and my new married name. So, Shay Blainey became Sharon Soleymani, and her life was not at all what Shay had once imagined.

In fiction, I hand my characters endings sufficiently ambiguous that I don't get lumped in with romance writers and sufficiently redemptive that my readers multiply. It is a balancing act impossible in real life. There, Anahita has grandiose plans for some school project, doesn't leave enough time for it and gets into a snit when it doesn't go how she wants while I wind up yelling at her, "Why didn't you tell me last week you were going to need pipe cleaners?" and feeling guilty for yelling and even more guilty when I realize that, when it comes to domestic ambition and time management, she is exactly like me. Or Al goes off to campus on a winter morning without shovelling the snow and I spend the day cursing his thoughtlessness until I am ready to boil over but when he comes home he reminds me he had that tenure committee meeting he was so dreading and I have completely forgotten to ask how it went. Daily life is fragmentary and irregular and it is only in fiction you can somehow make its halting and erratic course seem subtly symbolic of something.

At any rate, we did not live happily ever after. Our disagreements and hurts were legion; we would wait until the girls were in bed to have it out or, worse yet, we wouldn't have it out but just add it to the pile of unresolved arguments that accumulate in a marriage. And then Al did it again; he had an affair with one of his students. It used to be received wisdom among the smart women I knew—the Alexes and Beckys—that if you had an affair with a married man, the best you could hope for was to be the next wife he cheated on. But in the depth of the moment we all think our love is special and unique, unfathomable and infinite and then, in the misery of deception and divorce, we are convinced no one else has ever felt pain like this.

If Al and I are different, it is only because of cancer. He came back and we got a second chance and this time, to make amends, I wrote a story just for him.

The Dickens Bicentenary Serial: Chapter 15
Peckham, Surrey. May 11, 1870

"I was shocked by the last instalment you gave me to read."

"Shocked?"

"Well, maybe *hurt* is the better word."

"I've hurt you, my dear? I would never wish to hurt you with anything I wrote. What is it that troubled you?"

Nelly took a deep breath. The remains of their modest supper lay between them. She was never much of a cook but did not like to keep Jane late. They often had to content themselves with plates of cold food. Tonight there had been cheese and salad, and a nice wine. She had waited until they had eaten to speak but she felt she had to say something. She could not keep her feelings secret and lie when he asked her what she thought; surely she of all people had a right to an honest reaction beyond proof-reading marks or recommendations about structure.

At first, she had been hugely relieved that he was publishing another novel; it had been almost five years since she had coaxed him through the excruciating final numbers of *Our Mutual Friend* in the aftermath of the train crash and he had not written anything since. Or, at least, he had not published another novel. Of course, he had made contributions to his magazine, producing the much-anticipated Christmas story every year; he had done some more reporting for his *Uncommercial Traveller* series. But he had not really written. Instead, he had read.

Oh, how he had read, taking Nancy and Sikes up and down the country, travelling to America. The latest tour had almost killed him. She had thought he would expire on the spot that night in Manchester, but he had come back to consciousness in seconds and, despite her pleas for him to remain where he was, had struggled to his feet within minutes. He had brushed off Mr. Dolby's repeated suggestions they call a doctor and would not hear of cancelling the remainder of the tour; they begged him to at least rest for a few days but he had read the next day and honoured every commitment till he finished up the following month.

She sometimes thought the readings were a way of escaping writing, a way of assuring himself that his readers still loved him without actually having to produce any new stories with which to entertain them. He could have retired if he wanted, spent his time at Gad's Hill. No one would have thought the less of him. But she knew that he was too restless to ever stop working and too sensitive to ever be deprived of the delights of his own imagination.

Years before, she had taken a secret pride in *Great Expectations*, published during those happy days at Mornington Crescent, before she had to leave for France. They said it was his best work ever and she felt it was her love, her sacrifice, that had let him achieve it. If others might suspect there was something of Nelly in the heartless Estella, loved beyond reason yet declining to love in return, she only saw something of him in Pip, with his boyish infatuation lasting a lifetime. At any rate, she had rejoiced in that book and she had wanted another. However, the delivery of *Our Mutual Friend* had only proved excruciating, and she saw that their last chance was fast approaching. Perhaps if she were honest she would have to admit that for her to feel her power she needed him to feel his power. She needed him to be vital since neither of them could still pretend he was youthful.

The new story was a mystery. Safer to move in a different direction, not to attempt another sprawling *Bildungsroman*. Unusually, he had neither read out loud to her from his manuscript nor asked her to read the proofs as he began writing; she wondered a bit about that at the time but didn't ask any questions. His work on it seemed precarious enough that she did not wish to risk the balance. Perhaps, she thought sadly, their literary collaboration had been so polluted by the agony of *Our Mutual Friend*, he did not wish to renew it. At any rate, she was busy enough with the house, the dog, her mother's visits, her trips to town, her books and her music. So, when the first number appeared she had no idea what to expect. The novel was set in a cathedral town named Cloisterham, a place that would be quickly recognized to those who knew it as Rochester, the city of her birth. He himself had spent the early years of his childhood just next door, in nearby Chatham. And there had been a relationship in those first pages that made her queasy. Now, as she caught up with the story in a batch of manuscript pages he had finally left with her the previous week, her fears were confirmed. She was deeply unsettled by the shape the novel was taking. She did not wish to disrupt his progress, change his direction or risk him stopping and yet she felt too aggrieved to remain silent.

"You are telling the story of a man obsessed with a very young woman, still a girl really, and that man forces himself on her despite her obvious distaste and resistance." Nelly had just read Chapter 19 of *The Mystery of Edwin Drood*.

"You are not going to make the mistake of reading fiction as autobiography, my dear. I have warned you before . . ."

"No. There is nothing of you in Jasper. He is a man without compassion or generosity, animated only by envy. His pursuit of Rosa is grotesque. It would make me very sad to think you saw yourself that way."

"I am a storyteller. It's a story."

"Jasper is a villainous villain, fair enough, but it's Rosa I really object too."

"What's wrong with her?"

"Well, first of all her name. Rosa Bud."

"Yes. Rosebud. She is young and innocent."

"I was young when you met me . . ."

"Seventeen. Young and innocent."

"Young girls are not necessarily innocent. I certainly wasn't."

"My dear. Really. What can you mean?"

"I don't mean I wasn't pure. Before, well, before Mornington Crescent I was certainly a maid."

"I never doubted it."

"But I did know something of the world."

"Did you, indeed? And what did you know of the world?" He took a jocular tone, seeking more comfortable ground. It annoyed Nelly; despite the fancy dinners and expensive presents that marked her every birthday, despite the celebration of her thirtieth the previous year, he seemed to forget that she was no longer seventeen or twenty-one. In her anger, she spoke.

"I knew enough to take precautions, for starters. Otherwise, I might have borne you ten children instead of just one."

There was a silence between them.

"I'm sorry. That was unfair."

They never spoke of his wife; he spoke of his love for his daughters—Nelly had met both and was on cordial terms with them even if she had visited Gad's Hill but twice—and of his worries for the sons he had sent off to

India and Australia, but they never even acknowledged that these now adult children had a mother. Charles, seeking a fresh life with his true love, had taken the position that his wife no longer existed or even that she had ever existed; a large fancy to maintain with nine living children to his name. Nelly tended to relegate Catherine to the same forgotten corner of life, although, as the years went by, she came to realize that Charles was not always an easy companion and that his wife, whatever her faults, might have had some justifiable grievances. Nelly became less certain of her own superiority, less certain that she was his natural partner. Still, she did not dwell unduly on Catherine's fate and if it seemed cruel to deprive the woman of her growing children's company, the childless Nelly, who had motherhood so quickly snatched away from her, was only dimly aware of what a bitter punishment this might be. As for her, there was no longer any risk that she might have to remove herself to France again. Charles was old now. He kissed her lips, he stroked her hand and, on the occasional night he spent in the house at Peckham, he leant across to pat her thigh through the thick eiderdown before falling exhausted into what was often a loud and restless sleep.

"I just mean to say that Rosa has no character, no idea about anything, perhaps she has been sheltered and so knows little of the world, but she has no idea of herself either. She is just pure innocence. Such people don't exist."

"She has character; she is spoiled and petulant with Edwin."

Nelly dismissed that with a wave of the hand. "That is simply a decoration, like her hair ribbon or her shawl. It helps advance your plot but it is superficial and is a quality quickly abandoned once Eddy disappears. As a character, she does nothing but represent purity. She has no purpose at all; she simply reacts to Jasper. She is too good, innocence just sitting there waiting to be injured. There has to be something in between Estella and Rosa, some kind of real girl."

Charles drew himself up. Nelly saw his eyes were watering. "I am sorry you find my characters so poorly drawn," he said.

And, instantly, she felt deep remorse for having hurt him, for prodding him about his failings rather than accepting his gifts. She sat silent for a minute.

"Well, she had the good sense to break it off with Eddy; that shows strength of character, that is purpose," she said, making a peace offering. "I suppose she marries Neville Landless in the end, does she?"

"Or something like that. Youth will to youth."

"Perhaps. If there's youth around. You certainly did not take me away from any Eddy."

"But you will have your Neville in the end, Nelly. I promise you. You are not my creature and you will have your real life soon enough."

The Dickens Bicentenary Serial
An interlude

"I'll tell you a story that you'll prefer, shall I? What would you like? Something from *The Arabian Nights*?"

"Certainly."

"As I recall, you used to like the story about the Prince of Persia."

"A love story."

"Yes, but a rather dark one. It must be some years since I've told you . . ."

"Then tell it to me again."

"Yes. All right. And you can correct me if I get bits wrong."

"The Prince of Persia was a learned young man, schooled in astronomy, geography, law and arithmetic, fluent in five languages, trained to play several musical instruments and renowned for his mastery of the art of penmanship."

"I remember. A veritable prodigy. Proof of the importance of a good education."

"Yes. Although I seem to have managed without much of an education."

"Of course you have, dear. I interrupted you. Do go on."

"Such was his skill that word of it reached his father's ally, the King of Hind, who was determined to invite this young prodigy—your word, my dear—to his court. The King of Persia assented to his departure and the Prince set off with his retinue, loaded with gifts and messages for the King of Hind. Travelling by horseback they were set upon by bandits."

"I seem to recall they had to cross hostile territory."

"Don't we all."

"But there was a name for the place . . ."

"It hardly matters. 'Hold, we are messengers to the King of Hind. Harm us not,' cried the Prince, but the bandit chief called back, 'We know no King of Hind. These are not his dominions.' So, the bandits set upon the Prince, killed his servants, stripped him of his clothes and purse and left him for dead.

"Half naked and half starving, the Prince walked for many days until he arrived at the gates of a city and entered seeking help. There he saw a little tailor . . ."

"You missed a bit about him stripping the clothes off his dead companions and emptying their pockets for food."

"That's rather gruesome. Sometimes I leave out those unsavoury bits."

"Don't leave them out on my account."

"No? The whole unvarnished truth of it? Is that really what you want, my dear? All right, where was I? The tailor. There was the tailor, sewing outside his shop. The Prince greeted the little man, who, taking note of this stranger's . . . well, his strangeness, invited him inside and sat him down. When the tailor asked the Prince from what land he came, the Prince was so moved by a sympathetic inquiry that he told the tailor everything of his home in Persia, his father the King, his journey to Hind and his encounter with the bandits.

"'Take care,' said the tailor. 'Our King is the sworn enemy of your father. You must tell no one here of your identity, but you will need some money to buy food and clothes.'

"'I am learned in law and arithmetic; I can play several musical instruments and speak many languages,' offered the Prince.

"'We have no use of such learning here,' said the tailor. 'You should take up woodcutting. It is a surer way of providing for yourself.'"

"The woodcutting, already? I think you missed a funny bit there when he listed all his fancy skills and the tailor dismissed them one by one."

"Yes. Perhaps that was something I added. I was airing my prejudices against formal education. Look at my boys: I try, but the best schools don't seem . . ."

"No, no dear, of course. But do go on. Woodcutting, that's where you were."

"Yes. Right. So, the Prince borrowed an axe and set out the next day for the forest. As he swung at a tree, his axe struck something on the ground and loudly gave forth the sound of metal on metal. The Prince bent down, cleared away debris and discovered a brass ring attached to a trapdoor; he tugged and tugged and succeeded in shifting the door, revealing a hole opening into the ground. He climbed into the hole and discovered that a staircase led away from it, down into the earth. The Prince descended the stairs and found himself in a richly furnished chamber with cushions and carpets covering the floor. And who do you think he discovered there?"

"A beautiful maiden . . ."

"Yes, a beautiful young maiden stepped forward to greet him. She had skin as white as porcelain, hair as blond as straw and eyes as deep as the earth itself."

"Surely, if we are travelling from Persia to India, she has dark hair, not blond."

"Well, I suppose she resembled you, my dear. Except she wasn't half as clever. At any rate, have it your way. Skin as white as porcelain, hair as black as night and eyes as deep as the earth itself. 'Stranger,' she said. 'How do you find yourself in my chamber?'

"So the Prince explained the story of his journey from Persia, his attack by the bandits, his rescue by the tailor and his employment as a woodcutter. The maiden sighed and drew the Prince farther into the room, settling him on the cushions, washing his feet and feeding him dates and pomegranates.

"'How do you find yourself in this cave so deep under the ground, my lady?' the Prince asked, and the maiden explained that she was a princess betrothed to a prince when she was little more than a girl. On the eve of her wedding as she travelled to the prince's land, an evil genie had captured her and brought her to this cave. Every tenth night he took human form and came to her in the guise of a Persian and slept beside her, but the other nine nights he returned to his genie wife and ten genie children, who knew nothing of the maiden in the cave. So he had kept her for ten long years, and if the Princess ever needed anything or found herself in trouble, she had only to touch an ancient inscription carved in the wall of her cave and the genie would appear to her."

"I don't recall that the genie had a wife and children. You didn't mention that before. Do genies even have children?"

"They must have children. How else would the genie race propagate itself?"

"I suppose that's true. I'd never thought of it that way. Genies are magical beings, after all."

"Yes, well, this magical genie has a genie wife and ten children. I have no idea if they take after him and are magical too. That would be a different story. So, where were we? Yes, the Princess, as we now know she is. The

Princess says to the Prince, 'The genie was here last night. You are safe here for nine days.'

"And so the Prince stayed and entertained the Princess with stories and music and by nightfall the pair were in love. For nine days and nine nights, they loved each other with a passion that burned like fire, giving each other oceans of pleasure and mountains of delight."

"Oceans of pleasure? But surely the Prince calls up the genie right away?"

"No, I don't think so. I think the Prince and the maiden dally . . ."

"If they dally for nine days and nine nights, she's not much of a maiden."

"Really, my dear. Shall I continue or do you want to argue about it?"

"No, no, continue."

"So after the nine days and nights, on the morning of the tenth day, the Princess said, 'You must leave now, and hide yourself in the forest for the genie will come tonight. Then you can come back tomorrow.'

"'No,' cried the Prince. 'I will fight the genie and take you from this place.' And so saying, he marched toward the inscription.

"But the Princess stood in his path, pleading with him. 'My love, why be greedy? What is one night apart when I am yours the other nine?'

"'Fie,' said the Prince. 'You will be mine for always and forever.' He pushed past her and put his hand to the inscription. You see? Now he calls up the genie, after the nine nights.

"Instantly there was a deafening roar as though the earth itself was breaking apart, clouds of dust rose in the chamber and when they parted, the genie stood there. He was the size of two men with a bare chest like a table-top and legs like tree trunks. His expression, as he saw the Prince, was ferocious.

"'Who is this man?' he bellowed and he turned on the Princess. 'Harlot! This is your lover. Admit it. You have deceived me.'

"'Master, I know not this man nor where he came from,' the Princess replied. 'He only just arrived in my chamber.'

"'You lie. You have taken this mortal as your lover. Admit it!'

"'O mighty one,' the Prince interceded. 'I know not this maid. I have stumbled into this chamber less than an hour ago.'

"'It is true, Master. This man only walked in upon me but moments ago.'

"'Very well,' said the genie, eyeing the Princess. 'If he means nothing to you, you will not mind killing him.' And he drew a mighty sword from his belt, handed it to her and commanded her, 'Cut off his head.'"

"I don't remember this part at all."

"No? It's rather good. Bit gory, but you did say you wanted the unvarnished version. So, the Prince stands there silently, trying desperately to communicate with the Princess through his eyes, pleading with her to remember their love and spare his life.

"The Princess raised the sword, preparing to strike, signalling the Prince with her eyes that she loved him like no other but could think of no way out of this predicament. She stood for a long moment with the sword poised, ready to strike and then dropped her arm.

"'Master,' said the Princess. 'Why should I kill this man who has done nothing to me, has not harmed me, has barely spoken a word to me? It is not justice. Whoever this man is, he has committed no crime. I cannot kill him.'

"But the genie replies, 'You lying whore.' Oh dear, you'll excuse the language. He is an intemperate genie, as you'll recall. 'This man means everything to you and that is why you cannot bring yourself to slaughter him.' The genie now grabbed the sword from her slack hand and passed it to the Prince.

"'Here, contemptible man. If you have never seen her before this moment, you won't mind slicing off her head.'

"Now it was the Prince's turn to stand with the sword watching the Princess plead with her eyes for her life.

"'O mighty one,' he said to the genie, 'if a mere woman can argue for a greater justice than this, then what as a man might I answer but that this woman, whoever she might be, does not deserve to die. She has committed no crime; even though she is a stranger to me, I cannot take her life without reason.'

"The genie takes back his sword again. 'Both of you lie. You look on each other with the eyes of lovers, begging and pleading and promising with your gazes even as I stand here.' He snatched up the Princess now with both his hands and held her up in front of his furious face. 'You will confess this man is your lover,' he roared at her, 'and I will torture you until you do.'

"As the genie began to shake the Princess to and fro, she screamed in pain and terror. The room was soon filled with her piteous cries and, with their sound ringing in his ears, the Prince charged up the staircase, and bolted into the forest."

"He ran."

"Yes, he ran and ran, until he had no breath to go farther and finally he limped back to the tailor's shop for he had lost both sandals in the depths of the forest."

"But the Princess? She stays. Just the way she had stayed for ten years. Why?"

"I don't know, my dear. There the story is silent."

"Does she fight now?"

"Well, not exactly. That's a rather nasty bit. I was just coming to that but perhaps . . . Should I go on?"

"Well, we've come this far."

"So, the Prince stayed with the tailor that night and the next day, the man came to him and told him there was a visitor, a fellow Persian, who had come to restore his lost axe. The Prince went into the front room of the shop and greeted the visitor, a well-dressed fellow, a

Persian notable from the look of him but unknown to the Prince. The man held out an axe and a pair of sandals to the Prince and explained, 'I was travelling in the forest and found these. Are they yours?'

"As the Prince started toward him to reclaim his property, the man was suddenly enveloped in a puff of smoke and emerged as the genie with his chest the size of a tabletop and his legs like tree trunks. He seized up the Prince, delighted at the success of his trick.

"'I took the shape of a man to find you. You will come with me now and see what has happened to your love.' He grabbed the Prince up as a man might pick up a child, tucked him under his arm and flew through the sky toward the forest.

"The Prince found himself in the underground chamber once again and was horrified by the sight that greeted him. The Princess had been stripped naked, her arms and her legs had been tied to four stakes, blood had oozed from her sides as the genie had tortured her, but now she was cold and dead."

"But he loved her."

"Yes, madness, I know, but listen to the genie's plea.

"'She was mine,' said the genie. 'She was mine and she loved me. For ten years, on every tenth night, I left my magic realm, took the form of a handsome young Persian and came to her here in this chamber. I embraced her as a man, and every tenth night we loved each other as much as any human pair ever loved. She was mine until you ventured into this place. Women were ever perfidious: she betrayed me, so I killed her. You, however, are a man unknown to me; your crime is the lesser. I won't kill you. Instead, I will give you a choice of punishment. Would you rather be a dog, an ass or an ape?'

"The Prince stood there, uncomprehending of the genie's offer so numb was he with pain at the sight of the Princess and the thought that he was the cause of her death.

"But the genie quickly lost patience.

"'So, be it an ape then,' he said, raising a hand and muttering some incantation. Instantly, the Prince was transformed into a tailless baboon and hopped away into the forest."

"Does the story end there?"

"Well, the Prince had several more adventures before he takes the form of a man again, but I find I am growing tired. So, there you are. Don't ever get stuck living in a cave with an old genie."

"Or trust a young prince to save you."

"That too. But the genie does rather have the upper hand over the Prince, being magical and all."

"I suppose so."

"I don't think the baboon part was in the story I used to tell you?"

"No. It was a different story altogether."

"So, the storyteller can't help himself." Jonathan sounds uncharacteristically thoughtful over the phone the Thursday morning after I email him this latest instalment. "And finally he tells her the truth."

"Yes. I guess that's right. Or acknowledges reality. Which is a way of saying sorry, I suppose. Anyway, one more to go. Your big death-bed scene."

"Oh, ignore what I said. I was just joking. Finish it however you want. I trust you."

"Thanks."

The phone rings again a few hours later. It's Frank.

"I love it," he says. He's read the latest bit in *The Telegram*'s computer system, over Jonathan's shoulder, so to speak. "Did they tell you how we are doing?"

"They don't tell me much at all. Last I heard, we'd hit seven thousand copies. Seven thousand extra, that is."

"I heard nine thousand last weekend. Stanek must be kissing your feet."

"I haven't heard from Stanek, but Jonathan seems a lot more relaxed."

"Oh yeah, he would be. You are selling newsprint, Sharon, reams and reams of it."

"That's good, I guess."

"Sure is. I don't know if I told you this; I probably didn't want to spook you when you were just starting. The publisher took a flyer on newsprint; he got a great price two years ago on a ten-year contract." There was a moment's silence as he let this sink in.

"Ten years' worth of newsprint? He thinks print will last till 2020?"

"That's what he bet."

I laugh. Here I am worrying away about Dickens and *The Thousand and One Nights*, and apparently after all that I am just greasing a cog in the fish-wrap industry.

The next morning, I look over anxiously at Al and Saturday's thick stack of newsprint sitting on the kitchen table. Once he's finished reading, he begins with academic nitpicking.

"I think Nelly's objection to Rosa Bud is anachronistic. Victorian literature was filled with pure docile heroines of that kind; she wouldn't have seen her as unusual."

"Maybe not. But my Nelly wants a heroine with agency."

"A princess who will run up the stairs."

"Yes."

"But in the end neither Catherine nor Nelly resisted."

"No, they didn't."

He looks down at the paper in front of him. "'The Second Dervish's Tale' is a pretty ugly story to tell the woman you love."

"Yes."

"You're really enjoying this, aren't you?"

There's a pause between us. I summon up my courage and ask, "Did I go too far?"

"No," he replies. "I think it's the best one yet."

f I have a vivid memory of Tehran, an almost physical
recollection that proves I lived there once, then that
memory is of the sound of the fountain in my grandparents' garden.

They lived in a house on a small street in North Tehran
with a view of the Alborz Mountains if you craned your
neck out the bathroom window. The main windows of
the house all looked southwards toward the growing city.
A few streets from greater homes and larger gardens, it was
a modest but magic dwelling, two rooms downstairs, two
rooms up, a charmed place that my father was expected to
inherit and would have, if things had turned out differently.
Meanwhile, we lived a bit farther south in generous accom-
modations in a recently built block of flats. We had well-
proportioned rooms and a balcony where my mother
nurtured various flowering shrubs in plastic pots, watering
them profusely during the dry summer months and bringing
them indoors to clutter up the living room during the winter.

But my grandparents, they had a real garden, a little courtyard with enough sun that my grandfather could grow jasmine and cherry trees, planted in china urns and arrayed on either side of the blue-tiled fountain. Our school holidays at Nowruz, the Persian New Year that falls in late March, were celebrated with new clothes, spring cleaning and bonfires in the streets, but what we anticipated the most was the turning on of the fountain. My cousins, my sister and I would be invited over for tea or lemonade and cakes, maybe even ice cream if my grandmother were to indulge us, and my grandfather, with much huffing and puffing, would oil the valves and check the washers. After all his deliberations, he would finally say, "I believe we are ready," and the youngest, or the one who was about to graduate high school, or the one who had broken his leg skiing that winter, the special one deserving of a treat, would be invited to turn the spigot that would start the flow of water for the first time since the autumn before. We would listen, we children: could we hear the water in the line? We would wait and wait. Sometimes, there was a problem, a complication that would send my grandfather back to the source, turning taps, fretting a bit, scratching his head and then, always, miraculously, just as we were beginning to fidget and poke one another, water would issue forth. At first it complained, groaned a bit, then gurgled and finally gushed, bursting forth into the still cool air of spring. After that first effort, it would settle down and run along happily with the soft tinkling that formed a perpetual backdrop to any spring afternoon, any summer evening, the continual dancing of water on tile that played a theme song to my childhood.

The Old Persian term for a walled garden, *pairidaeza*, is the source of the word *paradise*. And indeed, we lived in some kind of heavenly state in those days. My grandfather was a rug merchant with a small but profitable export business down in the bazaar. When not engaged in sales or tending his garden, he composed verses in the Persian tradition that he read out loud to my grandmother, whether she wanted to hear them or not. Such was his success in business, his only son, my father, could aspire to make scholarship not merely a hobby but a profession: my father was engaged in a lengthy research project tracing the Persian threads in the Arabic tapestry of *The Thousand and One Nights* and taught literature at the University of Tehran. Continuing a family tradition, he read to my sister and me from the classic texts and prodded us about our homework, insisting we read not only Farsi and Arabic but also English and French. My mother, on the other hand, expressed no opinion about school other than to remind us we had to arrive there on time. A quiet soul who deferred to my father in all things, she kept the apartment, watered the shrubs and made the kebabs. I woke to her soft voice each morning; it was her sweet smile that greeted me every day when I came home from school and her quick kiss that sent me off to sleep. If she had some other ambition, some larger interest than to care for my father, my sister and me, it would be many years and other continents before it even occurred to me to consider what that might have been.

In this happy, balanced world, I was the neighbour-hood marble king. Having beaten all the local boys many times over, winning off them their agate and alabaster spheres, their tiger's eyes and their biggies, I had amassed a collection to rival the treasury of a shah. I carried it—or at least the part of it not so precious that I couldn't take it into the street and risk it in play—in a cloth bag my mother had sewn for me, with a braided cord for a drawstring at the top. I took it everywhere with me, even to church on Fridays, despite my father's stern if unen-forced prohibition and my mother's gentle pleading. Even if I could not play marbles on those days, merely the sight of that bag was enough, if I passed a schoolmate or neighbour on the street, to remind him of my prowess. Back at home, I would take them out and spread them on the floor, counting, categorizing and admiring. On week-days on the way home from school, I would prowl the streets looking for a game, although increasingly the other boys refused to play with me since they knew they would lose theirs to mine. I didn't care; my position was secure and some days, to prove my magnanimity, I offered to play free games for the mere fun of it, without penal-ties for the loser and loot for the winner.

I still have my marbles tucked away somewhere; it has been years since I have taken them out and admired them. In truth, I find them almost unbelievable, a tangible link to the intangible, a physical thing whose incredible existence is somehow more painful, more troubling than the faint memory of the sound of water in the garden on a summer evening.

Because this was a perfect world and we, its inhabitants, lived in it without sorrow, fear or deprivation, of course, I thought it rather dull and was convinced that somewhere else was better. The place I thought was better, the place I longed for, was England, or at least what I thought was England. I had an image of it, misty but persistent, in my mind's eye. It was London under snow, at Christmas, with a goose and plum pudding on the table and a tree in the parlour; it was a country road and a coach inn where the landlord might stir up some hot punch; it was Tiny Tim on his father's shoulders, Oliver Twist in the orphanage and Mr. Micawber fully certain that something would turn up.

I believe my introduction to Dickens was *A Christmas Carol*. Our Christmases in Tehran were small and private things; we were a handful of Eastern-rite Christians in a Muslim world, and we kept our beliefs and our practices to ourselves. Our celebration was merely a midnight mass in an ancient stone church and a supper afterwards during which the exhausted children inevitably fell asleep once they had opened the small gift or two provided by my parents or my grandparents. One year, in the midst of this personal, almost secret holiday, someone, I think perhaps it was one of my aunts, gave my sister and me a battered copy of *A Christmas Carol*, saying if my father was so insistent on us learning English, here was a lovely book we could read. In those days of the Shah, the Americans were our good friends and it was fashionable to study English. So, I did read it, haltingly, uncomprehendingly in places but gradually piecing together its fabulous story with my limited skills.

And from there I was launched. I was ten or eleven, and I read all the early Dickens: *The Pickwick Papers*, *Oliver Twist* and *The Old Curiosity Shop*. As the hot, dusty summer of the plain swirled around us, I dreamt of cozy pubs, ramshackle antique shops, gabled houses and cobblestone streets. I thought I saw in my grandmother's chador-wrapped cleaning lady the decency of the Marchioness or in the sleepiness of a heavy-breathing classmate the narcolepsy of the Fat Boy. I dreamt I was Oliver himself and imagined my outraged protests against the injustice of the orphanage, the exploitation of Fagin and barbarism of Billy Sikes. By the time the revolution arrived, I was reading *David Copperfield*.

At first, my father welcomed the revolution almost gleefully. Indeed, it was all my mother could do to stop him from running downtown to join the students in the streets. It was hypocritical perhaps, or maybe just foolish, since we profited from the relative economic security the Shah had delivered and we supported the Westernization of Iran, but my family members were all quietly opposed to the regime. Whatever the Shah had achieved, he was a dictator kept in power through intimidation and violence, aggrandizing and enriching himself at the expense of his people. The thuggery practised by his security forces, the personality cult surrounding his reign and the unearned wealth accumulated by the royal circle sat badly with my literate, middle-class family. For my father, justice was now being served; the people were finally getting their say. For him, it was a time of heady optimism. For me, on the other hand, it was a time of uncertainty and dawning fear: during the days, my parents would argue about whether or not my father should go in to the university; at night, my sleep was disturbed by the eerie calls of "Allahu Akbar" that resonated from the rooftops across Tehran as citizens denounced secularism in spontaneous, invisible protests the security forces were powerless to find and stop.

When the Shah first fled, my father was jubilant: finally we might get a government that did something for the poor. I think my grandfather was more aware of what lay ahead; with his headquarters down in the bazaar, he knew the gossip, saw how the bazaari, who had once backed the regime, had swung their power behind the ascendant clerics. As Christians, we were a minority among minorities; we were not even Armenian, like most of our Christian neighbours, but part of a yet smaller group of Orthodox Persians. We were largely invisible but also expendable. We needed to keep our heads down. My father, however, was not to be dissuaded from

attending the ongoing protests and also, most dangerously as it turned out, from making classroom speeches
about freedom and passionate assertions that it did not
matter whether his female students covered their heads.
He did not last long in the new Islamic state: it was only
a matter of months, as the new government took control
of the university, before he was hauled before a committee of colleagues he had once considered friends and
summarily fired. He sat at home, unable to understand
how a country he loved could not make room for his kind
of patriotism, how a people he so trusted could choose a
new kind of tyranny. My grandfather, seeking a solution
for him, decided he needed to expand his export business
to Canada. He worked his contacts at the bazaar, convinced the right people it was best if my father left and
got papers for the four of us. In 1980, nine months after
the revolution had swept the Shah from power, we
boarded a plane with as many rugs as we could possibly
fit in our bursting suitcases and left Iran for good.

I remember, arriving in Montreal, that we marvelled
at the broad streets and the huge North American cars,
my sister and I ate hot dogs and watched TV, and all
those things that today are so familiar and banal were
novel and exhilarating then. How quickly the beauty of
Persia was lost to us, and as a young man I did not seem
to regret it at all.

But now, sometimes, I think differently. On winter
nights in Toronto, I will sit cuddling with my daughters

around a wood fire, kissing the tops of their little heads and marvelling for the thousandth time at the blond hair they both inherited from their mother. How did I produce such creatures? My eyes will stray to the floor, admiring the reds and blues in the thick pile of the Persian rug that my forgiving father gave us as a present at my second wedding, and for a moment I will think I hear a fountain playing softly somewhere not far away.

A l is standing at the door of my office with the print-out I have handed him that morning. I can't tell if he's annoyed; his expression is dark and unreadable.

"So, the writer can't help herself." It reminds me of what Jonathan said about Dickens. The piece is presumptuous, but I actually intended it as a gift. I wait.

"You aren't planning to publish this, are you?"

"No. Of course not."

"I mean, it's not part of the serial or something?"

"God, no. We wrap up safely next weekend with a final bit about Nelly. No more dervishes, no more Dickens. I wrote that for you and the girls. I just wanted to get the family history down on paper. So it won't get lost."

"Well, thanks."

"You don't sound sure . . ."

"It's odd to read about yourself in the first person. I mean, I think of myself in the first person obviously, but to read someone else . . . pretending to be me."

"The novelist's art, pretending to be someone else."

"You're good at it, that pretending."

"Thank you."

"All that stuff. Did I tell you all that stuff? About my marbles and the revolution and my father?"

"Yes. You told me all that stuff. In bed mainly."

"Oh. Don't tell the girls that bit, will you?"

"No. But I loved those stories. I wouldn't want them not to know. It was part of what made me fall in love."

"Well, thank you for this." He gestures with the pages. "You made such an effort to understand me."

"I tried."

But we don't wrap up safely that weekend because I miss my deadline.

I phone Jonathan late Thursday morning, feeling stupid. I have spent the week somewhere else and haven't put pen to paper—or fingers to keyboard.

"I'm sorry. I just don't think I can deliver today."

"Not a problem," he says breezily. "It will raise suspense. We'll put a big mysterious promo in this weekend . . . due to unforeseen circumstances . . . and you can finish up next week."

"Oh, that's a good idea."

"When you didn't file last night I figured something was up; you are always so reliable. I pulled out some other stuff we had in the hopper and we'll stick that in instead.

The thumbsucker about judiciary reform will finally see the light of day. You've made our justice reporter a happy woman."

"I'm sorry to have left you to do that. I should have called last night."

"Are you okay?"

"Oh probably."

"I know it's hard. My mum . . . well, she died last year."

"I'm sorry to hear that."

"Yeah." There's a silence on the line. An honest silence. And then I hear him take a breath.

"I just wanted to say I have enjoyed working with you on this. You're very professional and I know Bob is really pleased with the results. He said he's going to send you a note. Handwritten. In the mail." He laughs. "I don't think we've saved newspapers single-handedly, but you've given everybody at this end lots to think about. Let's do another one next year."

"Sure. Next year. I'll get the last piece to you Tuesday."

I hang up the phone and sit at my desk thinking. It is not hard to write the end of Nelly's story. I just need to bring my mind around to it. It's how to tell Al about the doctor's appointment that is hard. I had my nine-month checkup two weeks ago; no big deal, I thought. They've tested me and poked me and X-rayed me so continually. Either you go into every appointment with a queasy stomach or a cold sweat expecting the worst or you choose to ignore the whole thing until somebody tells you otherwise. This time, they told me otherwise.

First it's an intern, his finger pausing as he examines my scar.

"Hmmm."

All of a sudden, I am paying attention.

"I'll just get Dr. Abate to take a look at this."

"Take a look at what?"

"Oh, um, there's just . . ." The intern looks at me panicked. He knows he has screwed up. He hurries out of the room and returns a few minutes later with my oncologist at his side. She's a tall, elegant woman and she practically glides in, calming words flowing out of her in a continuous stream as she repeats the examination.

"Sharon. Doing well? Scar healed nicely. Book coming along? Family well? Little nodule here, bit of fat maybe. Probably nothing to worry about but we'll just do a quick biopsy to be sure."

She glides out again and eventually another doctor appears and gives me a biopsy on the spot, sticking a needle into a bump on my scar that I had not even noticed. That night I tell Al the nine-month results are fine, repeating to myself that it's probably nothing. I proceed to a follow-up appointment Tuesday. They are fast these days, give them their due. They got some big donation at the breast cancer centre for the express purpose of getting the results back to patients within a week. No more nasty waiting around thinking about it. So, Tuesday, I sit there in one of those flimsy little gowns that provide a very small amount of rather unnecessary coverage. These people cut off one of my breasts; I hardly care if they see me naked. Dr. Abate inspects my scarred chest and the remaining breast with long-fingered hands; her touch is warm and very gentle. She tells me to get dressed and then we sit together in a pair of office chairs. I'm nervous, afraid of her somehow, like I'm the dumb intern and I am about to catch hell. She clears her throat.

"I'm afraid . . ."

I have to tell Al there isn't going to be a happy ending.

The Dickens Bicentenary Serial: Chapter 16
Peckham, Surrey. June 8, 1870

Nelly leant back against the wainscotting and tried to consider the situation calmly. She needed to call a doctor but she trusted neither the medical expertise nor the discretion of the local man. Charles had an excellent physician in Kent. He mumbled and she squeezed his hand again.

"Yes, dear. I'm here. Stay with me now. Stay with me." She wiped a hand across his forehead. His eyes fluttered open but he did not appear to see anything for he merely stared at the ceiling and then closed them again.

She suspected he was dying, and he needed to die at home.

"I'm going to get Jane, dear. I'll only be a second." She got to her feet and hurried out of the drawing room to the second floor where a doorway led to the attic. She opened it and called up the stairs: "Jane. Jane, are you awake? I need your help. Can you come downstairs? Mr. Dickens has taken ill."

He had seemed fine earlier that evening. Well enough to take a tour in the garden before dinner and admire the flowers. It was June and the roses were in full bloom. Jane had prepared roast beef and stayed downstairs until he arrived to make sure it was perfectly cooked and that she could see to the carving herself, something Nelly could never manage with her bad hand. Then, as always, she had discreetly withdrawn to her attic room. He had eaten almost nothing, but he had chatted amiably enough; his face was as lopsided as ever, but Nelly was almost getting used to that—it was the palsy that had come upon him months before—and he no longer complained of the numbness he had sometimes felt on the left side of his body. They had moved into the parlour after dinner and sat together on the sofa but he seemed to have nothing left to say. After a bit, he said simply, "I don't feel at all well."

"Will you not lie down, dear?" she asked, rising to take him upstairs or just make room for him to stretch out on the low sofa.

"Yes," he agreed and then said, "on the floor" as he slumped forward and fell onto the rug. He rolled on to his side as he fell and lay there, occasionally mumbling, occasionally opening or closing his eyes, as she held his hand and called to him: "Charles, Charles. Are you all right?" But clearly he was not all right.

"Oh, miss. What's happened to him?" Jane asked as

she came into the room, belting her thick dressing gown around her.

"He's had an attack. He should never have come out here. I shouldn't have let him."

"It's not your fault, miss. I'll go for the doctor."

"No." Her suggestion forced Nelly to concentrate on the present. "No, Jane. Go to the Rye and see if Archer or Smithers are sitting there with a cab. I need a hackney that can go to Kent this evening."

"You're not going to try . . ."

"I have to. I need a hackney with a strong driver. I'd prefer Smithers' coach; he's more sensible and that's two horses. We'll need them. If you find him, get him to come back to the house with you."

Jane returned about ten minutes later and Nelly could hear she had the driver with her. The man came into the parlour, doffing his cap as he did so.

"I hear you need some help, Miss Ternan."

"Yes. This gentleman has taken ill and we need to get him home. He lives in Kent, at Higham."

"That will cost you a pretty penny."

"I don't care how much it costs. I just need to know if you can drive me that far tonight."

"It'll take hours, miss. Would it not be better to call a doctor?"

At this point, Charles mumbled loudly.

"Had a few, has he?" the driver asked. "Well, we'll get him home."

Nelly was in no position to protest about her friend's sobriety. Probably best if the man just thought he was taking home an inconvenient drunk.

She turned to Jane. "I need to tell them to expect him. I'll write out a telegram for you. Once we are off, you go up to the post office and see if you can raise Mrs. Robertson. She shouldn't be asleep yet, I wouldn't think."

Nelly rose from Charles's side and slipped into the chair in front of her small writing desk that sat in the far corner of the parlour. She pulled out paper and wrote in block capitals: "MISS GEORGINA HOGARTH, GAD'S HILL, HIGHAM, KENT.

HE IS TAKEN ILL. RETURNING TO GH BY CAB. GET DOCTOR."

She debated how to sign the thing. She could hardly hide her identity from Mrs. Robertson, who knew Jane, but the telegram office in Higham had no call to know who was sending the message. She simply wrote N at the end and handed the paper to Jane. "Nunshead as the return address; not my name," she said quietly.

She, Jane and Smithers then began the difficult process of lifting Charles to his feet and getting him out to the coach. It might have been easier if they had carried him as if he were a patient or a corpse with the women taking his head and Smithers his feet but the driver, assuming he was dealing with a drunk, simply hoisted up his torso as though his passenger might be trusted to put an arm over his rescuer's shoulders and at least shuffle his feet a bit.

"Oi. Here we go. Look lively, sir. There's a chap . . ." Smithers kept up a steady stream of such encouragements as he dragged Charles toward the door with Nelly doing her best to help on his other side.

The drive was slow as Smithers wended his way through the countryside south of London, moving eastwards but seemingly with no particular route in mind. Inside, Charles lay slumped against the side of the small coach covered with a blanket Jane had thought to hand out to them as they climbed in. He was no longer mumbling but Nelly could hear his breathing, heavy, laboured but encouragingly regular. "Not long, dear. Not long," she kept saying, although she suspected it was going to take hours. In the dark, she could see little out the small window and soon after they passed Greenwich she lost all track of where they were. She tried to concentrate on Charles and trust in Smithers to find his route but at the point where she swore they had passed the same church tower twice, she lowered the window and leaned out to talk to her driver.

"Can you find the way, Smithers? You're looking for the Gravesend Road; we must cross it at some point."

"Right you are, miss. Not used to going cross-country, most of my fares just go to and from the city."

"Perhaps if we pass a pub you could pull in and ask," she suggested.

"Right you are, miss." Smithers was large and steady, but the journey was taking him miles out of his known territory.

———

They travelled for another quarter of an hour, with her scanning both sides of the road for any inn or pub. As they approached what seemed like a large crossroads, she saw a pub sign swinging from a small gabled inn and she felt Smithers pulling the coach toward it. She was just wondering whether it would still be open and scanning the premise for any sign of light when they both glimpsed the same thing: a signpost on the larger road they were approaching, indicating London and Gravesend to their left and Rochester and Canterbury to their right.

"There it is, miss." Smithers turned the carriage to their right and they continued on their way. After half an hour, Nelly was wondering when they would ever get there and again scanning the countryside anxiously. The moon had now set and she couldn't make out where she was. She had only been to Gad's Hill on a few occasions when she could be safely invited to large parties with her sisters or mother, and she had come by train. Nothing that she could make out looked the least familiar. It was when she saw lights of a sizeable town in the distance that she realized they must be approaching Rochester itself and it dawned on her that they had overshot their mark and had passed Gad's Hill already. She banged on the wall in front of her urgently and opened the window again.

"Smithers, I think we're already past it; that's Rochester ahead. We should have turned left at the crossroads instead of right. We need to turn back."

"Right you are, miss." He turned the coach around and headed back the way they had come, with Nelly now glued to the window. They passed the crossroads where they had turned the wrong way and, within a few minutes, she spotted the little white pub, Sir John Falstaff's, that sat right on the road across from the house.

"We're here," she called out to Smithers. "Turn left here. Where the lights are on."

They had started out about nine and it was now well past two in the morning. It belatedly occurred to Nelly that she needed to pay Smithers and had, at best, three shillings in her purse. In her anxiety she had failed to negotiate the fare, but he had just driven her a good twenty-five miles in the middle of the night and would certainly need a sovereign if not two. She supposed she could ask Georgina if she had any ready cash, but she didn't like to; it would feel as though she was humbling herself somehow. Nelly had always found Georgina an intimidating figure, clever, supremely well organized, unwilling to suffer fools and ferocious in both the efficiency of her household management and in her protection of Charles and his reputation. Nelly often suspected that it was she who insisted Charles keep his life in Mornington Crescent, Slough or Peckham completely secret. Over the years, there had always been those occasions when he was ready to defy convention and, alarmingly, wanted to introduce Nelly around, but after a trip home to Gad's Hill he would repent of his reckless- ness and tell her "Soon" or "Perhaps another time." Well, that was all water under the bridge now. As the coach crunched across the gravel and came to a stop out- side the house, Nelly leaned toward Charles and reached inside his jacket. She found his wallet in his pocket and slipped out four one-pound notes, for it also occurred to her she would need to pay her own way home too. The front door of the house opened, spilling light into the drive, and Georgina hurried toward them.

"How is he?" she asked without preamble as she pulled open the coach door.

"He doesn't seem fully conscious," Nelly replied. "He was speaking a bit at first. Just mumbling really, but he has been quiet for hours now."

"What happened?"

"He just said he didn't feel well and then he col- lapsed on the floor."

"Rathborne and Evans will help get him into the house. I've made up a divan in the dining room. I thought that was easier than trying the stairs. The doctor's wait- ing inside."

Rathborne and Evans, a hulking man and a more slender lad who Nelly supposed were the gardener and his boy, appeared out of the darkness and carried their master toward the house. Nelly turned to her driver.

"We did not set the fare. Here's two guineas," she said as she handed him two of the notes and two coins of her own.

"Oh, miss, that is far too much. I only need half of that, Mr. Dickens being sick and all."

Somewhere along the way, Smithers had figured out the identity of his passenger. Perhaps there were rumours in Peckham about her regular visitor.

"Please, take it," Nelly said, pressing the money into his hand. "You have to drive all the way back to Peckham too."

"Did you not want me to stay and see you home, miss? . . . Since you have paid for it," he added.

"That is very kind of you, but no, I will stay for a bit."

She saw him off, went into the house and found the dining room off the main hall. Charles was lying on a low divan under the window, his head and torso blocked from her view by the doctor who bent over him, while the gardener and his boy were just retreating through the service door at the back of the room. Georgina hurried up to her and led her back into the hall. Hers, as always, was an inconvenient presence.

"Thank you. For the telegram and for bringing him here. We owe you a large debt. It must have been a difficult journey."

"It seemed the only thing to do."

"It was very thoughtful of you, and sensible. Will you wait in the drawing room until the doctor leaves?"

So Nelly waited in the drawing room for hours. A maid brought her a cup of tea but otherwise no one disturbed her. Finally, toward dawn she heard noises in the hall as the doctor took his leave and Georgina came back into the room.

"I'm sorry I've been so long. The doctor is just going home to sleep for a bit but he'll come back in the morning. I'm afraid . . . " and at this her voice wavered and broke. She bit her lip and blinked away tears. "He says there is no hope. It's only a matter of time. As soon as it's light, I have to get a message to Charley or he won't see his father again. The doctor says he won't last the day."

"Can I see him?"

"Of course. Kate is with him now. Mamey has just gone to lie down for a bit."

Nelly followed Georgina across the hall and back into the dining room. Charles lay under blankets in about the same state as he had been all night. His daughter Kate was sitting beside him on a straight-backed chair.

"Nelly," she said, rising and taking her hands. "Thank you, thank you for everything."

Nelly wasn't precisely sure what everything included, but she nodded and took her place on a second chair. She sat there for a bit, holding his hand and stroking his forehead from time to time and then, as the room grew light, she rose to leave. More visitors would be arriving soon and she had no wish to embarrass the family.

She knelt down now to be close to his ear and, remembering she had read somewhere that hearing is the last sense to leave the dying body, whispered to him.

"You're safe home now, dear. I need to go. So . . . goodbye. Goodbye and thank you."

She got up and left the room with Georgina at her heels.

"I could get the coachman to run you down to the station. It's just down the hill in Higham . . ." she offered hesitantly.

"I remember where it is," Nelly replied. "I'll walk. It looks to be a beautiful morning."

So Nelly walked downhill toward Higham station in the first light, calculating there would be a train into the city by seven and that she would be back in Peckham in time for a late breakfast. The birds were singing, on gentler notes than they did in Italy. She waited at the train station until the ticket office opened and bought herself a first-class ticket, plucking one of Charles's notes out of her purse and wondering at it as though it were a relic of what was already a bygone era. Had it been but a few hours since she had taken it from his pocket? She took her change, deftly plucking the coins off the counter and placing them in her purse with none of the usual awkwardness in her right hand. When the train arrived, ten minutes later, she joined a few early commuters on their way into the city.

"Beautiful morning," the gentleman in her compartment nodded amiably before he buried himself in his paper.

She looked out the window, watching a soft mist slowly lift and evaporate to reveal a gentle green landscape, and considered the events of the past night. He was not going to last long; that was clear. And once he was gone, then there would be a great deal of fuss, newspaper reports and eulogies, some grand funeral that she would not be able to attend, she supposed. She wondered if they would invite Mrs. Dickens. Probably not.

And so her mind turned finally now to truly consider Catherine. She saw her once again, the heavy woman trapped in the little vestibule of Park Cottage. In those early days, it had been easier to dismiss her, to view her as a pathetic and foolish figure who probably deserved her fate, not being clever, lively or pretty enough to hold on to the mercurial Charles. It had been easier than considering the alternative, that perhaps he was neither patient nor kind enough to hold on to her. And then, over the years, Nelly had come to feel a certain kinship with this invisible soul; the private Charles was not a comfortable person, dark, restless, regretful, and his closest companions often bore the brunt of that personality. Today, Nelly imagined Catherine's sorrow and her desperation; she felt them almost as her own; they had loved, they had forborne. They had seen a greater need than their own, and they had been erratically rewarded.

She shook herself, almost physically the way a dog does when it comes in from the garden or gets up from a nap, dismissing this fantasy and smiling to herself at the path her thoughts had taken: She didn't suppose any sympathy she felt for Mrs. Dickens could possibly be mutual.

As the train shuddered its way toward London, she barely noticed the time passing, and when they arrived at Charing Cross less than an hour later, she realized she had completely forgotten that she was always nervous on trains. She smoothed her skirt, a sensible summer linen she had worn to walk about the garden the previous afternoon, and rose from her seat, pausing before the compartment door. She nodded at the stranger across from her, took a deep breath, grasped the handle firmly in her right hand, pushed open the door and alighted onto a platform already bustling with morning commuters. She shook out her skirt as though to brush off the grime and walked unhesitatingly into the crowd. Within a moment, she was lost from sight.

She reappeared about an hour later in Peckham, home in time for a late breakfast as she had promised herself, but when she arrived at her own front door, Jane was standing there, looking grim and holding a telegram in her hand.

"This just arrived, miss. You probably crossed the boy in the street."

The telegraph had proved faster than the train and the news had beat her home: he must have died before she had even arrived in London. She crumpled Georgina's telegram in her hand and sat down heavily on the sofa in the parlour, the sofa where he had been sitting only twelve hours before.

"I'm very sorry, miss," Jane said, guessing at the news. "He was a great man. All England will mourn him deeply."

Nelly tossed her head at the platitudes and stared down at the floor.

"I suppose it will," she replied finally, but she was thinking more about how she would mourn him. Very privately, no doubt. She didn't look up at Jane and spoke more to herself than to her servant.

"I'd known him since I was seventeen. All my adult life."

"He meant the world to you, miss."

"Yes."

"You knew him better than anyone."

"I suppose so."

"You should write a memoir, miss."

"Oh, no. I don't think so." Nelly looked up now, roused from her thoughts and outraged at the suggestion.

"Of course not, miss. I wasn't thinking."

"No, I am not much of a writer," she said, more pensively.

"No, miss."

"And of course, I really didn't know him."

"No, miss."

"After all, I was only a very little girl when he met my family. My sisters knew him better; they are older than I am, but I was just a little girl and he was just a family friend."

"Yes, miss."

"I was quite small, just a child." She was staring at Jane now.

"Yes, miss." Jane sounded puzzled.

"I mean, I'm young yet, not even twenty-one."

"That's a story, miss."

"Yes," Nelly replied, drawing herself up straight and raising her chin, "but it's a good story."

My darling daughters:

Your father did keep this text safely for you. Last year, with your birthdays coming up, he finally read it and then he gave it to me. He wanted my advice, or my permission perhaps. Your mother intended you to read this, she wanted you to know our pasts. And who are we to interfere in her decisions about her relationship with you just because we can? I love you both and have always enjoyed being your stepmother. I know things have not always been easy between us; you girls were so sad and confused when I first arrived in the house. I wanted to spend every day hugging away all the pain in your little faces but I wasn't your mother; I couldn't make it up to you. And later? I guess adolescence is never easy for anyone.

My solution, the only solution I could think of, has been to love you as much as I possibly could through the years, for your father's sake, but also because I felt I owed that to your mother. She may have had her reasons to resent me, but I never felt any hostility toward her. In truth, there was a period where I just wanted to be her, which may sound silly since I think I only met her once, at a party or something, but I used to long to be her. I guess what I really mean is that I longed to be your father's wife. It was odd reading what she had written; I certainly knew what it felt like to be Shay and then the bits about marriage really struck home. Long marriages are often more complicated than they look from the outside.

Your mother has taught me things about your father that I didn't even know. Somehow it's hard to picture the great Dickens scholar as a little boy playing marbles in the streets of Tehran, isn't it? Even when we went back there last year, he never mentioned the marbles.

I know when you ask him about his childhood and Iran, he always says it was a different life; that he is Canadian now, but sometimes when he talks about a rug or says a few words in Farsi, you can see he is still half Persian.

But, most of all, you have to realize how proud he is of you both. It was a big reason why he wanted to go back to Iran. He just wanted to be able to tell his cousins and his aunts: "This is Goli, some day soon she will be president of the bank; this is Anahita, she fills in for the main newscaster on weekends but soon enough they will see that he has to go so that she can take over the job." He would never say such things in Canada. I know it made you both squirm but he loves you to pieces, both of you, even if he doesn't always say it.

Last year, I asked him if he wanted to go back to Iran again this summer and do you know what he said? He said, "Goli and Anahita and Hope are my country." He stressed each of our three names so emphatically and so equally. It was the most beautiful thing he had ever said to me. It so confirmed for me that I was part of you.

So, now you can read your mother's last story. As she herself told you, it is yours to do with as you wish. You always call me Mum and that means a lot to me but I know if people ask you directly, you say "Hope is our stepmother. Our real mother died when we were eight." You explain your mother grew up in Halifax and moved to Toronto as a student; that she was a popular novelist who had published several best-sellers before she died of breast cancer at thirty-eight. And you say that your father is an Iranian immigrant and an English literature profes-sor at the university who specializes in the works of Charles Dickens. But Sharon has given you another truth, and you should cherish it: if people ask where you came from, tell them your father was a prince of Persia and your mother a storyteller from Samarkand. And no one could ever really say which one seduced the other.

H.

Acknowledgements

Charles Dickens was a man of many biographers. To create a fictional version of Ellen Ternan, I have drawn primarily on Peter Ackroyd's *Dickens* and Claire Tomalin's *Charles Dickens: A Life*. Of course, Tomalin is also Ternan's biographer. Her groundbreaking 1990 book, *The Invisible Woman*, was part of what inspired me to imagine how exactly Nelly managed the compromises she did; a postscript to the paperback edition floats the intriguing hypothesis that Dickens suffered his final stroke not in his own home at Gad's Hill but at Peckham with Nelly.

The neglected Catherine Dickens is the subject of an excellent biography and social history by Lillian Nayder, *The Other Dickens: A Life of Catherine Hogarth*. Nayder is the person who actually calculated that Dickens and his wife were probably practising abstinence around the period of his first American tour. Mrs. Dickens' menu book was originally published as a pamphlet, but it can be found today, reproduced in full, in the culinary history *Dinner for Dickens* by Susan M. Rossi-Wilcox, a book that explains how the family ate and entertained.

We do know that in childhood Dickens read and enjoyed what he called *The Arabian Nights*; he makes numerous references to its characters and settings in his novels. He would have known the stories through popular English translations of the early eighteenth-century French translation by Antoine Galland. There are many versions of *The Thousand and One Nights*—the text is fluid and much disputed—and numerous contemporary reissues of the more scholarly English-language translations that began appearing in the mid-nineteenth century. (I used a recent Penguin edition of Richard Burton's 1880 translation.) But for the contemporary reader who just wants to sample the tales, by far the most delectable taste is to be had in Hanan Al-Shaykh's 2011 retelling, *One Thousand and One Nights*, which features a mere nineteen of Scheherazade's stories.

When it came to fashioning the contemporary characters in *Serial Monogamy*, Hamid Sodeifi, Azar Masoumi and Pegatha Taylor helped me create Al by commenting on the section about his childhood in Tehran. Meanwhile Andrew Taylor advised about academic careers, Hannah Carolan provided information about triple-negative breast cancer and Jane Coults helped with proofreading. I am also indebted to the Toronto Arts Council for a grant that allowed me time to complete a first draft, while much of my research was conducted at various branches of the ever reliable Toronto Public Library.

My agent Dean Cooke was an enthusiastic advocate for the novel from the start, as was editor Nita Pronovost, who originally acquired an early draft for Doubleday Canada. There it was skilfully massaged by Martha Kanya Forstner, whose wisdom about fictional characters was indispensable. I am always indebted, for their loving support, to my parents, J.H. and Mary Taylor; my husband, Joel Sears; my son, Jed Sears; and my much-missed friend Teresa Mazzitelli, who died while I was researching this book.

About the Author

KATE TAYLOR was born in France and raised in Ottawa. Her debut novel, *Mme Proust and the Kosher Kitchen*, won the Commonwealth Writers' Prize for best first book (Canada/Caribbean region) and the Toronto Book Award. Her second novel, *A Man in Uniform*, was nominated for the Ontario Library Association's Evergreen Award. A recipient of the National Newspaper Award and the Atkinson Fellowship in public policy journalism, she also writes about the arts for *The Globe and Mail*, where she currently serves as lead film critic and writes a weekly column about culture. She lives in Toronto.